BETRAYAL AT IGA

Also by Susan Spann

Claws of the Cat

Blade of the Samurai

Flask of the Drunken Master

The Ninja's Daughter

BETRAYAL AT IGA

A HIRO HATTORI NOVEL

SUSAN SPANN

SEVENTH STREET BOOKS®
AN IMPRINT OF PROMETHEUS BOOKS
59 JOHN GLENN DRIVE • AMHERST, NY 14228
www.seventhstreetbooks.com

Published 2017 by Seventh Street Books®, an imprint of Prometheus Books

Cover design by Nicole Sommer-Lecht
Cover image © Shutterstock
Cover design © Prometheus Books

Inquiries should be addressed to
Seventh Street Books
59 John Glenn Drive
Amherst, New York 14228
VOICE: 716–691–0133 • FAX: 716–691–0137
WWW.SEVENTHSTREETBOOKS.COM

21 20 19 18 17 • 5 4 3 2 1

Library of Congress Cataloging-in-Publication Data

Names: Spann, Susan, author.
Title: Betrayal at Iga : a Hiro Hattori novel / by Susan Spann.
Description: Amherst, NY : Seventh Street Books, an imprint of Prometheus Books, 2017. | Series: A Shinobi mystery ; 5 | Description based on print version record and CIP data provided by publisher; resource not viewed.
Identifiers: LCCN 2017005189 (print) | LCCN 2017011773 (ebook) | ISBN 9781633882782 (ebook) | ISBN 9781633882775 (softcover)
Subjects: LCSH: Ninja—Fiction. | Samurai—Fiction. | Murder—Investigation—Fiction. | GSAFD: Mystery fiction.
Classification: LCC PS3619.P3436 (ebook) | LCC PS3619.P3436 B45 2017 (print) | DDC 813/.6—dc23
LC record available at https://lccn.loc.gov/2017005189

Printed in the United States of America

For Christopher

AUTHOR'S NOTE

Although the characters in this book are fictitious (even when based on historical figures), I have tried to portray the time and its people as realistically as possible. Since Japanese names and terms can be tricky for readers unfamiliar with the time and culture, I've included a cast of characters—and a brief glossary—at the back of the book. Where present, Japanese characters' surnames precede their given names, in the Japanese style. Western surnames follow the characters' given names, in accordance with Western conventions.

Thank you for reading—I hope you enjoy the adventure!

CHAPTER 1

AUTUMN 1565

Hiro Hattori leaned into the wind that swept down the hill and across his face. He pulled his kimono tighter and glanced at the Portuguese priest beside him. "Remember, you must eat everything set before you—"

"—because leaving food on the plate offends the host." Father Mateo smiled. "I have attended Japanese feasts before."

"Not like this one." The words came out more sharply than intended.

Father Mateo stopped short. "You're nervous."

"And you should be." Hiro faced the Jesuit. "This is not a 'welcome the foreigner' feast in Kyoto, with samurai willing to overlook a stranger's breach of etiquette."

The sun had dropped below the horizon, filling the air with the chill of mountain twilight. Hiro gestured toward the top of the hill. "That house belongs to Hattori Hanzō, leader of the Iga *ryu*. Everyone inside is a trained assassin, half of them visitors from Koga and thus not under Iga's control. If you can think of a less advisable place to cause offense, feel free to enlighten me."

"But . . . isn't Hanzō your cousin?"

Hiro frowned. "That fact will not protect you."

Father Mateo looked concerned. "If attending is truly so dangerous, why didn't you try to prevent me from accepting the invitation?"

"Would you have listened?"

"No," the priest admitted.

Hiro shrugged. "That answers your question."

"It never stopped you before."

Hiro ignored the comment and continued up the hill.

Father Mateo fell in step beside him. "I've wanted to meet Hattori Hanzō from the moment I learned he sent you to protect me, back in Kyoto."

"The client who hired the Iga ryu to guard you is responsible for your protection," Hiro corrected. "Hanzō merely chose me for the job."

Father Mateo smiled. "Do you realize fear makes you peevish?"

"I am not frightened," Hiro snapped. "I'm focused."

"Either way, you're peevish."

They rounded a curve, and Hiro shivered as the wind rustled through the leaves of the pines and colorful maples that crowded against the earthen path. His favorite gray kimono wasn't warm enough to block the autumn chill.

"Why did Hanzō invite me tonight?" the Jesuit asked. "I know he wanted you to keep an eye on the Koga emissaries, but I'm not part of the peace negotiations."

"The commander of the Iga ryu has an obligation to welcome every guest who arrives in the village. Important guests must also be given a feast on the night they arrive."

"So the Koga *shinobi* arrived today as well?"

Hiro nodded. "Unfortunately, they did not reveal their arrival date in advance, placing Hanzō in the awkward position of needing to welcome multiple guests on a single . . ."

He trailed off as he realized the priest was no longer beside him.

Father Mateo stood on the path staring up at Hanzō's mansion, which had finally come entirely into view.

Solid walls of earth and stone rose ten feet high around the compound, giving it the appearance of a fortress. Black-glazed tiles topped the walls and arched across the massive wooden gates that marked the entrance. Beyond them, the mansion's sloping roof rose up like the back of a sleeping dragon.

"It looks like the shogun's palace." Father Mateo was awestruck.

"A reminder to all that Hattori Hanzō is more than a village chieftain. Hurry up, we can't be late."

"Shouldn't there be someone here to greet us?" the Jesuit asked as they passed between the gates and entered the courtyard. "Guards, or someone?"

"In peacetime, Hanzō needs no guards." Hiro looked around. "I would have expected some tonight, with Koga emissaries in the village. Apparently, Hanzō believed them unnecessary."

As he crossed the yard with Father Mateo, Hiro observed how barren the compound seemed, compared with Kyoto's samurai mansions. No Buddhist statuary or flowing koi ponds filled the space. A Zen dry garden in the corner offered an interesting view, but only to those whose eyes were trained to understand its austere beauty.

Carved stone lanterns stood on either side of the wooden steps leading up to the covered veranda that surrounded Hanzō's home. In the gathering darkness, their flickering light illuminated a row of crimson maples, dwarfed by pruning to prevent intruders from using them to scale the roof. The maple leaves glowed like coals, surrounding the house with living flame.

The mansion's roof soared high overhead, with finials carved in the shape of tigers. Twilight hid the details, but Hiro remembered them all too well.

He passed the lanterns and stepped onto the porch, frowning at the line of sandals sitting by the door. "The Koga delegation has arrived, which makes us late."

The heavy, wooden door swung open, revealing an ancient, wizened woman barely as tall as Hiro's chest. Wrinkles obscured her features, and her ears resembled apricot slices left in the sun too long. Golden hairpins glimmered in the coil of snow-white hair atop her head, while embroidered autumn leaves flowed down the side of her silk kimono, shimmering in brilliant shades of scarlet, gold, and orange.

The wrinkles around her mouth drew back, revealing a set of shockingly healthy teeth.

She did not bow, but Hiro did, more deeply and with more respect than Father Mateo had ever seen him show. As Hiro straightened, the priest made a slow, equally respectful bow.

The woman's smile grew. "Welcome home, Hiro-*kun*."

Father Mateo looked at Hiro, surprised by the ancient woman's use of the diminutive.

"Thank you, it is nice to be back." Hiro gestured to the priest. "May I introduce Father Mateo Ávila de Santos, a priest of the foreign god, from Portugal."

The woman nodded.

Addressing the Jesuit, Hiro added, "My grandmother, Hattori Akiko."

Father Mateo bowed again.

"You are late, Hiro-*kun*," Akiko warned. "The meal is ready. Everyone is waiting."

"Is that why you answered the door?" Hiro asked.

She shrugged, and her formality fell away. "Hanzō sent his wife into the mountains, with their infant son." She dropped her voice to a whisper. "Betraying his assertion that he trusts the Koga, and needs no guards, because the delegation comes in peace."

"He didn't send you to the mountains?" Hiro asked.

Akiko made a dismissive gesture. "I refused to go. I'm old. Nobody wants to hurt me, and if they tried, I wouldn't care. It's been too long since I had a decent fight."

She stepped away from the door. "Follow me, and hurry. You know how Hanzō-*kun* dislikes delays."

Almost as much as he hates the nickname "Hanzō-kun," Hiro thought as he left his sandals by the door. A wave of discomfort washed over him as he followed Akiko into the house. The last time he had seen his cousin Hanzō, things had not gone well.

Behind him, Father Mateo whispered, "She's your *grandmother*?"

The Jesuit spoke in Portuguese, so Hiro replied in kind. "Yes, and don't be fooled by her innocent act. She has killed a man with nothing but a chopstick."

CHAPTER 2

Hiro and Father Mateo followed Akiko down a narrow passage lined with paneled sliding doors and covered by a low, carved ceiling designed to prevent the use of swords.

Underfoot, the wooden floorboards creaked.

Father Mateo looked down. "Nightingale floors, like the ones in the shogun's palace."

"To warn of intruders," Hiro confirmed. "Iga had them first."

At the end of the building the passage made a sharp left turn. Just past it, Akiko knelt in front of yet another paneled door. She laid her hands on the frame and looked expectantly at Hiro.

He knelt beside her and gestured for the priest to do the same. "Hanzō holds with protocol. The feast has started, so we must enter the room from a kneeling position."

Akiko smiled approvingly as Father Mateo joined them on the floor. When Hiro nodded, she slid the panel open.

A knee-high rectangular table sat at the center of the feasting room, the only furniture in the space. At the head of the table, facing the door, knelt a man about Hiro's age. He wore a kimono of dark blue silk, and his hair was bound in the samurai style. His features bore a strong resemblance to Hiro's; strangers often mistook them for brothers. Although the other man wore no swords, Hiro had no doubt that Hattori Hanzō—and everyone else in the eight-mat room—was fully armed beneath his silk veneer.

Four strangers knelt along the left side of the table. They turned their heads to the door in unison, faces revealing veiled suspicion, but no alarm, at the sight of the foreign priest.

The visitor closest to Hanzō wore a silk kimono patterned with the crest of the Koga clan. His hair, also bound in a samurai knot, had a greenish tint that suggested dye. Between his uncommonly pale skin and the sheen of sweat across his forehead, he appeared both nervous and uncomfortable.

To the sweating stranger's right knelt a man in his twenties, distinguished mostly by his cleanly shaven head and surly scowl. At the sight of Hiro and the priest, he leaned toward the even younger man who knelt on his other side and whispered something. Given the look in the bald man's eyes, his words were not polite.

The emissary in the lowest position, closest to the door, was a woman. Her hair fell down her back in a single braid so long the end of it rested on the floor. Defying tradition, she wore silk trousers and a tunic belted at the waist instead of a formal kimono. Although she knelt in the junior place, and wore the clothes of a commoner, she looked at ease in samurai company, suggesting a noble birth.

Unable to delay any longer, Hiro shifted his gaze to the woman who knelt on the opposite side of the table, directly across from the female Koga emissary.

His breath caught in his throat.

Neko's slender face was even lovelier than he had remembered, jet-black eyes and narrow eyebrows strikingly dark against her pale skin. She wore her hair in a feminine version of the samurai knot, with the back piled high atop her head, and the front hanging loose in a fringe around her face. She wore a violet kimono embroidered with a flight of shimmering phoenixes, a daring choice for a season that called for muted, or at least autumnal, hues.

But then, Kotani Neko was impossible to mute in any season.

Given their history, Hiro had hoped he would no longer find her attractive. Unfortunately, his body betrayed that hope.

"Hiro." Hanzō broke the silence. "How nice of you to join us."

Hiro placed his hands on the threshold and bowed his forehead to the floor. After holding the obeisance for a calculated moment, he pushed himself back to a kneeling position and entered the room, remaining on his knees.

Behind him, Father Mateo repeated the bow and followed Hiro onto the *tatami*. To Hiro's relief, the Jesuit remained on his knees, remembering that etiquette did not permit a guest to stand when the host and other guests were already seated.

"Good evening, Hattori-*sama*." Hiro opted for a higher honorific than the usual -*san*, in recognition of his cousin's status. "I deeply apologize for our tardiness. May I introduce Father Mateo Ávila de Santos, a priest of the foreign god, from Portugal."

Hanzō nodded, accepting the introduction, and addressed the sweating man to his right. "Koga-*san*, this is my cousin Hattori Hiro. He and his companion have just arrived from Kyoto, on their way to the foreign settlement at Yokoseura."

The sweaty man nodded. "I am Koga Yajiro. Allow me to introduce my companions." He gestured first to the bald man, and then to each of the others in turn as he named them: "Koga Fuyu, Koga Toshi, and Koga Kiku."

Hiro found it strange that the Koga ryu, which consisted of at least a dozen clans, would send four emissaries from a single family. More likely, they merely used the surname of the ryu's most powerful clan as an alias to hide their true identities and ranks.

Kiku bowed her head in respectful greeting, but did not lower her face to the floor, confirming Hiro's suspicion that she was of samurai birth. He wondered why she insulted Hanzō by wearing commoner's clothes to a formal feast.

The bald shinobi—Fuyu—sneered at Hanzō. "How convenient that your best assassin happened to arrive the same day we did."

"Actually," Hanzō replied with a tight-lipped smile, "Hiro is Iga's second-best assassin."

Fuyu scowled, but the woman across the table spoke before he could respond.

"At least Hattori Hiro is his real name." Neko narrowed her eyes at the bald shinobi. "Can you say the same, *Koga* Fuyu?"

"Neko!" Hanzō bent his head toward Fuyu. "Please accept my apology. I invited Hiro and Neko—two of my best operatives—as a show of respect for your delegation. You are my personal guests in Iga, as safe in this village as you are in Koga Province, if not more so. Now, let us begin the feast."

Hiro's grandmother bowed from the doorway. "We will serve the first course at once."

Hiro and Father Mateo approached the table as the door slid shut behind them.

Neko indicated the cushion next to Hanzō. "Our foreign guest should take the place of honor."

She met Hiro's eyes, and the scars on his shoulder burned beneath his robe. The pain was imagined, though the fire in the woman's eyes was not, and Hiro wasn't certain which one caused him more discomfort.

As Father Mateo took his place beside Hanzō, Hiro settled beside the priest, uncomfortably aware that his position placed him in the middle of the table, hampering his ability to rise and draw a blade.

Worse, it seated him next to Neko. The scent of her jasmine hair oil sent a rush of heat through his body, which once again reacted to her against his will.

She gave him a sideways glance, but he looked away.

"Thank you for accepting my invitation," Hanzō told Yajiro. "Treaty negotiations will begin tomorrow morning—"

"Koga has not agreed to a treaty," Fuyu interrupted. "We know you only invited us here to steal our independence. Do not think we will fall for your verbal tricks!"

CHAPTER 3

"Fuyu, be silent!" Yajiro rested his hand on his stomach. "Do not make me apologize for your behavior at a welcome feast."

The door slid open, revealing Hiro's grandmother, along with a slender teenage girl who Hiro didn't recognize. The girl wore dark blue trousers and a tunic, like a servant—but there were no servants in Iga village. More likely, the girl was training to become a female assassin—a *kunoichi*.

Hiro wondered what prompted Akiko to take a new apprentice, since his grandmother had retired from teaching several years before.

The women carried lacquered trays with plates of sashimi beautifully garnished with thin-cut vegetables in the shape of flowers. Each plate's garnish differed from the others, to better display the creator's skills.

The women moved along the sides of the table on their knees, serving the guests in order of rank. Akiko served the Koga emissaries, starting with Yajiro, while her apprentice set plates in front of Hanzō and the Iga side of the table. The girl focused on her tray with intensity, never raising her face or looking directly at anyone in the room. When placing a plate in front of Father Mateo, she started visibly, almost dropping the dish at the sight of his pale, scarred hands. Fortunately, she recovered the plate without spilling and set it carefully before the priest. She bowed her forehead to the floor, as if in silent apology, before following Akiko from the room.

Hanzō gestured to the plates. "Please enjoy a selection of Iga's delicacies."

Father Mateo dipped his head in momentary, silent prayer and raised his chopsticks to his plate. "This looks delicious."

Koga Toshi nodded agreement. "Thank you, Hattori-*sama*, for your generous welcome."

The comment drew a disapproving glance from Fuyu.

Yajiro sampled a piece of the garnish. Hiro followed suit. The vegetables tasted crisp but tender, gently steamed and lightly pickled to enhance their flavors.

"Forgive my ignorance," Father Mateo said to Yajiro, "but does your family lead the Koga ryu?"

Before Yajiro could answer, Fuyu set his chopsticks down and hissed, "No single clan controls the Koga ryu."

"The foreigner meant no harm." Hiro's tone held both a warning and a promise. He would not start a fight at the feast, but would gladly teach the Koga shinobi a lesson in manners, should it be required. He glanced at Yajiro, wondering why the delegation's leader did not intervene.

"Foreigners are like children," Neko added. "They are curious, but mean no insult."

Fuyu scowled at the Iga woman. "Even a child knows when to hold his tongue."

"Koga is the name of our home province," Yajiro told Father Mateo, ignoring the others' hostility, "as well as that of my—our—family. The clans who compose the Koga ryu govern the province, and the ryu, by cooperative efforts."

"Thank you," Father Mateo replied in formal Japanese, "and I humbly apologize. I did not intend my question to cause offense."

"Then you should not have asked it," Fuyu said.

In the awkward silence that followed, Hiro focused on his plate. The sashimi tasted cold and pure, like the river from which it came, and the vegetables provided a perfect palate-cleansing complement.

He noted that Kiku and Toshi enjoyed the food without hesitation, but Fuyu sniffed each bite and inspected it carefully before raising it to his mouth. Yajiro ate slowly, though not unwillingly—more as if something had ruined his appetite.

The door slid open. Akiko entered on her knees, balancing a tray that held a set of covered lacquer bowls. Steam escaped around the lids, and Hiro caught the faint but unmistakable scent of fish in savory broth.

His stomach rumbled. Despite its lack of noodles, the dish was one of his personal favorites.

The middle-aged woman who followed Akiko into the room was not an apprentice. She wore a brown kimono embroidered with a pattern of green and silver bamboo stalks. The undersides of the delicate leaves were an almost perfect match to the silver strands in the woman's hair. She kept her face turned toward the floor, but Hiro knew her instantly.

Like all sons, he'd recognize his mother anywhere.

"Koga-*san*, may I present my aunt, Hattori Midori." Hanzō nodded at the woman in the bamboo-patterned kimono. "She prepared the dishes we enjoy tonight."

Hiro's mother set her tray on the floor and executed a lovely bow. "Welcome to Iga. Please enjoy our local specialties."

This time Akiko served the Iga side of the table, while Midori served the visitors, placing new dishes on the table and removing the empty sashimi plates. When finished, they bowed and left the room.

Hanzō raised the lid from his bowl, and everyone else did also.

Hiro inhaled the fragrant steam, which carried a briny tang along with the slightly musty scent of the mushrooms that floated atop the pale broth. A piece of fish sat half submerged in soup, its flesh pale white beneath a paper-thin layer of crispy skin.

They ate in silence. When Hiro raised his bowl to drain the last of the savory broth from the bottom, he looked around the table, noting that everyone but Fuyu had finished the dish.

Yajiro looked down at his empty bowl, made an awkward noise—half burp, half swallow—and vomited his meal across the table.

Chunks of fish and bits of vegetables showered the tabletop and spattered Father Mateo's face and kimono. The acrid odor of bile filled the air.

Fuyu leaned back to avoid the spray as Hanzō jumped to his feet with a cry of disgust and alarm. Yajiro retched and sent a second pungent wave across the table. He clutched his stomach, leaning forward, his face a mask of pain.

A dagger appeared in Fuyu's hand. Hiro reached for the *shuriken* in his sleeve, but stopped as he realized Neko was already on her feet and brandishing a *tanto* of her own.

Kiku pushed Toshi and the bald shinobi aside and crawled to Yajiro. "Toshi, get my box from the guesthouse, now!"

Toshi glanced at Fuyu as if for instructions.

"*Now!*" Kiku commanded.

Toshi started for the door.

Father Mateo slowly wiped his face with his hand, and lowered the hand to his kimono, all the while staring in horror at Yajiro, who continued to retch and heave.

Bile dripped from the emissary's mouth. Strings of saliva dangled from his lips. He trembled, teeth chattering as if from cold, although the room was warm.

Hiro doubted Toshi would return in time, assuming he even remembered the way to the guesthouse.

Yajiro's shaking intensified. Kiku helped him lie on the floor and rolled him onto his side mere moments before his body began to seize. His eyes rolled backward into his head, and his back went rigid. He bucked and shuddered. Foam appeared at the corners of his mouth.

As the seizure passed, Yajiro's lips turned blue. His breathing faltered. He blinked, and his eyes flew wide as he clutched his throat and gasped for air. He tried to speak, but Kiku laid a hand on his chest.

"Lie still." She sounded calm, but Hiro saw the terror in her eyes. "Relax and breathe. Toshi has gone for my medicine box."

Yajiro tried to nod. He struggled to breathe and attempted to roll over.

"Keep him sideways," Hiro warned. "He'll asphyxiate on his back."

Kiku looked over her shoulder, as if surprised.

"He's choking." Hanzō gestured. "Sit him up. We'll pound his back and free the food."

"He isn't choking," Kiku said.

"He's poisoned." Hiro and Kiku spoke together—earning him yet another startled look from the kneeling woman.

Yajiro gagged and moaned as bile trickled from his lips. He clutched his chest again and flopped on the floor like a fish on a riverbank.

A second, stronger seizure arched his back. His body went rigid, and his arms flew away from his chest as if no longer under his control.

Kiku grabbed a pair of chopsticks off the table and forced them between Yajiro's teeth. Fortunately, he didn't bite through them, but as the seizure ended his jaw fell slack and the chopsticks fell to the floor.

Yajiro's breath escaped with a sigh. His eyes went dark and still as the spirit left them.

"No!" Kiku shook her head, and then his body. "Breathe! You have to breathe!"

Father Mateo made the sign of the cross and bowed his head in prayer.

"What is he doing?" Fuyu pointed at the priest. "Stop that!"

"He is praying," Hiro said. "It cannot hurt Yajiro-*san*."

Nothing anyone did could hurt Yajiro any longer.

"No. . . ." Kiku's voice held a strangled plea. Her eyes grew red, though she struggled to control her emotions. She pounded a fist on Yajiro's chest. "You have to breathe!"

"With respect," Hanzō said gently, "you cannot help him. He is dead."

"Dead?" Venom dripped from Fuyu's voice. "He is not merely dead. You murdered him."

CHAPTER 4

Toshi returned, clutching a wooden medicine box. He paused on the threshold, struck by the scene, and hurried to Kiku without a word.

Moments later, Akiko appeared in the doorway. She stopped short at the sight of the dead man and the table in disarray, and then withdrew.

Toshi knelt and extended the box to Kiku. "I brought . . ." He trailed off at the sight of Yajiro's body.

Hiro leaned toward Father Mateo. "We should go."

"Stay where you are!" Fuyu raised his dagger. "No one leaves this room."

"You were right, Fuyu-*san*." Toshi looked up, face stricken. "It was a trap, and now he's dead!"

"Nonsense." Hanzō sounded unusually relaxed for a man whose guest had just collapsed and died at the dinner table. "It wasn't a trap, and it wasn't poison. The way Yajiro-*san* clutched his chest, it's clear his heart gave out."

Hiro looked at the vomit strewn across the table. Half-chewed vegetables, bits of fish, and other slimy fragments floated in a pool of soup and bile. He saw no poisonous roots or leaves, but, even so, he disagreed with Hanzō.

"Yajiro's heart was healthy," Kiku said. "He showed no weakness on the journey."

Fuyu gave the woman a look that Hiro couldn't read, but the glare she returned required no translation.

"Lack of an obvious weakness tells us nothing," Neko countered, "as shinobi don't complain of minor pains."

Kiku leaned over the table and inspected the vomit, nudging the chunks around with the end of a chopstick. She poked at a slimy leaf. "What did your people use to prepare the garnishes?"

"Vegetables and edible flowers," Hanzō replied, still calm. "My relatives prepared this feast. I assure you, you will find no poison here."

Hiro noted the response did not exactly deny the use of poison.

"Koga-*san* did not look well," Father Mateo said. "I saw him sweating."

Hiro gave the priest a warning look.

"You murdered him!" Fuyu shook his knife at Hanzō. "I demand immediate vengeance!"

Neko leaped across the table and pressed her dagger to Fuyu's throat. "No one threatens Hattori Hanzō! As he said, there was no murder. Clearly, your companion's heart was weak."

"I will tell you only once: withdraw that blade." Kiku had risen up on her knees, and the point of her eight-inch tanto rested against the other woman's ribs.

Neko narrowed her eyes as if evaluating Kiku's fortitude.

At that unfortunate moment, Toshi coughed.

Neko jumped away from Fuyu, slashing her dagger down toward Kiku's neck. The Koga woman somersaulted backward, barely avoiding the lethal strike.

Hiro jumped over the table, knocking Neko to the floor so she could not assassinate the Koga woman. He felt the rush of air as Fuyu's dagger passed above his head.

As he landed on top of Neko, Hiro pinned her hands to the tatami and rested a knee atop her chest. She thrashed like a viper. Behind them, angry shouting filled the room.

Expecting a blade in his back at any moment, Hiro tried to strip the knife from Neko's hand. Suddenly, she shifted her weight and pitched her hips toward the ceiling. He counterbalanced—awkwardly, and barely fast enough to hold her down.

"Lie still," he hissed through gritted teeth.

She smiled. "That's not what you said the last time."

Against his will, his mind returned to that night—and the sight of Neko, naked, covered in his blood.

She bucked again and shoved him hard, rolling out from beneath him as he fell, off-balance, to his side.

Neko rose to her hands and knees, still in possession of her knife.

"*Enough!*" Hanzō's furious shout rang out above the chorus of angry voices.

Hiro stood up cautiously and backed against the wall.

The Iga commander glared at Neko, face flushed angry red. "You shame yourself, and the Iga ryu, fighting on the floor like a wild beast!" He turned to Hiro. "You as well!"

Neko smoothed the wrinkles from her kimono and executed a graceful bow. "I sincerely apologize, Hattori-*sama*, for obeying your order to protect your life."

Hiro bowed as well. "Thank you for a most unusual evening. Regrettably, Father Mateo and I must go."

Fuyu blocked the exit. "I told you, no one leaves until Yajiro is avenged."

"How, precisely, do you plan to avenge him?" Hiro asked. "Legitimate vengeance would require proof of the killer's identity."

Fuyu pointed his knife at Hanzō. "He poisoned Yajiro!"

Hanzō sighed. "I am not in the habit of murdering guests with whom I wish to negotiate an alliance."

"Even so," Kiku intervened, "he was your guest, which means, by law and custom, you are responsible for his death."

"Whoever killed him is responsible, not me." Hanzō made a dismissive gesture. "Put away your weapons. I want no violence—"

"You began the violence!" Fuyu yelled.

"With respect, and without intending offense," Toshi said softly, looking to the others as if for support, "we must insist on justice."

Neko made a derisive noise. "You'd die before your finger touched the hem of Hanzō's robe. But, if you *insist*, feel free to try."

"Neko!" Hanzō snapped. "The Koga emissaries have the right to ask for justice."

"This has nothing to do with justice," Fuyu said. "Yajiro's murder is an act of war."

CHAPTER 5

"This was not an act of war." Hanzō's voice now held a warning. "We do not know what happened here, and though I do respect your rights, no man threatens me in my own home."

Hiro noted with relief that Father Mateo had backed away from the table, but everyone in the narrow room remained within the reach of several blades.

"If you will listen," Hanzō added, "I would like to offer a solution."

"Your death is the only solution acceptable to me," Fuyu replied.

Hanzō smiled. "Then I fear you will be disappointed."

"Perhaps we could hear his proposal?" Toshi offered.

Fuyu glared at the youth, but Kiku nodded. "I agree. Listening does no further harm."

"You have no right—" Fuyu began.

"I have as much as you have, if not more." Kiku cut him off with force. "I have decided. Let him speak."

Fuyu and Toshi blinked, mouths open, but said nothing more.

"My cousin"—Hanzō gestured to Hiro—"specializes in the investigation of suspicious deaths. With the help of the foreign priest, he has captured a number of murderers in Kyoto."

"Leave us out of this," Hiro began, but Fuyu's derisive laughter drowned his words.

"You expect us to trust an Iga assassin to find the truth?" the bald shinobi scoffed.

"With great respect, I must agree—it is impossible," Toshi said.

Kiku nodded. "An Iga agent cannot conduct an impartial investigation."

"Let the foreigner lead the investigation," Hanzō proposed. "He has no loyalty to Iga."

Hiro opened his mouth to object, but Kiku spoke before he could.

"I would like to discuss the matter with my fellow emissaries—privately."

"Of course." Hanzō started across the room. "We will return when you have reached consensus."

Fuyu stepped away from the door. "Take the foreigner with you."

Hiro waited for Hanzō and Father Mateo to leave, and then backed slowly through the door behind them.

"The matter is far too risky, and the politics too complex, for him to investigate." Hiro gestured to Father Mateo, who knelt to his right in Hanzō's private study. The Jesuit's kimono had large damp patches on the front from Akiko's efforts to clean the vomit after they left the feasting room.

Returning his gaze to Hanzō, Hiro continued, "I will search for the killer, if you require it, but the priest will not."

He had no intention of risking the Jesuit's life to solve Yajiro's murder—no matter what Hattori Hanzō said.

"I have given my word, and I will not break it." Hanzō knelt across from the priest, with his back to a decorative alcove. The scroll that hung in the *tokonoma* showed a winter scene of snowy mountains, rendered with expert skill.

"If you didn't want the priest involved, you should not have brought him to Iga." Neko stood to Hanzō's left, on guard and alert even though the four of them were the only ones in the room.

Hiro drew a long, slow breath before responding. "Father Mateo came to Iga at Hanzō's invitation, not my choice, and the ryu has a contractual obligation to keep him safe." He shifted his attention to Hanzō. "Surely you would not want the man who pays to ensure the foreigner's safety learning that you put his life in danger?"

"Do not test my patience." Hanzō glared at Hiro. "My guest has just been murdered on the eve of a vital negotiation."

"As vital as ensuring the ryu's financial future?" Hiro asked. "How many clients will hire us if we risk the lives we are paid to protect?"

"While I appreciate your concern for the clan's well-being," Hanzō replied, "you should worry more about the personal consequences of disobedience."

"Pardon me," Father Mateo said. "I am willing to investigate this murder."

"You are not." Hiro faced the priest. "The facts will reveal that Hanzō, or an Iga assassin acting on his orders, killed Yajiro. Revealing that fact to the Koga delegation will cause the very war that Hanzō allegedly asked them here to prevent."

Hanzō scowled. "*Cousin*, once again you go too far."

"I merely acknowledge the facts," Hiro said. "Either you ordered Yajiro's death, we have a traitor in Iga, or the Koga emissaries executed him themselves. Between those options, which do you find most compelling?"

Father Mateo raised a finger as if in sudden realization. "The messengers who summoned us here from Kyoto mentioned an assassination attempt on Hattori Hanzō. Could that traitor remain at large in Iga?"

Hanzō's scowl deepened. "They should not have revealed that information. However, that assassin is no longer a threat to anyone."

"Perhaps another—" Father Mateo began.

"We have no traitors in Iga," Hanzō declared. "I order you both to investigate the death of Koga Yajiro."

"Gladly," Father Mateo said. "Do you know with certainty that this delegation truly came from the Koga ryu?"

The question struck Hiro as unusually insightful. Although he had no intention of investigating the murder, he decided to let the conversation continue a while longer.

"Last week I received a letter," Hanzō replied, "signed and sealed by the head of the Koga clan. It named the emissaries and described them in detail. This delegation matches that letter, and has no connection to the plot against my life."

"An assumption we will not rely on," Hiro said. "If we investigate."

"You *will* investigate," Hanzō repeated, immovable as the mountains that surrounded Iga village. "I remind you that you swore an oath of loyalty to the Iga ryu."

"I also made an oath to protect the priest." He met his cousin's stare.

"Pardon me," Father Mateo said. "Did no one hear me agree to investigate Yajiro's death?"

"Thank you." Hanzō looked triumphant. "That resolves your conflict."

Despite his concerns, Hiro found the mystery compelling. He had not yet solved the murder of any person whose death he had actually witnessed.

"*If* we do this," he said slowly, "it must be a true investigation. No restrictions, and we tell no lies, no matter what the evidence reveals."

Hanzō nodded. "I expect no less."

Hiro pointed directly at Neko, the gesture rude but intentionally so. "And you will keep her on a leash. No more starting fights or baiting others to attack."

"What happened, Hiro?" She feigned a frown. "You used to be such fun."

"You heard him, Neko." Hanzō didn't hide his amusement. "Stay away from the delegation. You will serve as my personal bodyguard for the remainder of their stay."

Hiro felt an unexpected flicker of jealousy, followed by a rush of hot chagrin. Returning to Iga with Neko present, and his cousin in control, was proving even harder than he expected.

"I told you inviting the Koga here would only end in trouble." Neko tossed her head. "We never needed this alliance, Hanzō. Now we face a war."

"If I want your political insights, I will ask for them." Hanzō waved a hand toward the door. "Leave us. I no longer need you here tonight."

Neko looked Hiro up and down. "I anticipate seeing more of you before the week is over." She crossed to the entrance, bowed, and left the room, closing the door behind her without a sound.

Hiro exhaled audibly. "She hasn't changed at all."

"On the contrary." Hanzō stared at the door. "She's far more lethal than she was before."

CHAPTER 6

Hiro followed Hanzō and Father Mateo back to the feasting room. As he reached the threshold, the sour odors of vomit and decomposing fish assaulted his nose, along with the salty tang of nervous sweat. He breathed through his mouth, but it helped far less than he hoped.

"We have discussed your offer," Fuyu said as Hanzō entered the room. "We have conditions."

"Then you accept my offer?" Hanzō asked.

"I did not say that," Fuyu snapped. "We demand an immediate change of lodging."

"Yajiro-*san* deserves a proper place to rest until we leave for Koga," Kiku said. "The guesthouse serves that purpose well enough—"

"But we will not share a roof with his corpse," Fuyu finished.

"That is acceptable," Hanzō replied. "Yet Iga has only two guesthouses, and the second is currently occupied by Hiro, Father Mateo, and their servant."

"We discussed that issue also," Kiku began, but once again Fuyu interrupted.

"We will not stay in any Iga guesthouse. Your assassins would attack us in the night!"

"Have you an alternative request?" Hanzō sounded remarkably calm, given Fuyu's insulting tone.

Kiku nodded. "We wish to stay in the home of the woman who cooked the welcome feast."

Father Mateo looked startled, but to Hiro the choice made sense.

"They think she poisoned him," he whispered under his breath, in Portuguese. "A killer does not set traps in her own home."

"Speak Japanese!" The dagger appeared in Fuyu's hand again.

Father Mateo raised his hands as Hiro took a half step forward, placing himself between the bald shinobi and the priest.

"We agreed, Fuyu," Kiku warned.

Slowly, the bald shinobi returned his dagger to his sash.

"Do you agree to our first condition?" Fuyu asked. "We stay in the house of the woman who cooked the feast—without her present—and we will kill anyone from Iga who approaches the building without permission."

"I am certain Midori will open her home to you," Hanzō replied.

"Second," Fuyu continued, "we want the killer delivered to us promptly. No delays. Yajiro's body must reach home in time for a proper burial."

"Also acceptable," Hanzō said. "The foreigner will need, at most, three days to find the killer."

The irony of yet another three-day window in which to solve a murder was almost enough to make Hiro believe in gods. It certainly felt like a deity's cruel joke, although, more likely, Hanzō's spies in Kyoto had reported how quickly Hiro and Father Mateo had solved their previous cases.

"Finally . . ." Fuyu raised his chin in challenge. "The foreign priest will stay in the house with us, so we can monitor his progress."

"You mean, so you can hold him hostage," Hiro retorted. "Unacceptable. The Jesuit stays with me."

"I'll do it," Father Mateo murmured in Portuguese.

Fuyu took a step toward Hiro, hand on the hilt of his dagger. "These conditions are not negotiable. If you refuse we will leave at once, and Iga will answer for its act of war."

"I said, I will do it," Father Mateo repeated, louder and in Japanese. He stepped to the side, away from Hiro. "I will stay with the Koga delegation until we find the killer."

"Unless the killer finds you first," Hiro replied in Portuguese. "You cannot risk it."

"Japanese only!" Fuyu snapped. "No conspiring in his foreign tongue!"

Hiro slowly turned to face the Koga shinobi. "I cannot let the foreigner go with you. The Iga ryu was hired to ensure his safe arrival at Yokoseura, and assigned me as his bodyguard. We have already accepted payment. . . ."

"Our terms are not negotiable!" Fuyu repeated. "You cannot—"

"Clearly, Hiro-*san* must stay with us as well," Kiku interrupted.

"I will not share a roof with an Iga assassin," Fuyu objected.

"If you're frightened, you may share a room with Toshi." Kiku shifted her gaze to Hiro. "But be warned: if you attempt to harm us, or do anything suspicious, I will kill you—and the priest as well." She paused as if awaiting his consent.

Despite the danger, Hiro nodded.

"I will also need his help with the investigation," Father Mateo said. "I do not know your customs well, and find your language difficult."

"You do not need to lie about our language to request his aid." Kiku gave Hiro an appraising look. "I expected Iga to insist on a representative. He will do as well as any other."

"Then, it is decided," Hanzō said.

"Not quite," Kiku countered. "Have you a local monastery that follows Pure Land teachings? We must arrange for priests to commence Yajiro's funeral prayers."

"We have, and I will summon a priest in the morning," Hanzō said.

"I will arrange the prayers—alone. It's not a woman's job." Fuyu stared at Kiku as if daring her to argue.

She clenched her jaw but did not reply.

Hiro wondered, once again, about her status within the Koga ryu.

"Shouldn't we move Yajiro-*san* to the guesthouse?" Toshi bit his lip. "Before he . . . stiffens?"

"Excuse me," Father Mateo said, "but I would like to examine the body here, before you move him."

"Absolutely not!" Fuyu exclaimed. "I forbid you to defile his corpse with prodding."

"With apologies, I must insist," the Jesuit added, "but I give you my word, we will not harm your friend."

Hiro didn't believe that Fuyu considered Yajiro a friend any more than the Koga shinobi truly thought examination would defile the corpse.

"I will stay and supervise them," Kiku said, "while you and Toshi take possession of Hattori Midori's home. After they finish their inspection, I will move and wash Yajiro's body—unless, of course, you would rather handle his corpse yourself."

"That part *is* a woman's job." Fuyu looked down his nose at Kiku.

"I will show you the way to Midori's home," Hanzō said, "and spread the word, so no one will disturb you."

Fuyu followed the Iga commander from the room, with Toshi on his heels.

CHAPTER 7

As he knelt to examine the body, Hiro remembered Kiku's actions during Yajiro's final moments, her reaction to his death, and her offer to wash the corpse.

He glanced at her. "You knew him well."

"I knew Yajiro for many years." She knelt beside Hiro. "I cannot say I truly knew him well."

Father Mateo regarded her earnestly. "I am sorry for your loss."

"The loss is his family's," Kiku replied, "and that of the Koga ryu. I accept your sentiments on their behalf."

Yajiro's empty, red-rimmed eyes had already begun to dry and lose their luster. The edges of his lips and the tips of his fingers showed a hint of dark discoloration.

Hiro leaned over the corpse and inhaled carefully, fighting the urge to cough at the stench of fishy vomit flooding up his sensitive nose. He noted only a trace of voided bowels, and no scent of any poison he could recognize.

"What did Yajiro-*san* eat today?" he asked.

"Essentially nothing," Kiku said. "He didn't like the food at inns, and refused the morning meal completely."

Father Mateo looked at the body. "Perhaps a sign of illness?"

Kiku shook her head. "He seemed unusually well today."

"Unusually?" Hiro repeated.

"Eager to arrive in Iga." Kiku's cheeks flushed pink, though her expression did not change. "Why does it matter what he ate? This is the meal that killed him."

"He may have ingested the poison before this evening," Father Mateo suggested. "Earlier today, or even yesterday."

"Unlikely." Hiro stared at the corpse. "He would have shown more symptoms if the poisoning did not occur today."

"You know a great deal about poisons," Kiku said pointedly.

"It isn't exclusively a woman's art." Hiro bent over the table to examine the vomit, trying to ignore the sour stench that rose from the slimy pools.

"Are we certain it was poison?" Father Mateo asked. "Yajiro-*san* looked pale and sweated profusely during dinner, both of which are signs of a weakened heart."

"The importance of this occasion made him nervous," Kiku said. "His heart was fine."

"Yajiro-*san* consumed no food or drink at all before this evening?" Hiro found that difficult to believe.

"Nothing . . ." Kiku's expression darkened. "He drank the tea and ate the welcome cakes Hattori-*sama* sent to the guesthouse when we arrived in Iga."

"Did the rest of you consume them also?" Hiro asked.

"Fuyu said the cakes were probably poisoned."

Hiro noted the nonresponsive answer, but let it pass. "Yajiro-*san* ate nothing else today? You're certain?"

"I was not beside him every minute." Kiku's tone acquired a hostile edge. "I recommend you focus on the contents of this feast."

"Rapidly acting poisons taste too bitter to conceal in sashimi or a simple broth." Hiro gestured to the table. "Nothing in this feast would mask them."

"Moreover," Father Mateo said, "every plate appeared the same. How could a killer have ensured the proper person got the poisoned bowl?"

Hiro didn't mention the elaborate garnishes on the sashimi, any one of which could easily mark a poisoned plate.

"A simple task for a poisoner," Kiku said. "Especially if she served the meal."

Hiro stood up. "The women who served tonight would not have done this."

"Not even if Hattori Hanzō ordered them to do it?" Kiku's words hung heavily in the air.

"We have learned all we can from the body," Hiro said. "It's time to go."

"May we help you move Yajiro to the guesthouse?" Father Mateo asked.

"Thank you, but while you were gone Hattori Akiko offered to summon men who have experience moving the dead in accordance with Buddhist custom. I prefer to wait for their assistance."

The door slid open, revealing Akiko.

Hiro suspected she had been listening outside the room since Hanzō left.

"Forgive my intrusion." The elderly woman bowed. "The men have arrived, whenever you are ready."

"Please show them in." Kiku turned to Hiro and the priest. "If you have finished, you may go."

"I can't believe the Koga delegation chose your mother's home." Father Mateo raised his lantern to illuminate the road before them as they passed through the center of Iga village. "How could they believe it safe, if they think she tried to kill them?"

Hiro eyed the moonlit landscape as he thought about the Jesuit's question.

Dense forest covered the land to the north of the road. To the south, segmented rice fields spread across the gently rolling landscape. Narrow berms of piled dirt made wavy paths between the fields, their patterns broken here and there by thatch-roofed houses rising from a patch of higher ground. Curls of smoke rose lazily from several of the village chimneys, sending the perfume of wood smoke wafting through the night.

Hiro inhaled the chilly air, spicy with the scent of pine, the musk of smoke, and traces of a grassy sweetness from the empty rice fields spreading out beyond the road. Only stubble filled them now, the harvest finished several weeks ago.

"It makes no sense," the priest repeated. "I would never choose Midori's home."

"I would have," Hiro said, "in their position."

"Truly?"

"Killers don't set traps in their own houses," Hiro explained again. "Not unless they know you're coming, anyway."

"Do you believe Midori poisoned Yajiro? And where will she stay now?"

Relieved the Jesuit's second question let him ignore the first one, Hiro answered, "Probably with Neko. She's the daughter Mother always wanted."

"Is that jealousy I hear?"

Frustration blossomed in Hiro's chest at the priest's amused response. Forcing it away, he changed the subject. "Hopefully we'll arrive in time to claim the room I shared with my brothers when I lived in Iga."

He turned onto a narrow path that led north, into the trees. Though wide enough for a pair of people to walk abreast, they would have to separate if anyone approached from the other direction.

Father Mateo raised the lantern higher. "Doesn't your mother live in the village?"

"The forest is part of the village," Hiro said. "My mother does not work a farm."

The path wound in and out among the trees. Although the darkness hid them, Hiro knew that houses lurked among the pines.

"Are the farmers also shinobi?" Father Mateo asked.

"Everyone in Iga is shinobi," Hiro answered. "Some tend farms between their missions; others lack the skills to fight, and farm to feed the clan. Rank and skill, as well as birth, determine a person's role within the ryu."

"Does your mother cook for Hanzō all the time, or just tonight?"

Hiro laughed. "My mother is among the highest-ranking members of the Iga ryu."

"Then why—"

Hiro pointed to the glow of a tall stone lantern, just now visible through the trees. "My mother's house is there."

He hurried toward his childhood home, hoping the priest would not renew the question.

CHAPTER 8

Father Mateo followed Hiro through the forest. "Why would Hanzō ask your mother to act as a servant, if she has rank within the Iga ryu?"

Hiro frowned. He should have known the diversion wouldn't work. "Because he trusts her to protect his interests—and his guests."

Or poison them, depending on the plan, he added silently, though he doubted Midori would have placed his life, or that of the priest, in danger.

"It's not dishonorable then?" the Jesuit asked. "To serve?"

"Members of the Iga ryu are duty bound to follow Hanzō's orders. Refusal, not obedience, brings dishonor."

A surge of emotions flowed through Hiro as the familiar, shadowed form of his childhood home rose up before him, slatted windows glimmering from firelight within. A chest-high lantern shone beside the covered porch, a beacon to his past.

The best, and worst, of who he was had formed inside those cedar walls.

Hiro lowered his voice and switched to Portuguese. "Before we enter, you should know: there isn't room in this house for Ana, and I don't think she's safe here anyway."

"She won't like that," Father Mateo said. "You have to tell her."

Hiro didn't blame the priest for wanting to avoid a confrontation with his aging, cranky housekeeper. He didn't relish the thought of breaking the news to her himself.

Fortunately, he had a plan.

"I'll tell her Midori won't allow a cat inside the house, and ask her to keep Gato at the guesthouse."

"Better you than me." The Jesuit hurried toward the house.

Like many village houses, Midori's lacked a formal entry. Hiro opened the door and stepped directly into the common room.

Father Mateo followed him inside.

A fire blazed in the sunken hearth at the center of the floor. Braziers in the corners filled the room with golden light. Hiro inhaled the familiar smells of clean tatami and cedar planks. The scent of Midori's favorite autumn tea perfumed the air like a peaceful ghost.

Memories haunted the room as well, for the most part equally benign.

Hiro indicated a sliding door to his right, in the southern wall. "That leads to Mother's room."

A paneled door in the wall directly across from the entrance opened with a rattle. Fuyu stepped up into the common room from the kitchen, which sat lower, at ground level.

Hiro noted the bald shinobi wore a sword he had not brought to dinner.

"Why does this house have a kitchen as well as a cooking hearth in the common room?" Fuyu asked.

His entrance through the dirt-floored kitchen explained why Hiro had not seen his sandals by the outer door.

"My father added a separate room for cooking, along with the storeroom and second sleeping chamber, after my younger brother's birth." Hiro crossed the common room to a door in the wall to the left of the entrance. "Father Mateo and I will sleep in here."

Toshi followed Fuyu in from the kitchen.

"I guess that means we sleep in here," the young shinobi commented, "since Kiku said she wants the owner's room."

"Unacceptable," Fuyu snapped. "As visitors to Iga, we should get the private rooms. Hattori Hiro and the priest can sleep beside the hearth."

Hiro decided not to point out that Father Mateo was also a guest in Iga. "The priest and I will gladly sleep in the common room. I merely thought you would object to an Iga assassin blocking your route to the house's only exits."

Fuyu glanced at the entry door. "I've changed my mind. Toshi and I will sleep beside the hearth. You and the priest will use the room without an exit."

"As you wish." Hiro opened the door and stepped into his childhood room.

The six-mat chamber seemed unchanged in the years since he left for Kyoto. Clean tatami covered the floor. A futon chest sat opposite the entrance, under a slatted window covered with oiled paper. Next to the chest stood a wooden cabinet that doubtless held his old kimono, along with those of his younger brother, Kazu.

Father Mateo followed Hiro into the room and stopped in front of the decorative alcove in the wall to the left of the door. The priest examined the scroll displayed in the tokonoma: a monochromatic landscape showing a set of distant, snow-capped mountains.

The Jesuit stared at the painting. "That looks like the one in Hanzō's study."

"Indeed." Hiro nodded, impressed by the priest's discernment. "My father painted both."

"He was an artist?"

Hiro smiled. "Among other things."

"That reminds me. I thought Hanzō would be older."

Hiro couldn't see the connection, but humored the Jesuit's inquiry. "Hanzō's father was the older brother, but my father married first."

A swirl of chilly air flowed through the room as someone entered the house.

"What are you doing here?" Fuyu's demand carried clearly through the open door.

Hiro stepped back into the doorway just as Midori entered the house with Ana, the Jesuit's housekeeper, behind her.

"I came to retrieve my belongings," Midori said, "and to show the foreigner's maid the way."

"Show her back to wherever she came from," Fuyu ordered, "and be grateful we don't kill you both for entering this house without permission."

Hiro bowed from the doorway in an exaggerated show of respect. "Thank you, Mother, for allowing the Koga shinobi to use your home."

Midori returned the bow with a look of annoyance, reminding Hiro of a similar backhanded act of politeness he had used to humiliate his brothers many years before.

"Beware the arrogance of pointed manners," Midori had warned the six-year-old Hiro. *"In shaming your brothers, you shame yourself as well."*

He felt his cheeks grow warm, but reminded himself that, on this occasion, his was not the worst behavior in the room.

Midori's attention had shifted back to Fuyu. "I gladly surrendered my home for your use, and will comply with your demands, but need to retrieve some personal items in order to stay away for the duration of your visit. You may watch as I retrieve them, if you wish."

Fuyu flung a hand toward Toshi. "List the items you require. He will fetch them for you."

"This is still my mother's home." Hiro felt his patience with the bald shinobi wearing thin. "I overlooked your rude behavior at the feast, because defense of Hattori Hanzō's honor does not fall to me. Insult my mother again, and you will answer to my blade."

Fuyu's hand dropped to the hilt of his sword.

Midori caught Hiro's eye, glanced at the floor, and raised her eyes again with a silent but unmistakable message: *Don't you dare get blood on my tatami.*

Thankfully, Toshi broke the silence. "We apologize for the insult, Hattori-*san*." He bowed. "Please gather what you need, and I will watch."

Hiro expected Fuyu to argue, but the surly shinobi had transferred his attention to Ana.

"What about her? We have no room for servants here."

"Please, allow me to handle this," Father Mateo called. "Ana, may I speak with you alone?"

Hiro stepped back into the sleeping chamber, and Ana joined them a moment later.

CHAPTER 9

As Hiro closed the chamber door, the Jesuit gave him a pleading smile, clearly hoping for help . . . or rescue.

"Hm." Ana turned and fixed an angry glare on Hiro. "Not three hours we've been in Iga, and already you're mixed up in another murder!"

Few commoners would risk their lives by castigating a samurai, but age and position made Ana act more like Hiro's relative than the Jesuit's servant.

For the second time in less than ten minutes, Hiro felt his cheeks grow warm.

"Don't worry, Ana," Father Mateo said. "We are in no danger. Please, return to the guesthouse and enjoy yourself for a couple of days. You worked so hard in Kyoto. You've earned a rest."

"Rest?" Her face contorted as if the priest had ordered her to leap into the nearest gorge. "I've no intention of lying around all day like a spoiled teahouse girl."

Hiro stifled a smile at the thought of ancient, wrinkled Ana in an entertainer's silken robes. At least, he thought he stifled it—her scowl suggested otherwise.

"Hm," she grumbled.

"Please, Ana," Father Mateo repeated. "I cannot permit you to sleep in the kitchen, and all of the other rooms in the house are taken."

The door to the common room slid open. Midori stood on the threshold, carrying a lumpy quilt that apparently held a number of other objects.

"Please forgive my interruption. I will gladly escort the housekeeper back to the guesthouse, if you do not wish for her to stay. She is also welcome to sleep at Neko's house, with me."

Hiro found the invitation strange, and a bit suspicious. "Thank you, Mother, but Ana will stay at the guesthouse. I will escort her back myself when we finish here."

Surprisingly, Ana did not argue. Hiro wondered whether the housekeeper did not trust Midori or merely wanted her to leave so Ana could renew the debate about the guesthouse.

Midori nodded. "Please use anything in the house or storeroom that you wish." She turned to Toshi, who stood behind her in the common room. "The same applies to your delegation."

"We have no intention of eating your poisoned food," Fuyu declared, from out of sight.

The front door opened, letting in another swirl of chilly air.

Kiku entered, carrying a cloth-wrapped bundle in her arms. She wore a longbow and a quiver across her back.

She looked around. "Which room is mine?"

Toshi nodded. "That one . . . on the far side of the room."

"*Her* chamber." Fuyu's tone suggested he had pointed to Midori. "As you wished."

Kiku disappeared across the room.

"Please excuse me. I should go." Midori bowed and left the house.

Ana looked reproachfully at Hiro. "I should start my long, cold walk as well."

"It's only for a couple of days." Father Mateo looked and sounded guilty, despite the housekeeper's clear intent to lay her full reproach on Hiro.

"I will return at dawn to make your breakfast." Ana narrowed her eyes at Hiro. "Yours as well, although you don't deserve it."

"I'll walk with you to the guesthouse," Father Mateo said as Hiro followed the housekeeper from the room. "I haven't had my evening walk tonight."

Hiro expected the priest had more in mind than an evening stroll.

The first half of the walk to the guesthouse passed in silence. A waxing moon flooded the path with a silvery glow that eliminated the need for Ana and Father Mateo's lanterns. Even so, Hiro didn't mind the extra light. Until they knew who killed Yajiro, preventing an ambush was a prime concern.

They passed through Iga village with the forest on their right and stubbly rice fields spreading away to the left of the path. Although it rarely saw a horse-drawn cart, the road was broad enough for two such vehicles to pass abreast.

"You are certain she'll be safe alone?" Father Mateo asked in Portuguese. He gestured to the moon to hide his meaning.

"Safer than she is with us," Hiro replied in kind.

"No use plotting to stop me making breakfast," Ana said. "I've no intention of lazing around that guesthouse like a hibernating bear."

The housekeeper spoke no Portuguese, but knew the Jesuit well enough to suspect the reason for his unusual switch to his native tongue.

"The walk to Midori's isn't short," Father Mateo said in Japanese. "You needn't—"

"Shorter than a trip to the Kyoto market." Ana sniffed. "And neither of you can cook a single grain of rice worth eating."

Father Mateo didn't argue. Neither did Hiro. On both points, she had them dead to rights.

CHAPTER 10

Iga's guesthouses sat on the western end of the village, north of the road and near the top of a low, forested hill.

When they reached the proper path, Hiro led the others off the road and through the trees. Towering bamboo grew between the pines and cedars, silvered by the dappled moonlight shining through the canopy. Ordinarily, Hiro loved the silent mountain forest after dark; tonight, he looked over his shoulder almost as often as he watched the path ahead. In his imagination, every shadow hid a blade.

As they approached the guesthouse door, it rattled faintly on its hinges, as if someone touched it from inside.

Hiro froze and raised a hand for silence. Ana and Father Mateo seemed confused, but when he signaled for them to wait, they stopped on the path and asked no questions.

Alone, he crept toward the guesthouse.

The one-room structure had only a single entrance and two slatted windows, one in each of the walls adjacent to the entry door. Neither window opened, and the slats prevented anyone from using them for ingress or egress. Inside the house, a pair of painted wooden screens allowed for semiprivate sleep or storage spaces, but aside from those the guesthouse had no place to hide.

A person lying in wait within would have to attack the moment the door swung open.

Hiro stopped at the edge of the narrow veranda that ran around the house. It lacked the usual roof, and the boards intentionally squeaked, preventing anyone from sneaking up on the building from outside. Earlier that afternoon, Hiro found these architectural details reassuring. Now, he regarded the door as he would a viper.

Once again the paneled door rattled in its frame, though the air was still.

Hiro's heart beat faster. Carefully, he slowed his breathing.

He reached into his sleeve and retrieved a shuriken, grasping the metal star so the points protruded between his fingers. After drawing a preparatory breath, he leaped across the porch, depressed the latch, and threw the door open.

Gato trotted out of the guesthouse, purring, tail high.

A rush of delayed adrenaline shot through Hiro's knees as the black-and-orange tortoiseshell cat rubbed up against his shins with a happy trill. Reversing course, she leaned against his legs, looked up, and mewed.

Hiro peered through the open door, half wishing to spot an assassin in the shadows. Instead, he saw only an empty room, lit by the glow of a brazier and a dying fire in the hearth.

As he bent to pick up the purring cat, he sighed.

"All clear at the guesthouse?" Father Mateo called softly.

Hiro turned as Gato settled in his arms. "All clear."

The Jesuit laughed as he reached the porch. "Not quite the threat you anticipated?"

Hiro extended the cat to the priest. "Perhaps you'd like to hold her?"

"I take it back." Father Mateo raised his hands and stepped away.

"Poor, sweet Gato." Ana swept the creature from Hiro's arms, slipped out of her sandals, and entered the guesthouse. "You're starving, and these men just stand and talk."

Hiro raised an eyebrow at Father Mateo. The Jesuit shrugged.

Ana set the cat by the hearth. "Are you coming in?"

Hiro ducked his head inside and looked around. The brazier's flickering light, though dim, left no significant shadows, and the wooden screens stood flat against the wall. The basket Ana brought from Kyoto sat beside the hearth, but nothing larger than Gato would fit inside it.

Recognizing Hiro's concern, Ana walked to the only piece of furniture in the room, a wooden chest designed for holding quilts and futons. She lifted the lid, revealing a pile of bedding. The elderly housekeeper made a fist and thumped the quilts with a vigor that belied her age.

She turned. "No uninvited guests in here."

"Except for the moth," Hiro added, as a small, winged insect flew in through the door, attracted by the light.

"Last one of the season." Ana watched the creature flutter silently across the room. "And even this one won't last long."

Gato executed a spectacular leap and struck the hapless moth to the floor. She fell on top of the creature, sniffed it once, and swallowed it alive.

"Does she do that often?" Father Mateo didn't spend much time with the cat, because she made him sneeze.

"She's an excellent hunter." Ana bent down and ran a hand over Gato's black-and-orange fur. The cat arched up and purred.

"Thank you for watching Gato while we're staying at Midori's," Hiro said.

"Hm." The housekeeper's smile faded as she glanced at Father Mateo and then back to Hiro. "I expect the same of you, Hattori-*san*."

Father Mateo shivered as he walked back through the village at Hiro's side. "Iga feels colder than Kyoto."

"Fewer buildings and higher altitude," Hiro said. "We'll find you a warmer kimono in the morning."

"At least Akiko-*san* managed to get this one passably clean." The Jesuit paused. "I wonder what happened to the clothes we left in Kyoto. Father Vilela promised to watch the house. . . ."

Hiro shrugged. The facts surrounding their departure from the Japanese capital could easily prevent the Jesuit leader from carrying out that promise. However, Hiro saw no point in making an issue of it at the moment.

A short time later, Father Mateo said, "Something bothers me about this murder."

Hiro bit his lip to stifle his initial response.

"The name 'Hattori Hanzō' is known, and feared, throughout Japan," the Jesuit continued. "His power in Iga is said to be absolute. Shouldn't he have known, or at least suspected, someone planned to murder Koga Yajiro?"

"I believe I mentioned that very issue, or something close to it, before we agreed to investigate."

"Also, he didn't seem alarmed by Yajiro's death," the Jesuit added.

"We cannot judge what Hanzō knew, or did not know, by his outward reaction," Hiro said. "For shinobi, as for samurai, revealing emotion is a sign of weakness."

"But you agree it's strange he had no warning of the plot against Yajiro?"

"He would not have needed warning if he was involved," Hiro replied.

"Do you think he was?"

"I think," Hiro said, "that I know better than to trust assumptions. They get people killed."

"Then Hattori Hanzō is a suspect." Father Mateo nodded.

"One of several." Hiro slowed his pace as they left the road and started north on the path that led to Midori's home. "Including possible traitors within Iga or in the Koga delegation."

"A traitor in Iga makes more sense," the Jesuit said. "All of the ambassadors are members of the Koga clan."

"As Neko pointed out at dinner, Koga would not send four emissaries from a single clan. More likely, everyone but Koga Yajiro is merely using the surname as an alias."

"Why 'everyone but Yajiro'?" the Jesuit asked.

"The head of a delegation normally comes from the most influential family. The Koga do not rule the ryu, but they are its strongest clan."

"Why would the others want to kill him?"

"That is why we need an investigation." Hiro regarded the glowing windows of his mother's house, ahead through the trees. "Until we know for certain . . . don't trust anyone."

CHAPTER 11

Hiro entered Midori's house to find Toshi and Fuyu laying out futons on the floor of the common room.

Toshi looked up as Father Mateo followed Hiro through the door. "We found these in the storeroom—"

"You don't need to explain to him," Fuyu interrupted. "We can use whatever we want."

Toshi ducked his head as a flush of embarrassment colored his cheeks.

Hiro felt a rush of compassion for the younger man. "You are welcome to them. Please excuse us, we should sleep as well." Halfway to his room, he added, "The foreigner's housekeeper will return in the morning, to cook and clean the house."

"Not without permission," Fuyu said. "We made that clear."

Hiro turned to face the bald shinobi. "Are you afraid of an elderly woman?"

"You can't fool me." Fuyu sneered. "You think I'll give permission so I will not seem afraid."

Hiro shrugged. "If you would rather clean the house yourself, it's fine with me."

"Only the housekeeper," Fuyu said, "and she leaves when she's not working."

"Understood." Hiro followed Father Mateo into their room and closed the door.

The Jesuit used the coals from his lantern to light the brazier near the door, as Hiro crossed the room and lifted the lid of the futon chest.

"Lay this out by the window." Hiro handed the priest a narrow mattress and a quilt. "I'll sleep by the door."

"In case of attack?" The Jesuit looked at the sliding panel as if expecting someone to burst through it.

Hiro removed a second futon from the chest and didn't answer.

As they laid the mattresses on the floor and spread the quilts on top, Father Mateo whispered, "If there is a traitor in Iga, how will we identify him?"

"Identify *her*, more likely," Hiro whispered back. "Hanzō aside, the logical Iga suspects are all female."

"You mean Neko?" Father Mateo asked.

"Neko, Akiko, and Midori. All experienced assassins, though I doubt my mother or Akiko would kill an emissary except on Hanzō's orders."

"Making Neko our primary suspect?"

"Unless Hanzō is involved." Hiro raised his quilt and slipped beneath it, fully clothed. "We need to examine the evidence and use the facts to reveal the truth, just as we do with every investigation. For tonight, let's get some rest. Today was long. Tomorrow will be worse."

He closed his eyes and exhaled softly, clearing the tension from his muscles. The rustle of a quilt across the room indicated that Father Mateo had also decided to sleep in his clothing. Hiro approved, given the chill in the air and the Koga shinobi in the adjacent room.

He had almost fallen asleep when Father Mateo whispered. "You named the cat for her, didn't you? *Gato* and *Neko* . . . they have the same meaning."

Hiro didn't answer.

"I know you're awake," the Jesuit added. "Your breathing gives you away."

"Gato's name has nothing to do with her."

"You loved her, didn't you?" Father Mateo whispered. "Do you still?"

"We are not having this conversation." Hiro rolled onto his side, away from the priest.

"Back in Kyoto, you didn't seem happy to hear her name, and the way you fought with her tonight . . ."

"Perhaps you didn't hear me say 'We are not having this conversation.'"

Across the room, the other futon rustled as the priest sat up.

"I'm not just idly curious. Your relationship with her could impact our investigation, especially if you're not honest with yourself about your feelings."

"I have no relationship with Neko," Hiro growled, "and no intention of talking about my feelings."

"Fine." The futon shifted again. "Don't tell me what happened. I'll ask your mother tomorrow."

Hiro sat up. "You will not."

"You're not the first man to love a woman who didn't love him back, you know."

"That's not what happened."

"Then tell me the truth." Father Mateo sat up again and folded his hands in his lap like a child waiting to hear a bedtime story.

"Fine. But only so you understand this has no impact on the investigation—and no interrupting me with questions."

Memories swirled in Hiro's mind like a swarm of angry bees. He'd tried to avoid them for most of a decade, yet the moment he set them free they flooded back as painfully as if they happened only days before.

"Neko and I grew up together. Each of us wanted to become the best assassin Iga ever trained. As children, we were rivals, but as we aged—"

"You fell in love with her," Father Mateo said, "but she didn't return your affections."

"Actually, she did." Suddenly, Hiro felt an inexplicable need to share the entire story. He found himself continuing like one of the Jesuit's Christian converts, confessing his sins in the hope of finding peace. "And you are correct, I loved her also. During our final year of training we were inseparable, day and night."

"I don't need *all* the details," Father Mateo whispered.

Hiro ignored him. "When I was seventeen, Mother told me in confidence that Hanzō—not my cousin, but his father, who was then commanding the Iga ryu—believed I could become the best shinobi Iga ever trained. Later that day, I shared the news with Neko. Her mother was away from the village—her father had died the year before—and she invited me to her house that night, alone, to celebrate the news."

"I really don't need—"

"Let me finish," Hiro insisted. "You will understand."

Father Mateo looked dubious, but nodded.

"That night, when everyone else was asleep, I sneaked out of the house and went to Neko's. She opened the door wearing only a thin kimono, which she dropped to the floor the moment I came inside.

"She led me to a futon by the hearth and helped remove my clothes. I lay down beside her . . . and suddenly felt a burning in my shoulder and my thigh. When I looked down, I was covered in blood. She had hidden a set of *neko-te* beneath the futon, lured me in, and used the claws to cut me."

"The scars on your shoulder . . ." Father Mateo's eyes went wide.

"I have a matching set on my inner thigh." Hiro clenched his fist. "Had she been anyone else, I would have snapped her neck."

"Why did she do it?"

"In her words: to prove who truly was the best in Iga. Worse, the moment she said it, Hanzō and Mother stepped out from behind a screen at the edge of the room."

"Your mother?" Father Mateo sounded shocked, but also confused. "Which Hanzō?"

Hiro sighed. "Both of them—my cousin *and* his father. Neko set me up."

"But why was your mother there? And why your cousin, if he wasn't in command?"

"Hanzō is a title," Hiro said, "not just a name, and at that time my cousin was in training to take over both his father's name and control of the Iga ryu. As one of Iga's senior captains, and Neko's main instructor, Mother insisted on being present to ensure the test was fair."

"She didn't try to stop it? Or to warn you?"

"Hanzō commanded her not to," Hiro said. "Neko had gone to him in secret and made a serious accusation—that I was vulnerable. He had to know the truth."

Father Mateo frowned, as if struggling to understand.

Hiro did not find the priest's reaction odd. Even other Japanese people had trouble understanding shinobi ways, and, despite his unusual empathy, the Jesuit came from a very foreign land.

Eventually Father Mateo asked, "What happened then?"

"Fortunately, Hanzō believed me when I swore I would never again let feelings cloud my judgment. He said my scars would suffice as a reminder—and a punishment."

"I meant with Neko."

"Clearly, she got what she wanted. Hanzō considers her Iga's best. The morning after betraying me, she left the village on her first assignment. I never saw her again until tonight." After a moment, Hiro added, "I assure you, I have no feelings for her that will compromise our investigation. And now, if you don't mind, I'm going to sleep."

CHAPTER 12

Unfortunately, sleep refused to come.

The fire in the brazier slowly died, and darkness filled the room. Hours passed as Hiro stared at the rafters, listening to Father Mateo's even breathing.

"*Hiro . . .*"

The whisper came from outside the slatted window.

Hiro pushed the quilt aside, stood up, and crossed the room without a sound.

As he reached for the window frame, he hesitated. The last time he answered this voice by night, his body and his pride had suffered scars.

He looked at Father Mateo, sleeping soundly on the floor, and at the narrow sliding door that separated them from the Koga assassins in the room beyond. He doubted the emissaries meant the Jesuit any harm, whether or not they killed Yajiro.

Even so . . .

He doubled back across the room and lifted the lid of a decorative box sitting on the tokonoma shelf. As he hoped, it still contained the bamboo caltrops he had left there on the morning he departed for Kyoto. He scooped them into his hand, pricking his palm on the sharpened edges in the process.

"*Hiro . . .*" Neko's whisper came again.

Silently, Hiro scattered the caltrops across the doorway, ensuring that Father Mateo would have warning if anyone entered the room. Nobody stepped on a cluster of sharpened bamboo spikes without announcing his presence, one way or another.

Hiro returned to the window, hoping the priest did not wake up and discover him missing—or, worse, have a barefoot encounter with the caltrops on the way to the latrine. Still, the risks of leaving Father Mateo unattended paled beside the prospect of a conversation—or, perhaps, a confrontation—many years past due.

He flipped a hidden latch beneath the slatted window frame, which pivoted open on silent, well-oiled hinges. Slipping out, he quickly pushed the window closed, securing it carefully while ensuring the lock did not engage completely.

Neko waited near the window, just beyond his reach. Moonlight washed the color from her cheeks and shimmered on her long, dark hair. She beckoned him to follow and started north into the forest. Her silence reminded Hiro of *yuki-onna*, the legendary spirit of snow that took the form of a beautiful woman.

Like the spirit, Neko's intentions were impossible to read.

Hiro noted that his sandals sat on the ground beneath the window. Neko must have brought them from the porch, which meant she knew he would answer her summons. Overriding his distaste for predictable actions, Hiro slipped on the sandals and followed her through the trees.

Neko carried no lantern but moved with confidence through the forest, using only the speckled moonlight that filtered downward through the branches. The muffled crunch of her footsteps had a light, irregular quality, more like a harmless forest creature than a human on the move.

Hiro reached into his sleeve and gripped his shuriken, doubly glad he hadn't removed the weapon before his attempt to sleep. The decision to follow Neko seemed increasingly foolish the farther they walked, but turning back would make him look afraid.

Eventually Neko left the trees and entered a clearing. A wooden bathhouse sat nearby, at the edge of a swiftly flowing river. Iga's only public bath stood on a raised foundation, with steps leading up to the entrance. Carved stone lanterns stood on either side of the door, but at this hour they were dark and cold. Given the time, the darkened lanterns, and the absence of a paneled *noren* hanging in the entrance, the establishment was clearly closed for the night.

Neko climbed the steps and laid a hand on the bathhouse door.

Hiro stopped walking. "Not a chance."

"Pardon me?" She faced him.

"Whatever you have to tell me, you can say it in the open."

Neko descended the wooden steps and returned to Hiro. A smile flickered across her face. "I wondered where you'd draw the line."

His temper stirred. "Was this a test?"

"No." She bowed from the waist. "It is a most sincere, and overdue, apology."

As she straightened, Hiro realized his mouth had fallen open in shock. He shut it quickly.

"I do not expect forgiveness," she continued. "In your place, I am not certain that I could, or would, forgive, but I sincerely regret my actions, and I do apologize."

Hiro stared at the lock of hair that had fallen across her forehead, mainly because it let him avoid her eyes. Internally, he struggled between the desire to believe her and the knowledge that she wanted him to do precisely that.

"What do you expect me to say?" His words came out more harshly than intended.

"I have no expectations," she replied, as calm as the forest on a winter morning. "I owed you an apology, and now I have delivered it. I know my words cannot change the past, yet I have nothing more than words to offer. They will have to do."

He met her gaze in silence, while inside he burned with anger—not at her, but at his own instinctive urge to raise a hand and brush the hair from her face. He clenched his fist and forced the desire away.

"I asked for you to come here." Neko searched his face. "When Hanzō ordered me to act as a guard for the Koga negotiations, I told him you were the only person I would trust to share the duty."

"Am I supposed to be grateful?"

"I would settle for polite." She tossed her head, clearing the hair from her face. "Did you follow me all this way just to insult me?"

Hiro drew a breath and exhaled slowly, reminding himself that hostility would not find Yajiro's killer. "Forgive me. . . ."

He trailed off, hoping Neko would relieve him of the duty to finish an apology he did not truly feel.

"I understand." She smiled. "You couldn't know what to expect from me. I didn't know what to expect from you, though I hoped. . . . I do regret what happened, Hiro. Had I the chance to live those days again, I would choose differently."

"Why did you wait until midnight to say this? Why lead me out here, and risk that I might not follow?"

"I am better at killing than apologizing," Neko said. "Your mother told me I shouldn't wait, that I needed to talk with you tonight, and I had to time it so you wouldn't bring the priest. I didn't exactly want to say all this in front of him."

Hiro remembered his earlier conversation with the Jesuit. *You and me both.*

"Did he truly help you identify murderers in Kyoto?"

Hiro shrugged. "It was that or listen to him preach."

She laughed—a low, spontaneous sound that triggered an avalanche of memories and a warmth in Hiro's belly that he tried to force away.

He changed the subject. "Do you know who killed Koga Yajiro?"

The laughter died on her lips. "No, but I'm glad it happened. An alliance weakens Iga's position in the coming war among the samurai."

"Allies make us stronger," Hiro countered.

"Incorrect." She shook her head. "Independence is Iga's greatest strength."

"If you believe that trusting others is a sign of weakness, it would seem your choices haven't changed as much as you believe."

Her expression softened. "I do not want to fight with you, especially tonight."

Hiro felt chastised, angry, and confused in equal measure. "I should get back to Midori's house. I must not leave the priest alone too long."

"I hope you find Yajiro's killer," Neko called as he walked away. "Iga does not need an alliance, but neither do we need a war with Koga."

CHAPTER 13

Father Mateo awoke as Hiro returned to the room. "The window opens?" He sat up. "But you told Fuyu—"

"What I wanted him to believe." Hiro shut the frame and secured the latch.

"Have we got an extra quilt?" The Jesuit shivered. "It's cold tonight."

Hiro lifted the lid of the futon chest, retrieved the last of the quilts, and laid it over Father Mateo's knees.

"What about you?" the priest inquired. "We can share it, if there's not another."

"I'm willing to share a room with you." Hiro knelt on his futon. "When it comes to sharing quilts, my preferences differ."

He lay down and closed his eyes.

"Where did you go?" Suspicion weighted Father Mateo's voice. "You wouldn't use the window just to visit the latrine."

"Out for a walk. I couldn't sleep." The answer skirted the edge of Hiro's promise not to lie to the priest, but was also completely true.

In the silence that followed, Hiro reviewed the encounter with Neko in his mind, examining each detail in an attempt to judge her motivation. If honest, her words suggested both remorse and a desire to renew their friendship . . . if not more. He also suspected a trap, but found it difficult to believe that Neko would reuse such an obvious tactic. Then again, attraction was a primary weapon of the kunoichi, and Neko had the skills—and looks—to use it more effectively than most.

Hiro awoke to the smell of steaming rice. His stomach growled.

Daylight glowed through the oiled paper covering the window.

Father Mateo knelt on his futon, head bowed down, hands clasped in prayer. His lips moved slightly, but no sound emerged. The words he spoke were for his god alone.

When he finished his prayer, the Jesuit opened his eyes. "Good morning, Hiro."

"And to you." Hiro stood and stretched to loosen muscles taut from sleeping. Something about his childhood room had lulled him into deeper rest than normal, and that bothered him.

"You could have warned me," the Jesuit said.

Hiro looked at the priest, confused.

Father Mateo gestured to the caltrops scattered by the door. "Was that truly necessary?"

Hiro shrugged. "It seemed a good idea at the time."

"Did you discover anything useful in the night, when you couldn't sleep?"

"No." Hiro thought for a moment. "But this morning, we need to examine the guesthouse where the emissaries received the welcome cakes and tea."

"Surely someone cleared the tray by now."

"Especially if the snacks contained the poison that killed Yajiro," Hiro agreed, "but it doesn't hurt to look."

Father Mateo nodded. "I need a few minutes to finish my morning prayers."

Hiro scooped up the caltrops and returned them to their box. "I'll see about breakfast." He opened the door and almost tripped over Toshi, who lay directly across the doorway, blocking the entrance to the common room.

Hiro nudged the young man with his foot.

Toshi startled awake. "Help! He's killing me!"

Fuyu leaped to his feet beside the hearth.

"No one's killing anyone." Hiro looked down at the young shinobi. "Why are you sleeping across my door?"

"So you can't sneak up on me."

Hiro gave the younger man an ironic look. "It didn't work."

Toshi scrambled to clear the doorway as Fuyu knelt beside the hearth and stirred the coals to life.

"What would you have done if I surprised you in the night?" Hiro asked.

"I would have killed you," Toshi said.

"You'd kill a man for using the latrine?" Hiro closed the door behind him, sighed, and started toward the kitchen. Fuyu's sour temperament, though irritating, seemed more understandable this morning. Training an eager but foolish young shinobi would try the patience of a bodhisattva, and though Fuyu had not identified himself as Toshi's teacher, their relationship seemed clear enough.

Hiro opened the kitchen door to see Ana standing in front of the earthen stove. A pair of pots sat over the fire, sending up coils of steam.

"I made enough for the visitors," the housekeeper said, "if they're willing to eat."

Hiro found Ana's description of the Koga shinobi vaguely amusing. She had no more connection to Iga than the emissaries did.

"We'll cook for ourselves," Fuyu answered from the hearth.

"You may, if you wish," Hiro said, "but you must clean the kitchen when you finish. The foreigner's housekeeper should not have to wash the dishes twice for every meal."

The door to Midori's room slid open, and Kiku entered the common room. She wore a practice tunic over pleated trousers, and her hair hung braided to her waist. "Do I smell rice?"

Fuyu faced her. "We're not eating anything they serve."

Kiku scoffed. "Starve if you wish, but I'm not going to. Iga's cooking carries a risk of harm, but at least it's edible, which is more than I can say for mine." She looked at Hiro. "If the housekeeper made enough to share."

"She did." Hiro paused. "How did you know that Ana returned this morning?"

"I doubted you or the priest could cook." She knelt by the hearth, and Hiro joined her.

Father Mateo entered the common room as Ana poked her head through the kitchen doorway.

"Who is eating?" the housekeeper asked.

Father Mateo seemed confused by Ana's breach of etiquette, but Hiro found it perfectly in character. Back in Kyoto, the housekeeper offered the Jesuit's "visitors" no more respect than she felt they deserved. Her master might not own this house, but Ana's behavior hadn't changed.

"The three of us." Hiro's gesture included Kiku, Father Mateo, and himself.

After Ana served the soup and rice, along with tea, Father Mateo bowed his head and asked his god to bless the food. During the prayer, Hiro caught Kiku's eye and extended his rice bowl, offering to trade. She pantomimed him tasting the food, and when the prayer ended Hiro took a bite from each of his bowls before passing them to her across the hearth.

"Thank you." Kiku handed her bowls to Hiro in return.

"Does she think it might be poisoned?" Father Mateo asked in Portuguese.

Hiro took a mouthful of soup. It tasted strongly of salty miso with a hint of bonito flake.

"Speak Japanese only," Fuyu warned. "We cannot understand your foreign tongue."

"We will speak Portuguese on some occasions," Hiro said. "The foreigner has only a basic grasp of Japanese." *And neither of us plans to let you hear our private conversations.*

"I'm sure the foreigner means no harm," Toshi ventured softly.

Fuyu rounded on the younger man, but Kiku changed the subject. "Have you a plan to find Yajiro's killer? Time is short."

Father Mateo took an enormous bite of rice—an obvious attempt to stall for time. Suspecting Fuyu would object to anyone else's answer, Hiro waited for the priest to finish chewing.

Eventually, Father Mateo swallowed. "I would like to inspect the guesthouse where Yajiro's body lies."

"You examined his corpse last night," Fuyu said. "You do not need to prod his body further."

"We did not *prod* the first time," Father Mateo countered, "and I wish to examine the guesthouse, not the body."

"But Yajiro-*san* was poisoned at the feast." Toshi's forehead wrinkled. "How can the guesthouse help you find his killer?"

"I see no reason not to let them look." Kiku set her rice bowl on the mat. "That is, if you go with them and observe."

"Us?" Fuyu leaned back. "But you—"

"You insisted we allow the investigation." She stood up. "So you can go and supervise."

CHAPTER 14

"You did not want an investigation?" Father Mateo asked.

Kiku shook her head. "It is a futile exercise. It will not bring Yajiro back to life, and the killer will not be punished. Meanwhile, we are heavily outnumbered, lightly armed, and surrounded by those who mean us harm. Toshi and Fuyu wanted this investigation. I did not."

"We will find the killer," Father Mateo said. "I promise you."

"He didn't mean that." Hiro switched to Portuguese. "In Japan, a man who gives his word and fails must offer his life as recompense."

"Then let's not fail," the priest replied in kind.

"I told you—" Fuyu began, but Kiku spoke over him.

"Have you an archery range in Iga?"

Hiro wondered at her behavior. Only a person of significant rank would dare to interrupt so rudely. "South of here, on the eastern end of the village." He gave directions to the place, but added, "I'd be glad to show the way."

"I can find it on my own." Kiku retrieved her bow and quiver from Midori's room and left the house.

The walk to the guesthouse passed in awkward silence. Hiro led the way with Father Mateo at his side. Fuyu and Toshi followed, several steps behind.

"Shouldn't we wait for them to catch us?" Father Mateo whispered. "It seems rude to walk ahead."

"Every time I slow my pace, they slow to match it," Hiro said. "I don't think Fuyu wants a conversation."

An elderly man walked toward them, carrying a load of wood. As he drew close, he turned to his right and left the road, walking across the roughened earth of the rice fields parallel to the path.

"Why did he leave the road?" Father Mateo turned to watch the old man trudging along beneath his heavy burden.

"The Koga delegation threatened to kill anyone who approached without permission," Hiro reminded the priest. "Hanzō doubtless spread the word, and everyone in Iga will obey."

As they approached the guesthouse where Yajiro's body lay, Hiro looked through the trees at the second, smaller house where Ana had spent the night. He wondered whether the housekeeper minded sleeping so close to a corpse. Many women would, but Hiro doubted Ana cared for popular superstitions, and he pitied any ghost that tried to haunt her.

He stopped beside the guesthouse door and bowed while the others removed their shoes and entered. After slipping off his own sandals, he stood in the doorway and surveyed the room.

Clean tatami covered the floor, and a pair of wooden screens blocked off the left rear corner of the space. A sunken hearth provided a place for guests to cook, and metal braziers in two of the corners waited to light the room by night.

A paneled door in the wall across from the entrance stood ajar; Yajiro's body rested on a futon in the center of the narrow room beyond. The emissary lay on his back, hands folded across his stomach as if to hide the stains that streaked his robe.

Father Mateo leaned toward Hiro. "As I thought, they took the tray."

"Shh," Hiro whispered. "Discuss it later."

"Well?" Fuyu asked from the hearth. "Don't you intend to investigate?"

"Did you set those up?" Father Mateo gestured to the wooden screens. The painted panels showed a bamboo grove in winter; snow hung heavy on the leaves and bent the narrow branches toward the ground.

"We set them up to make a place for sleeping," Toshi said.

"Has anything else been moved, or removed, that you remember?" the Jesuit asked.

"The tray." Toshi looked around. "The one that held the tea and cakes. It was here when we left for the feast last night."

"Would you recognize the person who brought the tray, if you saw her—or him—again?" Father Mateo sounded hopeful.

"Of course we would." Fuyu's voice dripped venom. "She is Iga's best assassin."

"Neko brought the tea and cakes?" Hiro asked. "You're certain?"

"In Koga, we don't send assassins to perform a servant's job," Fuyu replied, "unless, of course, they just pretend to serve."

"Perhaps Hattori Hanzō sent her as a sign of respect for Koga," Father Mateo offered.

"Or perhaps she came to kill us," Fuyu said.

The Koga shinobi's clear desire for a fight made Hiro determined to deny him one—at least for the moment. "Which members of your delegation drank the tea and ate the welcome cakes?"

"Yajiro had both tea and cakes. I drank some tea . . ." Toshi gave Fuyu a guilty look and quickly added, ". . . but not much."

"You should have known better," Fuyu scolded. "How could you forget my warning?"

"I inspected the tea before I drank it," Toshi began, but Fuyu cut him off.

"You lack the training to recognize poisoned tea."

"I learned last summer, in Mikawa." Toshi's reply held a hint of frustration, though he covered it admirably.

"On a mission where your instructor died," Fuyu scoffed. "The only thing you could have learned from him was how to fail."

Toshi's face reddened. "I learned enough for Father to send me here."

"As my shadow." Fuyu glared at the younger man. "Do not forget your place." Turning his back on Toshi, Fuyu asked, "Have you seen what you came to see? I need to speak with the monks about Yajiro's ordination. By this hour, they should have arrived in Iga."

"Yajiro wanted to become a monk?" Father Mateo looked at Hiro as if to confirm his understanding.

"Posthumous ordination plays a role in Buddhist funeral rites," Hiro explained. "Whether or not the decedent planned to become a monk in life."

Father Mateo looked at Toshi. "Did Yajiro-*san* seem well on your trip from Koga?"

Hiro approved of the Jesuit's choice to treat the younger man as an equal, especially now that Fuyu had refused to do the same. He half expected the bald shinobi to interrupt and forbid an answer, but Toshi spoke too quickly.

"He had a lot of headaches, and he didn't like the food at inns."

"Irrelevant gripes from a man unaccustomed to inconveniences," Fuyu snapped. "Do not mar his memory with slights."

"I didn't . . ." Toshi caught Fuyu's angry glare and lowered his face. "I humbly apologize. I meant no insult."

"Did he mention specific foods he didn't like to eat?" the Jesuit asked. "Or, perhaps, a food that made him sick?"

"What do you mean?" Toshi looked up.

"Sometimes certain foods, or animals, make people sick. Hiro's cat, for example: if I touch it, I sneeze and my eyes will itch."

"I have seen this illness." Fuyu's forehead furrowed. "A girl in my village died from eating roasted prawns. Her throat swelled closed until she could not breathe. She seized, but did not vomit. . . ."

"I am sorry about her death," the Jesuit said, "and, yes, that is the illness I refer to."

"I do not think this illness killed Yajiro. When he died, it did not look the same." Fuyu pointed at Hiro. "Your relatives poisoned the food, and now you try to trick us with distractions!"

"I'm not the one who suggested an illness," Hiro said calmly, "and I prefer you not accuse my relatives without cause."

"Statements of fact are not accusations." Fuyu took a step toward Hiro. "If you want to solve this crime, interrogate your mother and Neko. They, and Hattori Hanzō, are the only suspects here."

"Enough!" Father Mateo stepped directly into Fuyu's path. "*I* will decide who is a suspect here, and who is not!"

CHAPTER 15

Hiro stared. Fuyu froze, and even Toshi took a shocked step backward.

"You appointed me to act as your representative," Father Mateo said, "and I give you my word, as a servant of the Most High God, that I will discover who murdered Koga Yajiro. As it happens, I do intend to speak with the women who cooked the feast and served your welcome tea. However, I will not tolerate your inappropriate demands. Such behavior dishonors you and shames your clan."

Hiro shifted his weight to the balls of his feet, prepared for an attack.

To his surprise, it didn't come.

"You will report all new information to me immediately," Fuyu ordered. "Especially if it incriminates a member of the Hattori clan."

Without awaiting a response, he started for the door. "I must arrange the prayers for Yajiro. Toshi, come with me."

"But . . . what about them?" The younger man looked from Hiro to Father Mateo. "Will we leave them to investigate alone?"

"Iga shinobi will not speak honestly with us present," Fuyu said. "I do not trust them, and I do not like it, but we have no other choice."

From the guesthouse doorway, Hiro watched Toshi scurry down the path in Fuyu's wake. When the emissaries passed out of earshot, he lowered his voice and said, "We are no longer in Kyoto. Insulting samurai is foolish. Insulting shinobi . . . lethal."

"You didn't seem concerned last night, or this morning, when you defended your family's honor." Father Mateo stepped outside and into his sandals.

"My reputation will stay the hand of any man who knows my name. The same cannot be said of you." Hiro shut the guesthouse door.

"I will try to remember." Father Mateo's tone made no such promise.

Together they started down the sloping path.

"Does this village house the entire Iga ryu?" the Jesuit asked. "It seems so small."

"Iga has many villages," Hiro answered, "scattered throughout the province, both for safety and to hide our numbers."

"All of them answer to Hanzō?"

When Hiro nodded, Father Mateo asked, "Why don't people call him *Daimyō* Hattori?"

"Hanzō is not a samurai lord, although, like me, he is of samurai blood. Also, 'Hanzō' is a pseudonym. In childhood, people called him Masanari."

They reached the road that bisected the village and headed east along it.

Morning sunlight cast a pale glow across the stubbly fields south of the road. Low dirt berms divided the paddies, transforming the land into a tawny quilt. Here and there, the wooden houses rose between the fields like sentinels guarding the landscape.

Hiro inhaled the mingled scents of pine and grasses, with an undertone of sweetness from the rice fields drying in the sun.

The smell of home.

"Hiro, look!" Father Mateo pointed to an empty field just ahead, beside the road.

Inside the stubble-covered field, two young children circled one another like a pair of angry cats. Sunlight glinted off the daggers in their hands.

The children wore long tunics over midnight-colored trousers. Neither one was more than ten years old. The larger boy stood head and shoulders taller than the smaller child, who scowled like a tiger, unafraid, despite the difference in their size.

The big boy lunged. The small one backed away.

"Hiro," the priest repeated, far more urgently, "we have to intervene!"

"No. Wait." He raised a hand to calm the priest.

The larger child advanced again and struck. The small boy backed away.

"He's going to hurt the little one." The Jesuit started forward.

Hiro laid a hand on Father Mateo's arm. "Just watch and see."

The taller boy attacked with fury, but his diminutive opponent dodged his strikes with ease.

"The older one is losing focus," Hiro told the priest. "He's getting angry."

Sure enough, the larger boy began to swing his blade with less precision.

Moments later, when a strike flew wide, the smaller child ducked beneath the larger one's guard and shoved his side. Off-balance, the older boy staggered and fell to the ground with a cry of dismay.

The smaller one stood over him in triumph, dagger high.

"Told you." Hiro smiled at the priest.

Lowering his dagger, the victor extended his unarmed hand and helped the larger boy regain his feet. The children noticed Hiro and Father Mateo watching from the road. They bowed, and held the gesture long enough to show respect.

Hiro nodded and continued walking.

As they passed the children, Father Mateo glanced back over his shoulder. "Shouldn't we tell their parents they were fighting?"

Hiro raised an eyebrow at the priest. "The word is 'training.'"

"With daggers? They're only *children*."

"Blunted daggers." Hiro started up the path that led to Hanzō's home. "In Iga, children start to train as soon as they can walk. It is our way."

"And you approve of this?" Clearly, the Jesuit did not.

Hiro shrugged. "It made me who I am."

A frigid wind swept down the hill, reminding him that Father Mateo needed warmer clothing. His own old winter kimono hung in the cabinet at Midori's, but they would not fit the priest, and Hiro would not grant himself the luxury of warmth while his friend was shivering.

"Why doesn't the Koga ryu have a single leader," Father Mateo asked, "like Iga does?"

Hiro glanced at the priest, appreciating the artful—and deliberate—change of subject. "Koga has always operated by consensus of its member clans. Why, I cannot say."

"Yet some clans have more influence than others, like the Koga?" Father Mateo pulled his thin kimono tightly closed around his neck.

When Hiro nodded, the priest continued, "Unbalanced power often leads to jealousy. Perhaps one of the emissaries wants to start a war."

"Why would Koga want a war?" Hiro had a theory, but wanted to hear the Jesuit's explanation.

"Not all of Koga. . . . War with Iga could allow a lesser clan to seize control of the Koga ryu. Or control of Iga, for that matter."

"I note you mentioned Koga first."

"Not for any particular reason," Father Mateo said, "although you claimed no one in Iga would kill a guest, except at Hanzō's order."

Not Mother or Akiko, Hiro thought.

Father Mateo looked up the hill. "Why are we heading back to Hanzō's? Won't he be busy with Fuyu and the priests?"

"I hope so," Hiro said as they passed the gates, "because Hanzō is not the one we came to see."

CHAPTER 16

The door to the mansion swung open before they knocked, revealing the silent girl who helped at the feast the night before. In daylight, hollows underneath her eyes and shadows on her cheeks revealed malnourishment. Her hair hung down her back in a thin but tightly plaited braid. She stared at Hiro warily, and gasped as she noticed the Jesuit at his side.

Clasping her hands before her, palms together and fingers steepled in a perfect imitation of the Jesuit's Christian prayer pose, she bowed. As she straightened, she made the sign of the cross.

"Are you a Christian?" Father Mateo asked.

The girl's hands fell to her sides. She bit her lip and bowed her head as if suddenly aware of her breach of etiquette.

Hiro took pity on her. "We have come to see Hattori Akiko."

Relief washed over the thin girl's face as his words eliminated the need for either apology or explanation. She bowed again and disappeared into the house, leaving the door ajar.

Since she hadn't asked them to follow, the men remained outside.

"Does that girl seem odd to you?" the Jesuit asked.

"Aside from knowing your Christian symbols?"

"That's not so strange," the priest replied. "The Church has sent a number of missionaries into the hinterlands. I meant—"

Before he could finish, Akiko appeared in the entry. This morning she wore a gray kimono embroidered with a pattern of cascading maple leaves. Her hair was piled atop her head and secured with a set of enameled pins.

Hiro and Father Mateo bowed in greeting.

Akiko nodded. "Hanzō-*kun* just left with the Koga shinobi and a pack of monks."

Father Mateo looked over his shoulder. "We didn't see them on the road."

"They used the other gate. But I don't think you came to talk with Hanzō-*kun*." Without awaiting confirmation, she stepped away from the door. "Please come inside. I'll make us tea."

Hiro and Father Mateo left their sandals by the door and followed Akiko through the building and along a covered walkway that connected the first of the mansion's structures to a second, larger one beyond. Inside the second building, Hiro's grandmother stopped beside a paneled door. She slid it open, revealing a six-mat room.

Fine tatami covered the floor. A kettle hung above the hearth, steaming as if someone had already put the water on for tea. Beside the hearth a small cylindrical canister, a teapot, and a pair of egg-shaped teacups rested on a lacquered wooden tray.

Akiko turned down the hall and called, "Tane . . ."

The silent girl appeared at once.

"Retrieve another teacup from the kitchen for my guests," Akiko said. "We will delay your lesson until later."

Tane bowed to acknowledge the instructions. As she straightened she tapped her chest, clasped her hands together, and shook them as if casting an invisible fishing line. When she finished, she placed her palms together and wiggled her hands from side to side.

Akiko nodded. "Once you bring the cup you may go fishing, but no swimming. It is far too cold today."

Tane's face lit up. She bowed again and started down the hall.

Father Mateo watched her go. "The girl cannot speak?"

"Can't or won't." Akiko crossed to the hearth and knelt beside it. "Either way, she's never said a word. Yet, given her range of gestures, I believe you are correct: Tane is incapable of speech." She motioned to the hearth. "Please, make yourselves comfortable."

"You have never heard the child speak?" Father Mateo knelt across from Akiko, while Hiro placed himself between the Jesuit and the door.

"No one has, since she arrived in Iga several weeks ago." Akiko removed the teapot's lid. "A spy discovered her living alone in a burned-out mountain village near the border. She cannot read or write, but explained to us through gestures that Lord Oda's samurai burned the village and killed her family. She alone survived."

"He murdered an entire village?" Father Mateo's eyes grew wide.

Akiko nodded. "Oda Nobunaga will stop at nothing to control Japan, and he destroys what he cannot control."

"How did she identify the men as Lord Oda's," the Jesuit asked, "if she can't read or write?"

"We showed her the Oda *mon*, and her reaction to the symbol left no doubt." Akiko shifted her gaze to the priest. "You understand this word?"

"Mon?" he repeated. "Yes, I think it means a family crest."

Akiko nodded.

"Tane also recognized that Father Mateo is a Christian priest," Hiro said. "Is she a follower of the foreign god?"

Akiko shook her head. "She hasn't said so. Then again, she has not *said* anything."

"She made the sign of the cross when she saw me," Father Mateo explained. "A holy sign used by adherents of my faith."

"How interesting," Akiko replied. "I will have to ask her where she learned it."

"How did she survive the attack on her village?" Father Mateo asked.

Hiro approved of the question. Tane's survival seemed suspicious, and he hoped the explanation would reveal how a child escaped a fate that spies and assassins had not managed to avoid.

"Her parents trained her to hide when strangers appeared in the village," Akiko said, "a fact that reinforces my suspicion she is permanently mute."

"Why?" Father Mateo sounded puzzled.

"Your foreign companion overflows with questions, Hiro-*kun*." Akiko smiled. "Just like you."

Tane appeared in the doorway, holding a lacquered tray upon which rested a single teacup. She executed a deep and graceful bow, balancing the tray with care; the cup did not slide, or even rattle. Straightening, she entered the room, knelt, and extended the tray to Akiko.

Hiro's grandmother nodded approval and lifted the teacup from the tray. Tane's cheeks flushed crimson in response to the unspoken praise.

"Return the tray to the kitchen," Akiko said, "and you may go."

Tane rose to her feet and departed, bowing once again from the doorway before she disappeared.

Akiko set the teacup slightly apart from the others. "To answer your earlier question, Japanese families often keep disabled relatives out of sight. Hanzō had no knowledge of a mute girl in that village, so her parents hid her well."

"Is muteness shameful in Japan?" Father Mateo asked.

"Ignorant and superstitious people see a curse in every shadow." Akiko opened the wooden canister, and the scent of tea perfumed the air. Slowly, she spooned leaves into the teapot.

"How did the girl reveal her name," Hiro asked, "if she can neither speak nor write?"

"I do not know the name her parents called her." Akiko unhooked the kettle from the chain above the fire and poured a stream of boiling water into the teapot. "I named her Tane upon her arrival, to symbolize her new beginning here."

"*Tane* means 'seed.'" Hiro translated the name into Portuguese.

The Jesuit nodded. "Will you teach her to read and write, Hattori-*san*?"

"Among other things." Akiko returned the kettle to its chain. "She seems intelligent, although she doesn't care much for lessons. She's already a better thief than any child I've ever seen, and she can put a dagger through a squirrel's eye at fifteen paces."

She poured a cup of tea and offered it to Father Mateo.

"Her parents taught her to steal, but not to write?" The priest accepted the cup.

"It sounds to me as if she trained herself." Hiro extended both hands to receive his tea.

"Well deduced." Akiko filled the final cup—the one Tane brought—for herself. "The girl confirmed she had no formal training. What she knows, she learned through observation."

"Did Hanzō ask you to train her?" Hiro could hardly imagine his cousin deciding to have a mute child trained.

"No, he planned to sell her as a servant, in the capital." Akiko raised her teacup. "I refused to permit it. The girl is intelligent, no matter what he thinks."

"You defied his orders?" Father Mateo sounded impressed.

"My grandson may rule Iga, but he does not rule me." She raised her teacup, closed her eyes, and slowly inhaled the steam.

Hiro did the same, appreciating the autumnal tang of *sencha*, stronger and less delicate than the *ichibancha* he used to drink in Kyoto.

Akiko sipped her tea. "To business, then. You came to ask why I poisoned Koga Yajiro."

Father Mateo fumbled his teacup, barely recovering it before it spilled. "You killed Yajiro?"

"Does your friend take everything so literally, Hiro-*kun*?" Akiko smiled. "In fact, I did not kill him, but I helped Midori cook the meal, which makes me look quite guilty."

"What do you know about his death?" Hiro hoped she would tell the truth.

"Only what I saw when I cleaned the room." She sipped from her cup again. "With apologies for such an indelicate topic over tea, it appeared Yajiro died too soon to have been poisoned by the feast. The food we served would not disguise the taste of any toxin strong enough to work so quickly. Not one I would know of, anyway. . . ."

Hiro understood the words Akiko left unspoken. Although a highly proficient assassin, his grandmother did not specialize in poisons.

But Midori and Neko did.

"It was an unusually lovely fish we served," Akiko added. "Most regrettable that he had to die and spoil it."

Father Mateo switched to Portuguese. "How can she be so casual about murder?"

"Killing is as normal in Iga as tea ceremony in Kyoto," Akiko replied in perfectly accented Portuguese, "and we train for it with equal care."

CHAPTER 17

Father Mateo spilled his tea across his brown kimono. "You speak my language?"

"Where do you think my grandson learned it?" Akiko asked, again in Portuguese.

The Jesuit ran a hand through his hair. "I-I thought . . . that is, I didn't think . . ."

"He was a lazy student"—Akiko frowned at Hiro—"but it seems his skills, and accent, have improved with time and practice."

"How . . . where . . . ?" Father Mateo seemed too flustered to compose a sentence.

"How did I learn your language?" Akiko continued in Portuguese. "The first of the foreign traders wanted maids to clean their dwellings—older women who asked no questions and worked long hours for little pay. Many years ago, Hanzō's father sent me to Tanegashima as a servant. I lived among the foreigners for several years, learning both your language and your customs. Once I had acquired the knowledge I needed, I returned to teach the spies of Iga."

"Everyone in Iga knows Portuguese?" the Jesuit asked weakly.

"Hiro and I are the only ones in the village currently who know it." Akiko refilled her teacup, raised it, and inhaled the steam.

"Enough diversions," Hiro said. "What else do you know about Yajiro's murder?"

Akiko switched to Japanese. "I did not kill him, and Tane did not either."

Hiro found it interesting that she mentioned the girl.

"Also," she continued, "as I said before, the dishes we served would not have concealed the taste of a rapid toxin. Someone must have poisoned the emissary before the feast."

Akiko set her teacup on the tray.

"What about the garnishes?" the Jesuit asked. "Pickled vegetables might have hidden a poison's bitter taste."

"Midori made them." Akiko spoke as if this resolved the inquiry, though in Hiro's mind it merely raised another, far less pleasant one. "I inspected every dish myself before we served it. I saw nothing to suggest the food was poisonous or spoiled."

"You checked the dishes for poison?" Father Mateo asked.

"Hanzō ordered me to do so." She folded her hands in her lap. "He said the meal would impact the future of the Iga ryu, and that he wanted to ensure its safety."

Hiro kept his expression carefully neutral. He had no doubt Akiko knew her answer implicated Hanzō. Unfortunately, his grandmother obscured the truth as lethally as Midori measured poisons.

"What do you think about the proposed alliance with the Koga ryu?" Father Mateo asked.

"An interesting question." Akiko smiled. "I do not care, one way or the other."

"You don't care?" the priest repeated.

"I have watched the seasons change for many pleasant years—sixty-nine, when the *sakura* bloom again. The *kami* blessed me with healthy children and grandchildren, and I control my life in ways most women never do. I sit in comfort, drinking tea, while many beg for crumbs. I would rather not die, but when death comes I am ready to see what lies on the other side. So, you see, it truly does not matter whether Iga forms an alliance with the Koga ryu or not."

"But your relatives," Father Mateo said. "Surely you care what happens to them."

"Do you believe in your foreign god?" Akiko asked.

The Jesuit looked confused. "With all my heart."

"Do you believe he can control the fates of men?"

"I know He does."

"And if your god decides a man should die, can you prevent it?" Akiko tilted her head like a mother making an obvious point to a child.

Father Mateo raised a hand. "We still have an obligation to help others when we can."

"But I cannot." Akiko spoke matter-of-factly, as if discussing the weather or a meal. "I am merely an elderly woman. How could I stop a war?"

"By helping us," the Jesuit said. "Can you think of anyone with a motive to kill Yajiro?"

"Your friend asks excellent questions, Hiro-*kun*. Much better than yours."

"A fact which does not matter if you avoid them," Hiro countered.

She shrugged. "I'm just an old woman. What do I know?"

Hiro gave his grandmother a disapproving look.

"Hanzō has wanted this alliance since he learned of the shogun's death last summer," Akiko said. "Only a fool would try to prevent it, and Iga does not harbor fools. None that live long, anyway."

She stood. "I hope you find the answers you need in time to prevent a war."

Taking the hint, the Jesuit rose and bowed. "Thank you for the tea and conversation."

"Before we leave"—Hiro stood—"we left our winter kimono in Kyoto."

Akiko gave Father Mateo an appraising look. "I have something that should fit him. If not, I can let it out. I'll have Tane deliver it to Midori's house this afternoon."

"What about you?" the Jesuit asked Hiro.

"Mother left my old ones in the cabinet, but they'd barely reach your knees."

Akiko started toward the door. "Allow me to escort you out."

"Why didn't you tell me your grandmother spoke Portuguese?" Father Mateo asked as they started down the hill from Hanzō's compound.

Hiro stifled a smile. "It wasn't relevant."

"I might have revealed something confidential . . . or embarrassing."

"I would have stopped you. Probably."

Father Mateo shook his head. "Do you think she told the truth?"

"About the murder?" Hiro waited to answer until they reached the bottom of the hill. "I cannot see a reason she would lie."

"Which doesn't mean you think she told the truth."

"It means I do not know." Hiro considered how best to explain. "My grandmother's oath of loyalty to the Iga ryu predates both Hanzō and his father. By tradition, the oath transferred to Hanzō when he assumed the leader's role, but as far as I know Akiko never actually swore obedience to my cousin."

"She did mention going against his orders, training Tane," Father Mateo said. "Why do you think he let her overrule him?"

"She probably did it privately, so he could claim he changed his mind. As for why he didn't insist . . ." Hiro trailed off. "What do you think it would do to his authority if he ordered his own grandmother to kill herself? Especially if she refused to do it?"

"That would be awkward."

Hiro smiled. "Indeed."

They started east along the road.

Hiro remembered Akiko saying that Hanzō sent his wife and child into the mountains, presumably to keep them safe. That decision seemed suspicious now. He hoped the evidence would prove his cousin had not killed Yajiro, less because he cared for Hanzō than because he didn't want to choose between his oath to Iga and the Jesuit's promise to identify Yajiro's killer.

Were Father Mateo any other man, Hiro's loyalty to his clan would win that battle without question, but his friendship with the priest, and his oath to defend the Jesuit's life, created complications.

Hiro stepped off the road and onto a narrow footpath that led north into the forest.

"This isn't the way to Midori's house," Father Mateo said.

"Correct. It is the way to Neko's."

CHAPTER 18

Neko's home was hidden from view behind a stand of tiny maples, like a tiger waiting for its prey. Although the roof looked newly thatched, the wide veranda, solid, wooden door, and slatted windows looked unchanged since Hiro's childhood.

His hands remembered the splinters in the rafter beams and the prickly thatch atop the roof, where he used to perch in hopes of startling Neko as she left the house. He approached the veranda, lost in memory, and almost failed to notice that only a single pair of sandals sat beside the door.

Almost.

He stopped abruptly. "We should go. Midori isn't—"

The door swung open, revealing Neko. She wore a pair of pleated pants beneath a belted tunic, and her hair hung loose around her face. She smiled.

Hiro's chest grew tight, distracting and frustrating him in equal measure.

Neko bowed. Father Mateo returned the gesture, but Hiro merely nodded.

"Good morning." She gave no indication that she noticed the omitted bow, though Hiro also knew she hadn't missed it. "I didn't expect to see you again so soon, but I'm glad you came."

Father Mateo gave Hiro a look that promised an interrogation later.

"Good morning, Neko." Hiro looked straight ahead, avoiding the Jesuit's eyes. "We wish to see Midori."

"She went home to get some things she forgot last night." Neko stepped away from the door. "Please come inside. I've just made tea."

Father Mateo started forward, but Hiro remained at the edge of the porch. "We do not wish to inconvenience you. We'll wait outside."

"As you wish." Her face retained its pleasant smile, despite the slight.

To Hiro's increased frustration, Neko didn't return to the house or close the door.

After an awkward silence Father Mateo asked, "Do you know what happened to Koga Yajiro?"

"He died," Neko said. "At the welcome feast. I believe you saw it happen."

"I meant, do you know who killed him?" the Jesuit clarified.

"Hanzō would not have relied on poison, and no Iga assassin would dare to kill a guest in Hanzō's home." She shrugged. "Clearly, the Koga emissaries murdered him themselves."

"Or, perhaps, the killer did not act in Hanzō's home," Hiro said. "You didn't mention delivering the welcome tea and cakes to the delegation yesterday afternoon."

"You did not ask, and, as I did not kill Koga Yajiro, it's not relevant. If you want to find the assassin, do not waste your time on me."

"Hiro, what are you doing here?" Midori's voice came from behind them.

Chagrined by his failure to hear her approach, Hiro turned to see his mother carrying a wooden box. For a moment, he mistook it for his own, but as she drew closer he realized it simply had a similar size and shape.

"You went to retrieve your poison box?" he asked.

"Would you leave yours in the hands of Koga assassins?" Midori extended the box to Neko. "Would you put this in the house for me? I suspect my son has not come for a cup of tea."

Neko accepted the box. "Of course." She started to turn away but paused. "Hiro, beware of assumptions. They will cloud your judgment."

"Do not worry," Hiro said. "You taught me that lesson already, long ago."

She drew a breath as if to reply, but instead stepped into the house and closed the door.

Midori crossed her arms. "Your time in Kyoto has not improved your manners."

Hiro drew back. "Hanzō did not send me to the capital to learn deportment."

"A mother can still hope." Midori's expression softened. "Have you come to discuss my involvement in the emissary's murder?"

"Yes." Hiro started away from the porch. "But we want to speak with you privately."

Midori followed him to the edge of the path and waited as Father Mateo joined them.

"Do you know who poisoned Koga Yajiro?" Hiro asked.

"Not Neko." Midori looked at him sternly. "Do not allow the past to blind you, son."

"I haven't accused her." *Yet.*

"Those words might fool others, but not me," Midori said. "I do not know who killed the emissary, but the food we served contained no poison. He must have ingested the toxin earlier, maybe an hour or two before the feast."

"An hour or two?" the Jesuit repeated. "How do you know?"

"Hanzō said he vomited and seized before he died. To me, that indicates an herbal toxin. Plant-based poisons typically take at least an hour to kill when delivered in doses too small for the victim to recognize." She looked at Hiro. "You already know this."

He nodded. "Why did you help serve the second course, instead of Tane?"

"The girl had gone to the latrine." Midori hesitated. "Truthfully, I'm glad she did. Akiko believes in the child's potential, but I worried she would spill the broth on Hanzō or his guests."

"Have you an idea which specific poison might have killed Yajiro?" Father Mateo asked.

"Not without more evidence than vomiting and seizures. Did you notice any other symptoms?"

"He looked pale, and he was sweating," the Jesuit offered. "Once or twice, he clutched his stomach as if it hurt."

"A problem with his heart?" Midori asked.

"The other Koga emissaries rejected that theory," Hiro said.

Midori raised an eyebrow at her son. "And you believed them?"

"I recognize a poisoning when I see one," Hiro countered. "Did you know that Neko delivered a tray of tea and cakes to the emissaries' guesthouse yesterday, before the feast?"

"On Hanzō's orders." Midori nodded. "Orders, I will add, that she did not appreciate."

"Because she disapproves of the alliance?" Hiro asked.

"Because she objects to Hanzō treating her as a servant," Midori corrected. "Akiko offered to let Tane take the tray instead, but the girl disappeared—conveniently—when the moment came to deliver it."

"Neko thinks the other ambassadors killed Yajiro," Father Mateo said.

"Not an unreasonable theory." Midori spoke slowly, as if pondering the Jesuit's words. "Have you investigated that possibility?"

Hiro found the reaction strange. Surely Neko had already mentioned her suspicions to Midori. Briefly, he wondered whether his mother was involved in Yajiro's assassination. He trusted no one more than Midori . . . and yet, the circumstances of the case told him he could not trust anyone.

Not even his mother.

"We intend to," he said at last.

"I should tell you . . ." Once again, Midori hesitated. "Early this morning I met with Hanzō and offered to take responsibility for the emissary's death."

Hiro's stomach dropped.

"But . . . you said you didn't kill him," Father Mateo protested.

"Someone has to take the blame, and I prepared the meal at which he died." Midori gave Hiro a searching look. "You understand my reasoning. My life will save many others, including yours."

The chill that spread through Hiro's bones had nothing to do with the wind. "Did Hanzō accept your offer?"

"He said he would let me know in three days' time."

"Don't worry," Father Mateo said. "We will discover who killed Yajiro. You won't have to take the blame."

"I worry only about what I cannot control," Midori replied. "I chose this death, and if it comes I will accept it without fear."

CHAPTER 19

"I don't believe the other emissaries killed Yajiro," Father Mateo said as he and Hiro walked back to Midori's house. "I know I mentioned the possibility earlier, but I've thought it through again, and it makes no sense. If they murdered him, why let us investigate?"

"Perhaps only one of them is a killer," Hiro replied, "and didn't want to risk suspicion."

"Kiku did say she disagreed with the investigation."

"At this point, I find Fuyu equally suspicious," Hiro said, "and Toshi's innocence could prove an act. Still, Kiku has tried to deceive us in other areas. She dresses like a commoner, but there is nothing common in her manner or her speech."

"Fuyu doesn't snap at her the way he does at Toshi, either." Father Mateo slipped off his sandals and stepped up onto Midori's porch.

When Hiro didn't respond, he added, "Don't tell me you hadn't noticed."

"Of course I noticed." Hiro stepped out of his sandals and joined the priest. "I didn't expect you would."

Inside, the vacant silence of the common room told Hiro the house was empty.

"Ana?" Father Mateo crossed the room and checked the kitchen. "She's not here."

"The emissaries said she had to leave when she finished cleaning," Hiro pointed out. "She must have gone for a walk, or to check on Gato."

"Is she safe in the village alone?" The priest looked worried.

Before Hiro could answer, someone knocked at the door.

He swung it open, revealing Tane. The girl was looking backward over her shoulder, as if watching something in the woods, though Hiro saw nothing there.

Tane turned to face the door and startled, almost dropping the carefully folded kimono she cradled in her arms. Her eyes grew wide, but she recovered the moment she recognized Hiro's face.

She bowed and straightened, face cast down as if unwilling to meet his eyes. Extending her arms, she offered the kimono.

"Good morning, Tane." Father Mateo walked to the door. "Would you like to come inside?"

The girl looked up, eyes wide with shock. Ducking her head, she extended the clothing toward the priest.

Father Mateo accepted the garment. "Thank you for bringing this to me."

Tane pressed her palms together, touched the tips of her fingers to her lips, and then touched her forehead. She bowed again, as if to take her leave.

"Just a moment," Hiro said.

She straightened but looked on the verge of flight.

"Did you know that one of the Koga visitors died during last night's feast?" Hiro asked.

Tane glanced behind her, as if making sure that Hiro spoke to her and not to someone else. When she turned back, she looked at the floor and wavered slightly from side to side.

"She may not understand you," Father Mateo whispered in Portuguese.

"She understands." Addressing the girl, he repeated, "Did you hear about the man who died?"

Slowly, Tane raised her face and tapped her right hand to her ear as if to say "I heard."

"Do you know what killed the man from Koga?" Hiro asked.

Tane gave the priest a longing look, as if wishing she could speak to him instead.

"It's all right," Father Mateo said gently. "We won't hurt you. Do you know who killed the man last night, or how he died?"

She shook her head.

Hiro made a dismissive gesture. "You may go."

Tane bowed and left the porch at a measured walk that became a run the moment her sandals touched the path.

"I wanted to ask if she was a Christian." Father Mateo sounded disappointed.

"You can ask her later." Hiro closed the door. "For now, we need to find Yajiro's killer."

Father Mateo carried the folded kimono into the room they shared. A few minutes later, the priest emerged from the bedroom wearing a black kimono over a pair of pleated trousers that must have been folded in with the other garment. The borrowed clothing fit surprisingly well and looked much warmer than the Jesuit's lightweight brown kimono. Akiko must not have sent an obi, because the priest still wore his own brown sash, as well as the wooden cross that hung perpetually around his neck.

Hiro then entered the bedroom and quickly slipped into an old winter garment in the smoke-gray shade he favored.

When he returned to the common room, Father Mateo smiled. "Do you own any kimono that aren't gray?"

Hiro shrugged. "A man who wears only a single color never has to worry about fashion."

The Jesuit smoothed a wrinkle from his sleeve. "I appreciate your grandmother sending this to me." He looked at the door. "I also wish Tane wasn't so easily frightened."

"After living alone in a burned-out village, she's probably scared of everyone," Hiro said. "Or at least she pretends to be."

"Surely you don't think she could kill Yajiro? She's a child."

"Closer to a woman than a child," Hiro said, "and even a child can kill. However, I do not consider her a likely suspect at the moment."

Footsteps thumped on the porch, and the door swung open.

Toshi stopped on the threshold, clearly surprised to see them in the house. "Have you already found Yajiro's killer?"

"In the hour since we left you?" Hiro asked.

Toshi shrugged. "Fuyu says a guilty woman is easy to recognize."

"A prejudiced man is similarly obvious," Father Mateo murmured.

"Pardon me?" Toshi asked.

Father Mateo cleared his throat. "Fuyu-*san* did not return with you?"

"He wanted to observe the monks as they began the rituals. He sent me back to check your progress, but I didn't think to find you here. If you haven't found the killer . . . could I help you look?"

"Help us?" Hiro repeated.

"If I help you find the killer, maybe the treaty will still go through. . . ." Toshi flushed.

"You weren't supposed to admit that, were you?" Hiro asked.

The young man bit his lip. "Officially, my clan opposes the alliance, but my father wants it." He gave them a desperate look. "Please don't tell Fuyu-*san*."

"It's not my job to report to Koga." Hiro switched to Portuguese. "Stay here and try to get more information about the other emissaries, while I go to the archery range and see what I can learn from the woman."

"Is it safe to separate?" the priest replied, also in Portuguese.

"He will speak more openly without me present, and we may not have much time before the other one returns." Hiro shifted back to Japanese. "Forgive us, Toshi-*san*. I was explaining to the priest that, as your representative, he has an obligation to keep your secret. In return, he told me that he wishes to discuss our progress with you privately. So, if you will excuse me, I will leave you to speak alone."

"You can do that?" Toshi asked. "Hattori-*sama* will not object?"

"On the contrary"—Hiro started toward the door—"he understands, as I do, that the only way to ensure a man's candor is to speak with him alone."

CHAPTER 20

The archery range sat southeast of the village, in a field half screened by pines. To reach it more quickly, Hiro cut directly through the forest.

Sunlight filtered through the trees and dappled the ground, dimming periodically as clouds passed by the sun, which now stood almost overhead. Chilly winds whispered through the pines and shook the bamboo canes.

Something snapped in the woods to his right, stopping Hiro in his tracks.

Casually, he looked around as the wind died down and the trees grew still. Narrow pines stretched upward, trunks entirely bare of branches to a height of fifteen feet. Above that point, their bristling arms blocked out the sky. Clusters of green bamboo grew here and there among the pines, gathering where shafts of daylight penetrated the canopy. Interspersed between them, maples blazed with autumn's fire.

Hiro heard no songs in the trees. Even the forest crows had all gone silent.

He was not alone.

He closed his eyes, held his breath, and listened as a gust of wind blew past and set the trees to whispering. When it died the rustling faded, but he caught a tiny crackling sound—a snapping twig—that wind alone could not explain.

He opened his eyes and focused on the source, ahead and to the right. At first he saw only the empty trees, but a moment later he noticed a human figure pressed against the trunk of a cedar, twenty feet above the ground.

He didn't need to see a face to recognize the spy.

"I see you, Neko. Next time, watch the deadwood if you want to pass unseen."

In the blink of an eye she descended to the ground, landing with little more sound than a squirrel despite the carpet of needles and leaves that covered the forest floor.

"You think you could do better?" Her voice held a playful challenge.

"Could do, have done, will again." The childhood taunt jumped out unbidden. Flustered by his own reaction, Hiro started walking. "I should go."

"Hiro, wait." She laid a hand on his arm, but he shrugged her off.

"I'm on business, and I can't afford to be distracted."

She fell in step beside him. "Nice to know I'm still a distraction."

"More like a lesson, permanently learned."

"There's more to what happened that night than you realize."

He stopped. "You mean, last night? Yajiro's murder?"

"No. The other night. . . ." She spoke with unusual hesitation. "You must know . . . I didn't want to hurt you. . . ."

"Really?" He pulled his kimono off his shoulder, exposing the parallel scars. "Could have fooled me."

She took a step backward. "I did not realize the scars remained." She raised a hand as if to touch his shoulder, but pulled it back. "Hiro. Truly, I did not know."

"You expect me to believe you did not realize how deeply you cut me?" He shrugged the kimono back into place. "Now you do."

"I know it isn't fair to ask forgiveness—"

"Then do not." He kept his voice controlled to avoid appearing weak or angry. "Lives, like rivers, flow in one direction. Only fools attempt to change the course of either."

He continued through the trees.

"Hiro, wait—"

Though tempted to turn back, he forced himself to continue walking. Finding Yajiro's murderer was more important than fighting personal demons whose exorcism would bring him no relief.

Hiro emerged from the forest near the entrance to the archery yard. A teenaged boy walked toward him, carrying a pair of throwing daggers. The boy noticed Hiro, stopped, and bowed. He drew a breath as if to speak but let it out again, the words unspoken.

"Have you something to say?" Hiro's question granted the boy permission.

The youth glanced over his shoulder. "With apologies, one of the Koga emissaries is using the archery range."

"Did she ask you to leave?" Hiro asked.

The boy shook his head. "We were told we must not approach them. When I saw her there, I turned away. I'll practice later."

"A wise decision," Hiro said, "and thank you for the warning."

He continued down the path, trusting his rank and age would prevent the youth from following or asking any questions.

When he reached the open field that served as the village archery range, Hiro watched from the edge of the trees as Kiku emptied a quiver of arrows into a target made of reeds. Each missile struck the target's eye, clustering within a circle barely large enough to hold them all.

Hiro doubted the best of Iga's archers could do better. Privately, he felt relieved he hadn't brought a bow.

Watching was embarrassing enough.

Kiku looked over her shoulder and noticed Hiro.

He gestured to the posts for throwing weapons practice, which stood near the trees, too far from the archery line to pose a threat.

"You came to practice?" she called.

He nodded. "If you do not mind."

"Keep your distance." She started toward the target to retrieve her arrows.

So much for engaging her in conversation. Still, he could practice with his shuriken until she finished shooting, and then speak to her on the walk to Midori's house.

Hiro lined himself up with the nearest post and studied the divots that marred the wood. Constructed from a tree trunk cut to ten feet long and anchored in the ground, the post already bore the wounds of many weapon strikes. Narrow splinters littered the dirt around its base, while larger ones stuck away from the wood at awkward angles, split from the grain but not dislodged completely.

He drew a shuriken from his sleeve, sighted the target, and threw. The metal star struck the post three inches to the left of his chosen point.

Hiro winced. He preferred to use the shuriken as a fist-load weapon, throwing them only as last resort. Even so, he'd fallen badly out of practice.

He pulled the two remaining shuriken from his sleeve and threw them. Although slightly better aimed, they also struck off target. With a sigh, he retrieved them, threw another round, and then another. Slowly his aim grew more consistent, and his thoughts began to stray.

Neko's behavior weighed on his mind, especially her apology. He hadn't seen her in many years, but she had never been the type to feel regret. To acknowledge a misstep, maybe, but in her opinion awkward memories, like corpses, were better left entombed.

Unless, of course, she intended to distract him.

Hiro felt a rush of anger. Surely Neko did not believe that she could draw him in a second time. He threw two metal stars in quick succession. The first embedded itself in the post with a vicious thump that sent a spray of splinters through the air. The second struck the edge of the first and bounced away with a jarring clang.

Kiku lowered her bow and turned to look.

Hiro's cheeks grew hot as he bent to retrieve the errant shuriken.

Kiku approached with a knowing smile. "Only a woman makes a man that angry."

CHAPTER 21

"I'm not angry." Hiro straightened, shuriken in hand.

"If you say so." Kiku's smile revealed her disbelief.

Hiro retrieved his other shuriken. "Have you finished shooting?"

"I don't believe you came here to practice." Kiku turned away. "If you have something to say, you might as well say it while I train."

She headed back to the archery line, and Hiro followed. He chose a position far enough away to prevent interference, but close enough to talk without raising his voice. "You mentioned Yajiro-*san* seemed well on the journey. Are you certain?"

"That's a question only he could answer." She drew the bow and released an arrow.

"Perhaps he ate something spoiled at one of the *ryokan*," Hiro offered.

"We have had this conversation." Kiku sent another arrow into the heart of the bristling target. "Yajiro showed no sign of illness on the road from Koga. Yesterday morning, he refused the meal at the inn. He called the food inferior—his usual complaint. Upon arriving in Iga, he drank tea and ate the welcome cakes. Aside from that, and the food at the feast, he ate nothing yesterday."

"What kind of tea did Neko bring you?"

She lowered her bow and faced him. "*Sencha*—admittedly, bitter enough to hide a toxin, but Toshi, Yajiro, and I all drank it too. From that, you may draw your own conclusions."

"And the cakes?"

"I don't eat cakes. Fuyu refused to touch them and ordered Toshi not to eat them either. Yajiro ate the entire plate, so as not to offend our hosts." She reached for the quiver but found it empty. "Do you think Hattori-*sama* attempted to poison us with welcome cakes?"

"I think Yajiro consumed the poison before the feast, and that Hanzō is innocent," Hiro suggested, mainly to evaluate her reaction.

"Forgive me. I forgot a dog will never blame his master." Kiku started toward the target.

Hiro ignored the insult. "Loyalty has no impact on my reasoning."

She glanced at him but did not reply.

Hiro followed her to the target and helped her pull the arrows from the reeds.

"The evidence will tell us who assassinated Yajiro-*san*," he said.

"If not Hattori Hanzō . . ." Kiku stepped away. "You think we killed him. Either me, or someone else in the Koga delegation."

"That had not occurred to me," Hiro lied, "but since you brought it up: how well do you know your clansmen?"

She thrust a handful of arrows into the quiver. "Surely you have realized we come from different clans."

"It did seem odd to send four from Koga." Hiro offered her the arrows he'd collected. "However, that doesn't answer my question."

"I first met Toshi two weeks ago, shortly before we left for Iga." She accepted the arrows. "Fuyu, I knew by reputation only."

"And Yajiro?"

"How many times must I repeat myself?" She slung the quiver over her shoulder and started toward the path. "I did not know him well."

Hiro fell in step beside her. "Does Koga want an alliance or not?"

She pondered the question. "Our opinion is not unanimous. The Koga clan believes that we would benefit from a treaty with Iga. Some of the smaller clans agree."

"But Fuyu and Toshi's clan opposes it." Hiro used the singular "clan," hoping she would confirm his suspicion about the men's relationship.

"Fuyu's clan opposes the alliance vehemently," Kiku said. "As for Toshi's family . . . I'm not certain. Officially they oppose the alliance, and Toshi's uncle, who leads their clan, expects the boy to represent their interests."

"But you are not certain of his position?"

"I do not speak for Toshi, and fortunately I am not in his position." She smiled. "A fact that is fortunate for Fuyu also."

"You don't like him," Hiro observed.

"I have no tolerance for men who fail to respect a woman's skills."

"How far would Fuyu go to prevent an alliance?" Hiro asked.

"The man is a self-important fool, but he is not the assassin," Kiku scoffed. "The truth is, your friend Neko killed Yajiro."

"Neko?" The accusation startled him, but not as much as—or for the reasons—he would have liked. "Ten minutes ago you blamed Hattori Hanzō."

"She may well have acted on his orders."

The comment mirrored Hiro's own suspicions so closely that he opted for silence.

"I note you do not argue," Kiku said.

"I will make no accusations until I complete my investigation," Hiro answered. "I neither accept your theory nor dismiss it at this point."

She gave him a curious look. "I must admit, that's more than I expected."

Hiro kept an eye on the trees during their walk to Midori's house, but didn't see or hear any sign of Neko. Kiku walked beside him in a silence that he might have enjoyed, in different circumstances.

Back at Midori's, Hiro discovered Toshi and Father Mateo kneeling on opposite sides of the hearth. The Jesuit looked up as the door swung open. "Welcome back. You're just in time for tea."

"You're having tea together?" Kiku looked around the room. "Where's Fuyu-*san*?"

"He stopped by a few minutes ago to retrieve some rice from the kitchen for the rites," Toshi replied. "He's taking it back to the guest-house now."

"He let you stay here alone?" Kiku gave the younger man an unreadable look.

"I'm not alone." Toshi smiled at the priest. "Father Mateo has been telling me about his foreign god. Imagine: his god says there are no other gods at all!"

"Clearly, his god has not spent much time in Japan." Kiku set her bow beside the door and knelt to Toshi's right.

Hiro circled the hearth and took the place beside Father Mateo. As he knelt, he wondered if the priest had learned anything useful in his absence. Hopefully, the Jesuit hadn't spent the entire time attempting to convert the young shinobi to his religion. Hiro had no objection to Father Mateo's Christian faith but did regret its impact on the Jesuit's priorities.

Ana entered the room from the kitchen, carrying a tray that held a teapot, cups, a canister of tea, and a plate piled high with sweetened rice balls. Hiro's stomach rumbled as his own priorities altered course. Whatever the Jesuit knew could wait, at least until after tea.

The housekeeper knelt beside the hearth and set the tray before the priest. "Shall I bring more cups?"

"Please do." Father Mateo nodded. "Thank you."

Hiro examined the canister as Ana disappeared into the kitchen. "Is that Midori's tea?"

"Will she mind?" Father Mateo looked worried.

"No, but others might." He glanced at Toshi.

"I'm not worried," the young shinobi said.

Ana returned with a tray containing two more cups and a second plate of snacks. She set them down in front of Kiku and left the room once more.

Father Mateo spooned leaves from the canister into the teapot, unhooked the kettle from over the fire, and poured hot water over the tea. Curls of steam rose from the pot.

Hiro found it strange that neither Toshi nor Kiku had visible qualms about consuming food and drink, despite Yajiro's death the night before. On that one point, he would have agreed with Fuyu.

"Have the priests begun the prayers already?" Kiku asked.

"They should have," Toshi replied as Father Mateo poured the tea and passed the cups around. "Fuyu-*san* sent me away before they started."

Kiku's eyes narrowed in disapproval. "I should have made the arrangements personally."

Hiro closed his eyes and raised his teacup. He inhaled the grassy steam and noted a faint, bitter undertone, reminiscent of boiled radish.

His eyes flew open as Father Mateo raised the teacup to his lips.

"No!" Hiro struck the cup from the Jesuit's hand. "Don't drink the tea!"

CHAPTER 22

Tea spattered the front of Father Mateo's black kimono as the teacup flew from his hand and into the fire. Liquid sizzled on the coals.

Toshi and Kiku stared in shock.

"What's wrong with you?" Father Mateo demanded in Portuguese.

"Don't drink the tea," Hiro said in Japanese. "It's poisoned."

Toshi gave his cup a frightened look and set it on the mat.

Kiku raised her teacup to her nose and sniffed the steam. "He is correct." She narrowed her eyes at Hiro and slowly lowered the cup to the floor.

"It's poisoned?" Toshi asked. "You're certain?"

Kiku continued to stare at Hiro. "Yes, but only an expert would have noticed."

She reached across the hearth for the canister that held the tea. Slowly, she removed the lid and dumped the contents onto the tray beside her. Dark green leaves spilled over the lacquered surface, along with a powder the color of dirt and a scattering of brownish-purple petals.

Toshi wrinkled his nose. "The tea is old. The leaves are crumbling."

Kiku pointed to the petals. "That's not tea."

Hiro agreed, though he wished he didn't. "It looks like *torikabuto*."

"I concur." Kiku's expression grew dangerous. "Though, as I mentioned, only an expert would have known."

"Bird helmets?" Father Mateo asked in Portuguese.

"Japanese only," Kiku said. "If you speak, you speak to everyone."

"He asked about the poison's name." Addressing the Jesuit, Hiro continued, still in Japanese, "We call it torikabuto because its purple flowers look like helmets a bird could wear. Every part of the plant is poisonous, but the root is highly toxic, especially when dried and ground to powder."

Father Mateo drew back. "How toxic?"

"Had you tasted any, it would kill you within hours," Kiku said.

Toshi pointed at Hiro. "You tried to kill us!"

"An understandable accusation, but factually impossible. Neither the priest nor I have entered the kitchen since the morning meal, and we all know the tea was harmless then."

"The housekeeper," Toshi pressed. "She must have done it on your orders!"

Hiro snorted. "Ana wouldn't kill a spider on my orders."

"Your mother, Midori, is a poisons expert, is she not?" Kiku asked.

Hiro could almost see the kunoichi connecting the deadly tea with Yajiro's death, mainly because his thoughts had done the same. Not only had Midori cooked the feast, but she had recently retrieved, from this very house, the medicine box in which she stored her poisons. Hiro hoped the Koga emissaries did not know about that fact, and that Father Mateo had sense enough to keep the information to himself, at least for now.

"I asked about your mother's specialization." Kiku's voice took on a warning edge.

The most effective lies contained a grain of truth. "She is an herbalist and healer."

"You know as well as I do that a healer's training also covers poisons." Kiku narrowed her eyes at Hiro. "You recognize torikabuto because she taught you to."

"That doesn't mean she poisoned the tea," Father Mateo said. "My housekeeper spent the entire morning working in the kitchen. If anyone had tampered with the tea, she would have known, and would not have served it."

"Your mother prepared the meal that killed Yajiro-*san*," Toshi declared.

"The symptoms match," Kiku added, "sweating, vomiting, pain in the chest, and sudden death are all consistent with torikabuto poisoning. Dried and ground, it doesn't have much taste. However, it normally acts more slowly . . . the welcome cakes."

Hiro had thought of that as well.

"Who baked the cakes?" she asked.

Hiro raised his hands. "I do not know."

"How did you realize the tea was poisoned?" Father Mateo asked.

"I know the scent of sencha. When I smelled the steam, I realized something wasn't right."

Kiku looked at her cup. "I cannot believe I missed it."

Hiro didn't believe it, either.

The fact that she recognized torikabuto, and its symptoms, demonstrated her familiarity with poisons. She had gone to the archery range directly after breakfast, but could have returned while the house was empty, waiting until Ana left and sneaking in to taint the tea. He briefly debated asking to inspect her box of herbs, but doubted an examination would reveal anything amiss. Either the box would contain no torikabuto, proving nothing, or Kiku would claim that her possession of the deadly poison was coincidental, since every person trained in poisons carried a supply.

For the very same reason, he had no intention of checking Midori's poison box. He would need to find the answer another way.

"We must return to Koga immediately." Toshi's voice quivered. "Before the Iga shinobi kill us all!"

"Please, stay calm," Father Mateo said. "We do not know—"

Kiku cut him off. "I must agree with Toshi-*san*. Someone in Iga wants us dead." She turned to Hiro. "I note you have not spoken in Midori-*san*'s defense."

He returned her look without emotion. "No one believes a son who defends his mother."

"Even so, most sons would try."

"Midori has lost one son already," Father Mateo said. "She would never risk Hiro's life by poisoning tea that he might drink."

"How do you know this?" Kiku asked.

"He told me, after we rescued Ashikaga—" Father Mateo stopped abruptly.

"You rescued a member of the Ashikaga clan?" Kiku looked from the priest to Hiro. "When did this happen?"

"In Kyoto," Father Mateo said, "after Shogun Ashikaga's death."

"The child we saved was not in the line of succession," Hiro added quickly. "His survival makes no difference to the samurai clans' dispute about the shogunate."

He knew, though the priest did not, that Matsunaga Hisahide—the man who now controlled Kyoto over the protests of the Ashikaga clan—employed shinobi from the Koga ryu. While that did not necessarily mean that Koga supported Hisahide's bid to seize the shogunate, it made the Jesuit's innocent comment far more dangerous than it seemed.

"You lied to us." Toshi's expression darkened. "You claimed you hired the Iga ryu to escort you to Yokoseura. It takes a week, at most, to walk to Iga from Kyoto, yet the Ashikaga shogun died four months ago."

"Actually," Hiro corrected, "I was the one who told you about my mission to escort him to the foreign settlement."

"Hiro served as my translator in Kyoto for some time before we left the city." The Jesuit spoke calmly, as if nothing was amiss. "The decision to travel to Yokoseura was made more recently."

Kiku narrowed her eyes suspiciously but said nothing.

"You lied to us," Toshi repeated.

"We omitted," Hiro said.

"A sin of which no person in this room is entirely innocent." Father Mateo gave Toshi a look of gentle disapproval.

The young man reddened.

"At the moment," the priest continued, "the important thing is learning who put poison in this tea, and why."

"We know who did it!" Toshi insisted. "Whoever killed Yajiro-*san* intends to kill us all!"

"Not necessarily," Father Mateo said.

"Fuyu-*san* was right." Toshi clenched his fists. "We cannot stay in Iga any longer."

"Enough, Toshi." Kiku raised a hand like a samurai lord commanding silence. "We agreed to give the foreign priest three days to investigate—at your insistence, I recall."

"Fuyu-*san* required me to say it." Toshi reddened further.

"Even so, we gave our word," Kiku repeated firmly. "Breaking it would shame us."

"Staying here will kill us!" Toshi pointed at the poisoned tea.

"Only a coward runs from danger." Kiku crossed her arms.

"I am no coward," Toshi retorted.

"Then do not act like one," Kiku replied. "As it happens, the killer has done us a favor by threatening the foreign priest."

Toshi's forehead wrinkled in confusion. "How?"

"Iga agreed to protect the priest on his journey to Yokoseura," she said. "Now, the Iga ryu is honor-bound to identify and terminate the threat against his life."

"Not necessarily." Toshi nodded at Hiro. "He could also take the priest and leave for Yokoseura now. I wouldn't let the foreigner stay in a place where his life was threatened."

"You would choose to run away instead?" Kiku's tone revealed her disapproval. "I doubt Hiro-*san* will do the same. He does not seem the type to flee from danger."

Toshi scowled. "Fuyu will agree that we should leave."

"He would also agree that any further discussion of the issue should be private," Kiku hissed.

Toshi stood and bowed. "Please excuse me. I would like to take a walk."

He stalked to the door and left the house without another word.

CHAPTER 23

"I would apologize for his rudeness," Kiku said, "but, as between us, Iga's insult is the greater one."

Before Hiro could decide how to respond, the kitchen door slid open.

Ana entered the room with an expression that wavered between nervousness and horror. Clearly, she'd been listening at the door.

"Who entered the kitchen this morning?" Kiku demanded as the housekeeper approached. "Who touched this tea?"

"No one has been in the kitchen except for me." Ana kept her eyes on the floor, and her voice held none of its usual gruffness. "At least, not that I saw or know. I left the house after breakfast, and only returned a few minutes ago."

"Did you realize this tea was poisoned?" Kiku pointed to the tray of leaves.

Ana shook her head. "I never would have served it, had I known. I humbly apologize."

"She had nothing to do with this," Father Mateo said. "Ana has worked for me for years, and her loyalty is beyond question. She would never put my life in danger."

Kiku stared at the housekeeper suspiciously.

Hiro gestured to the tray of tea. "Dump that in the refuse bucket. Do not burn it. And sweep the tatami thoroughly, twice. When you finish, place the sweepings and the broom in the refuse bucket also."

Ana bowed, picked up the tray, and left the room.

Hiro stood. "Please excuse us, Kiku-*san*. It is time for us to demand some answers."

Father Mateo followed his lead, and the kunoichi nodded as they started toward the door.

"Where are we going?" the Jesuit asked as they left the house. "Is it safe for us to be on the road? What if the killer strikes again?" He looked around as if expecting attackers to burst from the trees at any moment.

Hiro started down the path toward the center of Iga village. "I believe the murderer will strike again, and soon, but not in the open and not against Iga. This killer wants to undermine the alliance. Fuyu, Toshi, and Kiku should worry. You and I are not targets." He remembered his promise never to lie to the priest. "Not yet, anyway."

"Targets or not, we were almost just victims," Father Mateo said, "and I confess, it has me worried."

"For your safety?" Hiro found that surprising.

"No—about revealing the killer's identity. No one in the Iga clan would risk us dying along with the ambassadors, and the Koga delegation wouldn't poison tea they planned to drink."

"Not all of them were there to drink it," Hiro pointed out. "What did Toshi tell you about the others—Fuyu, in particular?"

Father Mateo flushed. "Nothing . . . that is . . . he never had the chance. I thought he would open up to me after I told him about my faith—most people do—but you came back too soon."

Hiro wished the Jesuit would learn to keep better track of time when talking about his foreign god.

A woman approached them on the path. She carried a length of rope with a metal grappling hook affixed to the end, and wore a strip of cloth around her head. As they passed, she bowed in greeting.

Father Mateo turned to watch her go. "That woman knew you. I could see it in her eyes."

"I grew up here. I know almost everyone."

The Jesuit stumbled on a rock and recovered his balance. "Then why don't you introduce me?"

"Because although I know her, you should not."

"Do the people of Iga dislike foreigners?"

Hiro shrugged. "No more than other people do, and quite a bit less than some."

"Then why . . . ?" Father Mateo trailed off. "Do I embarrass you?"

"No more than other people do"—Hiro smiled—"and substantially less than some."

His smile faded. "A man cannot reveal the identities of those he does not know. I will not endanger the lives of my friends and family for the sake of curiosity—yours or anyone else's."

The Jesuit nodded in understanding. "No, I would not want you to."

They reached the road that bisected the village and continued west along it.

"Do you think your mother poisoned the tea?" Father Mateo sounded worried. "She did return to the house at the proper time."

Hiro avoided a direct answer. "We need to eliminate suspects in a logical fashion, starting with the most obvious: Hanzō and Neko."

"Hanzō I understand, but Neko?" Father Mateo clasped his hands. "Why would she put poison in the food she carried to the guests? And why would she poison Midori's tea?"

After an awkward silence the Jesuit added, "Hiro, wounds allowed to fester never heal."

"What do you . . . ?" Suddenly, he realized the implication. "I'm not festering."

"Neko seemed to want forgiveness, and God commands us to forgive others, as he forgives us, of every wrong."

"Your god never had a woman stab his thigh." Hiro started up the hill toward Hanzō's mansion.

"True enough. But a spear did pierce his side."

At the mansion, Akiko answered the door. When Hiro asked to speak with Hanzō, she led them to a room near the back of the enormous house.

Fresh tatami covered the floor of the six-mat room, perfuming the air with a grassy scent that reminded Hiro of summertime. A mural of painted cedars stretched across the paneled walls, their branches questing around the tokonoma opposite the entrance. In the decorative alcove, a monochromatic scroll displayed an autumnal scene.

Halfway across the room, Hattori Hanzō knelt behind a knee-high wooden desk with his back to the alcove. Chin in hand, he pondered a map laid out on the desk before him.

He looked up. "Good morning."

Hiro and Father Mateo bowed and entered the room on their knees. Behind them, the door slid closed with a silent whisper.

Hanzō nodded to Hiro, granting permission to speak.

Instead, Hiro opted for silence. Hanzō might have ordered Neko or Midori to murder the Koga emissaries, and then requested an investigation to distract the survivors from the truth. Hiro realized this was only a possibility, and thus not trustworthy, but even that knowledge could not quell his frustration.

The silence grew awkward, but Hiro did not break it.

"Have you something to report?" Hanzō demanded.

"I came to ask why you ordered Yajiro's murder," Hiro said, "and why you have endangered the life of the Jesuit you appointed me to guard."

Hanzō's face revealed nothing. "Those accusations would cost most men their lives."

"Fortunately, I am not most men."

"Only the most difficult of men," Hanzō muttered. "Why do you accuse me of threatening the priest?"

"Strange," Hiro said. "I understood that nothing happens in Iga without your knowledge."

"Did you come here merely to insult me?"

Father Mateo intervened. "No, Hattori-*sama*. We came because someone poisoned Midori-*san*'s tea with *torikatsu*. We almost drank it."

Hanzō stared at the priest. "I sincerely doubt that."

"Truly, it happened less than an hour ago."

"They poisoned her tea"—Hanzō paused deliberately—"with *torikatsu*?"

Hiro sighed. "Torikatsu means 'fried chicken.'"

"Oh." Father Mateo flushed.

"He meant to say torikabuto," Hiro clarified. "Someone attempted to murder us, along with two of the Koga emissaries."

Hanzō leaned forward slightly. "Was anyone poisoned?"

"Fortunately, no," Hiro said.

"But some of the ambassadors want to leave for Koga immediately," Father Mateo added.

"We cannot allow it," Hanzō said. "The Koga will interpret Yajiro's death as an act of war, especially if the survivors claim we tried to kill them also. You must stop them, persuade them not to leave."

"But we cannot make them stay," the Jesuit protested.

"Well, we could," Hiro quipped, "but not in ways that preserve any chance of a treaty."

"You will identify Yajiro's killer immediately," Hanzō ordered. "Then the delegation will not leave."

"We have not completed our investigation," Father Mateo said.

"All I need is a name." Hanzō gave Hiro a meaningful look.

Father Mateo switched to Portuguese. "Did he just order us to tell a lie?"

"I may not speak your language," Hanzō said, "but your face requires no translation. The need for an alliance with Koga outweighs the value of any single life. Hundreds will die if Iga and Koga go to war, including many elderly and young, who do not deserve that fate. Protecting their lives takes precedence over the truth."

Father Mateo raised his chin. "I will not blame an innocent person."

"Fortunately, I have not asked you to." Hanzō focused on Hiro. "Find a way to blame the Koga emissaries for Yajiro's death. If you cannot, select an Iga assassin . . . any one you wish, except for Neko."

"Why not Neko?" Hiro asked.

"Because I forbid it."

Hiro started to argue, but the Jesuit spoke first. "Neither Hiro nor I will blame an innocent person for this crime. We will not do it, and you cannot make us."

CHAPTER 24

Hanzō rested his hands on his knees. "No one tells me what I cannot do. Not the emperor. Not the shogun. And certainly not the servant of a weakling god who could not save himself from execution."

"I would not presume to tell you what you can or cannot do." Father Mateo spoke with the quiet calm of a winter lake. "I merely wish to explain what I will do. If you accuse an innocent person of killing Yajiro, I will speak the truth and expose your falsehood."

Hiro leaned back on his heels, stunned beyond speech.

"You will not," Hanzō replied. "I will not allow it."

"How, precisely, do you plan to stop me?" Father Mateo asked. "The Koga ambassadors named me as their agent. If you dismiss or silence me, you trigger the very war you wish to avoid. And if you choose to ignore that inconvenient truth and arrange an accident for me, you will answer to the man who pays you to ensure my safety."

Silence stretched between them, taut as a bowstring and equally lethal.

Hiro's chest thrummed with nervous energy. Hanzō had executed men for far less serious insults than the ones the Jesuit had just delivered.

Father Mateo looked over Hanzō's shoulder at the tokonoma. "That is a lovely painting."

Hanzō regarded the priest in stony silence for several seconds before replying. "One of my favorites."

Hiro looked at Father Mateo in amazement, partly because the

Jesuit had properly used a change of subject to offer a peaceful end to the argument, but mostly because Hanzō had accepted the foreigner's gesture. The issue remained between them, but etiquette no longer required an immediate resolution.

"Do you know who poisoned Midori's tea?" Hanzō asked.

"We suspect the same person who murdered Koga Yajiro," Father Mateo said.

"No one in Iga would murder an emissary against my orders," Hanzō replied. "However, the issue is not what I believe, but what the Koga ryu will accept. Since you have been unable to find the murderer, I must find an alternative solution."

After a moment, Hanzō continued, "Midori has offered to take the blame for Yajiro's death. In light of the need to resolve this situation promptly, it appears I have no other choice."

"You have many other choices," Father Mateo said, "choices that do not involve accusing an innocent person."

"I will not have to accuse her," Hanzō replied. "She will confess, and atone for the crime by suicide."

"No!" Father Mateo looked at Hiro for support, but Hiro's mouth had gone too dry to speak.

"I have decided," Hanzō said. "Unless you provide another name, it will be done."

Hiro found his voice. "How long do we have?"

"By custom the Koga emissaries must meet with me before they leave. Yajiro's killer will die at that meeting . . . one way or the other."

"How could you just sit there and not argue?" Father Mateo asked as they started down the hill. "Would you truly let your mother take the blame?"

"Silence is not agreement," Hiro said.

"It is when any reasonable man would protest."

"I know my cousin," Hiro replied. "Arguments will not persuade him. Only another name will change his mind."

"Surely he won't go through with it. Your mother is his aunt."

"By marriage only—and remember, she volunteered." Hiro clenched his jaw and looked away into the forest.

"How can he let her die when he knows she's innocent?" Father Mateo asked. "And how can you allow it?"

Hiro sought an answer that the priest could understand. "Doesn't your holy book say 'better one man should die to save the people'?"

"Yes. . . ." The Jesuit seemed to struggle for words. "But this isn't what that means."

"I see no difference."

Father Mateo opened his mouth but closed it again, the words unspoken. When they reached the bottom of the hill, he said, "You're simply going to accept his decision? Let your mother kill herself for a lie?"

Hiro turned so quickly that the Jesuit stumbled backward.

"I've no intention of letting my mother accept the blame for a crime she did not commit. However, unlike you, I recognize when argument is not only futile, but dangerous." His volume rose as his anger flared. "I pledged my life to keep you alive, an oath that will cost us both our lives if you do not learn to hold your tongue! Do you not realize, a single word from Hanzō means your death?"

Father Mateo started to respond, but Hiro hadn't finished.

"My speed and skills can save you from a samurai's direct attack, but Hanzō will not cut you down on sight, like a samurai lord. The death he orders comes by night. It gives no warning, makes no sound. I might prevent it once, or twice, or even a dozen times, but that won't matter. If Hattori Hanzō wants you dead, you die, and even I cannot prevent it."

The shock on Father Mateo's face made Hiro realize how wildly he had lost control. He took several deep breaths and continued in a softer tone. "You are my friend, and I do not want to bury you in Iga . . . or anywhere else, for that matter. So please, for the sake of our friendship, my oath, and our lives, do not speak to my cousin that way again."

Hiro continued walking. To his relief, the priest fell in step beside him. Knowing he needed to change the subject to break the awkward silence, Hiro said, "The only way to save my mother is to find the real killer."

Father Mateo shook his head. "Things were simpler back in Kyoto."

That's for certain, Hiro thought.

"I miss my congregation, and my work. How long, do you think, before we can return?"

Not for the first time, Hiro regretted his promise never to lie to the priest. "That depends on which samurai claims the shogunate."

"That could take years!" Despair filled Father Mateo's voice. "We never should have left."

"You would have died."

The Jesuit shrugged. "At least a martyr's death is useful."

"If that is so, then why object to Midori taking the blame for Yajiro's murder?"

"Because—" The Jesuit shook his head and continued, "I suppose it is no different, though I dearly wish it was."

"A man must allow the past to flow downstream, and wait for the future to reach him in its time. We cannot worry about Kyoto—the reasons we left, or when we might return. For now, we must focus on finding Yajiro's killer."

Father Mateo nodded. "And saving your mother from a fate she does not deserve."

Hiro hoped the priest was right, but a little voice at the back of his mind couldn't help but add, *That is, if she does not, in fact, deserve it.*

CHAPTER 25

A few minutes later, Hiro and Father Mateo approached the door to Neko's home. Hiro noted with relief that the only pair of sandals by the door belonged to Midori.

They knocked, and Hiro's mother answered several moments later.

"Good morning." Midori bowed to the priest and nodded to Hiro. "Come inside."

Neko's home consisted of only a single room with a sunken hearth at the center and tatami covering the wooden floor. Lacquered screens created a semiprivate sleeping space at the back of the room, and a line of wooden chests along the wall provided storage. Mingled scents of steaming rice and tea perfumed the air, along with the musky, dusty scent of chrysanthemums—Neko's favorite. Hiro found their stench almost unbearable. To him, the flowers smelled as if they died before they bloomed.

Worse, the odor unleashed another flood of unwanted memories: a teenaged Neko wearing chrysanthemums in her hair to see if Hiro would kiss her despite their stink; an even younger Neko chasing him with handfuls of the blooms; Midori explaining that Neko's teasing was actually a sign of friendship, something six-year-old Hiro found impossible to believe.

"Hiro?"

He looked up to see Midori and Father Mateo already kneeling by the hearth. She raised a teapot. "I asked, 'May I offer you some tea?'"

He crossed the room and knelt beside the priest. "Thank you, but we must decline."

"I see." She nodded. "Has something happened?"

He tried to decide how much to explain without offending his mother or revealing more than necessary.

"With apologies, Hattori-*san*," Father Mateo said, "the Koga ambassadors now believe you killed Yajiro."

So much for subtlety, Hiro thought.

"And you have come to tell me why." Midori looked expectantly at the priest.

As Father Mateo explained about the poisoned tea, Hiro tried to make sense of the doubts that swirled in his mind. Midori had always been the only person he could trust completely. He had not even blamed her on the night when Neko stabbed him—at least, not after Midori explained that she had been commanded not to warn him.

He loathed that he had to question her innocence, and hoped she hadn't murdered Yajiro and poisoned the tea. Personal love for her aside, Midori had taught him much of what he knew about poisons, deduction, and logic. She would prove a wily adversary.

"Do you believe I poisoned the tea?" Midori asked when the Jesuit finished speaking.

"Of course not," Father Mateo said. "The person who killed Yajiro must have poisoned your tea as well."

"Not that those are mutually exclusive." Midori glanced at the teapot and then at Hiro. "I trust the Koga emissaries' names are on your suspect list as well?"

"Why would they drink the tea if they knew it was poisoned?" Father Mateo asked.

"Are you certain they planned to drink it?" Midori countered.

"They certainly seemed about to," Father Mateo said, "but we will keep that possibility in mind. Have you any other suggestions?"

Midori nodded once. "Avoid the tea."

"Thank you, Mother," Hiro said drily. "How about something to help us find the killer?"

"If it's help you want, you should speak with Neko."

"Why?" Hiro asked. "Does she want to confess?"

Midori looked down her nose at him. "I thought I raised a more temperate man."

"I didn't think I'd ever hear you call me 'temperate,'" Hiro said.

"You still haven't." Midori's look conveyed her disapproval. "Neko overheard the Koga emissaries arguing. She may have information that can help you."

"Where is she?" Father Mateo asked.

"She went to practice in the forest." Midori raised an eyebrow at Hiro. "Someone said her camouflage needs work."

Hiro ignored the reprimand. "Just tell us what she heard."

"If you wish to learn what Neko knows, you will have to speak to her yourself."

"Mother, we have no time for games."

"Why such haste?" Midori tilted her head like a curious crow. "I see. You need to find the murderer before your cousin blames the crime on me.

"Don't deny it," Midori continued. "Hanzō deferred my offer this morning, but only temporarily. The Koga emissaries must not leave without a satisfactory resolution. If they do, it will mean war."

"But you're innocent," Father Mateo said.

Midori smiled like a parent entertaining the whims of a foolish child. "I do not know if you can comprehend my thoughts. Perhaps, in time, you will understand.

"Many years ago, I swore an oath to protect the Iga ryu, to place its needs before my own, and to obey its leaders without question. If Hattori Hanzō thinks my life—or death—will save this clan from war with Koga, I will give it willingly."

"You mustn't," Father Mateo protested. "An innocent person should never—"

"Innocent?" Midori laughed. "I am many things, but that is not among them."

"You said you did not murder Koga Yajiro," the priest persisted. "In that context, you are innocent, and should not bear the penalty for this crime."

Midori waved a dismissive hand. "I will gladly die for the Iga ryu. However, if you want the real murderer to answer for the crime, go speak with Neko."

Father Mateo rose to his feet. Hiro followed, noting with frustration that his mother had not actually denied involvement in Yajiro's death. He refused to think about what he would do if the evidence condemned her.

Truthfully, he did not know if he could watch her take the blame.

When they reached the path, Hiro started south toward the village center.

Father Mateo pointed to the trees. "Shouldn't we be looking for Neko there?"

"*We* aren't looking for her at all. I'm walking you back to Midori's house. While I find Neko, you must persuade Toshi to stay in Iga at least one more day."

"Why Toshi?"

"Kiku already seems inclined to stay, and one more vote will give them a majority," Hiro explained. "You're welcome to try for Fuyu if you'd rather."

"What argument could possibly overcome the poison in their tea? We would have left already, in their place."

"Unless you persuaded me not to," Hiro said. "I'm sure you'll think of something."

Father Mateo stopped and crossed his arms. "You don't want me there when you talk to Neko."

"That's not true." Inwardly, Hiro cringed at the broken promise. "Actually, yes it is—but that changes nothing. You're not going."

The priest leaned forward slightly. "Talking with women is not your highest skill."

"You think it's yours?"

"With this particular woman? I suspect I have an advantage, yes." The Jesuit raised a hand to his chest. "I'm not the one in love with her."

Hiro snorted. "I'll be fine."

Father Mateo's look said otherwise.

"Neko won't talk in front of you," Hiro added. "She does not trust outsiders."

"Then promise me you won't allow your emotions to obstruct the conversation. Listen to her. Don't let feelings blind you." Father Mateo made the sign of the cross in the air between them. "In the name of the Father, the Son, and the Holy Spirit, I pray that God will heal the breach between you."

When he finished the blessing, Father Mateo walked away along the path.

As he watched the priest disappear from view, Hiro considered his friend's unyielding belief that the Christian god truly cared about mortal lives. As always, it seemed strange, but then a lot of men—and women—put their faith in far more harmful things.

CHAPTER 26

Hiro stood on the path and pondered his options.

Given Midori's comment, he suspected he knew where Neko had gone to train: a glade near the river where they had spent many pleasant afternoons together in the past. He started into the trees, well aware that he could be walking into a trap. He had sent the priest away, in part, to minimize the danger, but could not avoid the risk himself.

If you do not enter the tiger's cave, you will not catch its cub. The proverb leaped to mind in Neko's voice.

He stayed on guard as he moved through the forest, searching for human forms among the shadows. He varied the length and pace of his steps and stopped frequently to listen. Despite his belief that Neko waited for him in the glade, he would not open himself to an ambush.

He inhaled deeply, enjoying the spicy scent of the cedars and the musk of fallen leaves, their scents distinct and sharp in the chilly air.

As he walked, his thoughts strayed back to Midori's involvement in Yajiro's murder. He did not want to consider what would happen if he failed to find the killer—or, worse, if the evidence proved her guilty. Emotions battered his chest like a bully's strikes. He clenched his jaw and tried to will his thoughts to calm. His breathing slowed, and his emotions faded, replaced by the realization that, regardless of what the investigation revealed, he could not let his mother die.

Overhead, a crow cried out in warning.

Hiro froze, alert and listening.

Years before, he and Neko created a system of coded cries, almost identical to those of real forest crows. In training exercises, they had used the calls to orchestrate opponents' swift demise.

A second *caw* echoed through the trees.

Hiro drew a breath to say he had no time for foolishness, but let it out again, the words unspoken. Neko never obeyed any orders but Hanzō's. The only way to ensure cooperation was to beat her at this game.

He cupped his hands to his mouth and tried to caw, but the sound that emerged reminded him more of the day the Jesuit accidentally shut a sliding door on Gato's tail.

Unsurprisingly, Neko did not reply.

His second attempt fared better, and a moment later Neko's answer echoed through the trees. Farther away, a genuine crow responded to her call.

Hiro continued through the forest, treading carefully over the shifting carpet of fallen leaves. He didn't bother to disguise his steps. He could not see her yet, but clearly Neko saw him well. Every time he strayed off course, a "crow" squawked to redirect his path.

He searched the trees each time her voice rang out but never found her. With intense frustration, he realized her weak performance in the trees that morning must have been a ruse.

He'd fallen for it, just as she intended.

The forest dimmed as a cloud obscured the sun.

Behind his back, a crow shrieked in alarm. He spun around, fists raised to fight, but saw only the empty forest.

Lowering his hands to his sides, he closed his eyes and listened for the slightest sound that might reveal Neko's true position. As long as he kept moving, she retained a tactical advantage. Hiro needed to change the game and make her come to him.

He inhaled the complex smells of the forest, allowing the familiar scents to calm the storm within him. Opening his eyes, he said, "I accept your apology, Neko."

Several seconds later, he added, "I spoke with Midori. I'm prepared to listen."

A gust of wind rattled through a nearby cluster of bamboo and sent a swirl of maple leaves cascading to the forest floor.

Neko did not appear.

Hiro's anger flared like glowing coals blown into flame. He would not beg, and would not let this woman make a fool of him again. He turned away, but froze at the faintest crackle of leaves behind him.

Without hesitation, he ducked and somersaulted sideways, feeling the rush of air as Neko flew past overhead. She hit the ground and rolled to her feet in a single, fluid motion.

Hiro rose to a crouch and raised his hands. "I did not come to fight."

"You expect me to believe you want my help?" She made a derisive noise.

He straightened. "I came to find you, didn't I? Midori said . . ."

"Hattori Hiro does not ask for help." She lunged, a dagger flashing in her hand.

He jumped away and raised his arm to block her counterstrike. She advanced and struck again. Once more he blocked and backed away, unwilling to fight back in earnest until she made her motive clear.

"You're slipping, Hiro." She smiled. "Has bodyguard duty made you soft?"

"I don't have time for games. I need your help."

She feinted, and he jumped away again.

"You used to be fond of games, when the stakes were high." She raised the tanto. "Disarm me, and I will help you. Unless, of course, you're scared to try."

He clenched his jaw.

She circled left. He matched her movements, keeping the distance even. He recognized her game as an attempt at manipulation, but it was also the fastest—perhaps the only—way to obtain her cooperation.

Hiro thought of the shuriken concealed in his sleeve. It would even the match but hinder his ability to strip her of the knife.

Sensing his distraction, Neko attacked.

Deflecting her strike with his left hand, Hiro counterattacked with his right. She stepped away, but the heel of his hand connected with her chest.

Clearly chagrined by her own miscalculation, Neko backed away farther. She circled, watching him carefully. Hiro mirrored her, step for step.

She sprang, but this time Hiro grasped her weapon hand and pulled her toward him. He felt a flash of concern as she stepped closer, instead of away.

Grabbing the back of his neck, she kissed him.

Hiro released her and pulled back. "That wasn't fair."

"Distraction is always fair." She smiled. "And you enjoyed it."

He wished that wasn't true.

"Also," she said with a taunting smile, "it appears you have not yet disarmed me."

Without hesitation, Hiro plowed his shoulder into her stomach, knocking her backward into the leaves. She landed hard, with Hiro on top of her, but he gave himself no credit for the takedown. The fact that she had fallen for it again so soon, after his successful use of the tactic at the feast, confirmed that she had always intended this fight to close the physical distance between them.

Neko dropped the knife. "I'm at your mercy."

Hiro leaned down over her until their faces almost touched and lowered his voice to a whisper. "Tell me what you heard while spying on the Koga emissaries."

Her smile vanished. "Let me up."

CHAPTER 27

"You really came out here to ask my help with your investigation?" Neko sounded disappointed.

Hiro stood and offered her his hand. "That's what I said."

Unexpectedly, she took it. As he helped her up, she said, "But you talked with Midori."

"About the investigation. . . . What did you think I meant?"

"It doesn't matter. Clearly I misunderstood." She bent to retrieve her dagger. "Has that foreigner made a Christian of you?"

"Why would I follow a foreign god? I don't even trust the Japanese ones."

She sheathed the dagger at her waist. "You've changed."

"Be glad I have." He nodded toward her obi. "Or that dagger would be sticking in a far more painful place."

She laughed. "That's the Hiro I remember."

"I really don't have time for this," he said. "If I don't figure out who murdered Koga Yajiro this afternoon, Hanzō will make my mother take the blame."

Neko shook her head. "He wouldn't."

"He told me he would, and he will. The emissaries have lost patience with our lack of progress." Hiro omitted the poisoned tea. "Now, they plan to leave at once, and Hanzō intends to punish Yajiro's killer before they go—one way or another."

"Why Midori?"

"She volunteered."

"I'm sorry, Hiro," Neko said, "but if she did, there's nothing we can do."

"We can find the real killer," Hiro countered.

"How?" She raised her hands. "It could be anyone."

"Mother said you overheard the emissaries arguing."

"Not about who killed Yajiro." Neko looked into the trees, remembering. "It happened right after I delivered the welcome tea and cakes. The kunoichi, Kiku, answered the door, and told me to set the tray beside the hearth. I offered to steep the tea, but the bald one—Fuyu—told me just to leave the tray and go. Based on his tone, he took me for a servant.

"After I left the house, I heard an argument through the window, so I doubled back and listened. Yajiro was in the sleeping chamber, arguing with someone—male, though I couldn't tell which one. The other shinobi called Yajiro unfit to lead and threatened to 'act' if Yajiro continued his 'charade.'"

"What kind of charade?" Hiro asked.

"That's all he said. The accusation made Yajiro furious. He threatened to ruin the other man when they returned to Koga."

"Through all this, you couldn't tell the other man's identity?"

"Yajiro never spoke a name, and they were whispering as if to ensure that no one overheard."

Hiro wondered how Neko managed to notice a whispered argument if she had really been leaving, as she claimed.

"As Yajiro finished his threat, I heard Kiku tell the men to come and drink the tea before it cooled. Yajiro complained of a headache, and she got angry. She said she hadn't prepared his tea for him to ignore it." Neko shrugged. "That's all I heard."

Hiro doubted her veracity. "Then you did not brew the tea."

"I already told you. I set the tray beside the hearth and left."

"Etiquette required you to brew it."

"Blame the emissaries." Frustration edged her tone. "They refused to allow it. I don't blame them. I would never let an enemy brew my tea."

"The Koga are not our enemies."

"Nor our allies," Neko countered. "Those who are not with us are against us. Ask your foreign priest. His sutras say the same."

"Now who sounds like a Christian?" Before she could answer, Hiro continued, "Mother said you had useful information. What do you think she meant?"

"Kiku made the tea, and poison is a woman's art."

"Then you believe Kiku poisoned the tea?" Hiro found the accusation interesting, for several reasons.

"Who else could have done it? Rapid toxins taste too strong to hide in the dishes Midori served. She chose the delicate flavors for that reason."

Hiro found that curious. "Did she say so?"

Neko nodded. "Yesterday morning Akiko-*san* recommended a heavier broth for the fish, something more appropriate for autumn. Midori refused to change the soup. She said she wanted delicate dishes, with flavors too subtle to disguise the taste of poison.

"Yajiro must have consumed the toxin after arriving in Iga, or he would have been too sick to attend the feast," Neko continued. "Kiku brewed the tea. . . ."

She trailed off, as if to let Hiro draw his own conclusion.

When he did not speak, she added, "Kiku is also the one who decided the delegation should stay at Midori's home."

"How do you know that?" Inwardly, Hiro winced at his own unintended admission. "Hanzō sent you home before that happened."

"He dismissed me," she corrected, "but he did not send me home. I hid near the mansion and followed Hanzō when he left the building. I had no intention of letting a Koga assassin put a dagger in his back.

"As they left the yard, Toshi asked Fuyu why he allowed the woman—Kiku—to choose their lodging. Fuyu silenced him and changed the subject, but the words were spoken." Neko smiled, as if at the memory. "He seemed angry to admit he took instructions from a woman."

She grew solemn. "It can't be coincidental that Kiku made the tea and also chose Midori's house."

"What does the house have to do with it?" Hiro thought of the other poisoned tea, but pretended ignorance.

"Taken together, the facts reveal that Kiku has far greater status than she wants us to believe. She probably comes from one of the other powerful clans in Koga, and assassinated Yajiro to increase her family's power within the ryu."

"At the risk of war?" Hiro found that doubtful, though the rest of Neko's argument made sense.

"Either Oda Nobunaga or the Ashikaga clan will start a war by spring, no matter what we do. Truly, does it matter whether Iga and Koga kill each other on our own account or at the whim of the highest bidder? Either way, we join the fight."

"Not against one another," Hiro said.

Unexpectedly, her expression softened. "I don't want to argue with you. We have spent too many years at odds already."

Hiro wanted to believe her, but her effort to blame Kiku seemed a bit too heavy-handed. Forcing away the desire to trust, he offered a deception of his own. "I'm going to need more evidence to prove that Kiku did this. Can you help me?"

"Anything I do would raise suspicion," Neko said.

Hiro started to leave but stopped to ask, "Is it possible the welcome cakes were poisoned?"

"Akiko-*san* baked them." Neko spoke as if this answered the question.

"Hanzō could have ordered her to poison them."

"If Hanzō wanted someone killed, I'm the one he would have asked to do it."

Given her tone, Hiro doubted Neko would offer any further information. "Thank you for helping. If you'll excuse me . . ."

She nodded. "You've a murderer to catch."

CHAPTER 28

As Hiro approached Midori's house, he noticed Father Mateo, Fuyu, and Toshi standing on the veranda.

"Hiro!" Relief washed over the Jesuit's face. "I hoped you would return before we left. Fuyu-*san* has granted me permission to say a funeral mass for Koga Yajiro."

"*Masso*?" Fuyu demanded. "No! I gave permission only for funeral prayers."

"Forgive me," Father Mateo said. "*Masso* is my people's word for 'prayers.'"

Fuyu looked suspicious.

"His prayers will help Yajiro-*san* receive a better judgment in the afterlife," Toshi said.

Hiro blinked in disbelief. In all the years he'd known the priest, their only serious argument had involved the Jesuit's vehement opposition to using religion as a ruse. Afterward, Hiro had promised never to exploit the Christian faith, or Father Mateo's god, for purposes of an investigation—and never to ask the priest to do so, either.

Yet now it seemed the Jesuit was doing precisely that.

"The prayers are lengthy"—Father Mateo spoke with unusual pointedness—"and will require quite some time to complete."

"We are going with him, to observe," the bald shinobi added.

"Not that we doubt his intentions." Toshi's comment drew an angry look from Fuyu.

Finally, Hiro found his voice. "All of you are going?"

It was precisely the type of obvious comment he often chided the priest for making, but also the first thing that came to mind.

"I promised Toshi's father I would keep him safe." Fuyu looked down his nose at Hiro. "Given the events of this morning, he is safer if he stays with me."

Hiro decided not to mention a skilled assassin could kill two men as easily as one. Irritating Fuyu, though enjoyable in its way, was not productive.

"Kiku chose to remain behind." Toshi nodded toward the door.

"She believes the foreign priest does not require supervision," Fuyu said.

"And, also, opposes this ritual," Toshi added.

"Silence!" Fuyu commanded. "No woman controls the funeral rites of a man who is not her relative, and no shinobi speaks of private matters in front of strangers."

Annoyance flickered over Toshi's face, but disappeared almost at once. The young shinobi hung his head. "I apologize, Fuyu-*san*."

The older man refused to answer.

Hiro felt another flash of empathy for Toshi. He had never suffered such an irritating master, but remembered the sting of bullying all too well. Although he wondered what made Fuyu agree to allow the Christian prayers, he didn't ask. The ritual had bought them time, and Hiro would not risk those precious hours with unnecessary questions.

"Your investigation is over," Fuyu said. "Soon we will meet with Hattori Hanzō to inform him of our decision to leave and to refuse the alliance he proposes."

Hiro felt a rush of concern. "When will this meeting take place?"

"As soon as the priest completes the funeral prayers. We would not even stay that long, but Toshi wants to appease the foreign god."

"You agreed as well. . . ." The younger man trailed off as if unwilling to risk another reprimand.

Fuyu ignored him. "At the meeting, we expect your devious commander to apologize for Yajiro's murder and offer reparations. Otherwise, there will be consequences."

"Is that a threat?" Hiro felt no genuine offense, but refused to let the insult pass unanswered.

Fuyu stepped to the edge of the porch and looked down his nose at Hiro. "Since you failed to understand, I will speak more clearly. If Hattori Hanzō does not hand over the person who murdered Koga Yajiro, as well as the one who tried to poison Toshi earlier today, every man, woman, and child in Iga will suffer Koga's wrath . . . beginning with you."

Hiro raised a hand to the hilt of his sword. "If you're so certain we're to blame, why wait?"

"You see, Toshi?" Fuyu retreated a step. "I told you this would happen. He wants to trick me into attacking, so Iga can excuse our deaths as well."

Hiro looked at Father Mateo. "When Hanzō asks, I started this." He took an aggressive step toward Fuyu. "You are a coward and a weakling. Only a man without true skill believes insulting others makes him strong. You are a peasant, not a samurai."

Fuyu attacked so quickly Hiro barely had time to duck the strike.

As soon as the sword passed overhead, Hiro stood and seized the bald shinobi's weapon hand. Gripping it tightly, he used his other hand to grab the back of Fuyu's arm and pushed his opponent's elbow upward, holding the wrist firmly in place as he extended Fuyu's elbow joint to its painful limit.

Fuyu froze, aware that any further movement risked a serious injury.

Hiro held his opponent fast, tempted to snap the rude shinobi's arm. He glanced at Toshi, half expecting an attack, but the young man backed away.

Returning his attention to Fuyu, Hiro ordered, "Drop the sword."

Fuyu scowled. "The fall might harm the blade."

"The lack of it will surely harm your elbow," Hiro said. "The choice is yours."

Fuyu's katana dropped to the ground.

"Now, let's see if you can learn a lesson," Hiro continued. "If I had meant you any harm, your arm would be broken, along with your neck.

"I am going to release you now, as a sign of my respect for the Koga ryu. In return, you will sheathe your sword as well as your tongue, and keep them both under better control for the rest of your time in Iga. I will not demand an apology—it would not be sincere—but if you speak a single insulting word in my presence, Toshi and Kiku will carry a second corpse to Koga along with Yajiro. Is that clear?"

"Yes," Fuyu grunted.

"Then we have an understanding." Slowly, Hiro released the pressure on the bald shinobi's arm. When Fuyu made no sudden movements, Hiro let go and stepped away.

Fuyu retrieved his sword from the ground. Rubbing his elbow, he stepped back onto the porch. "Toshi will supervise the priest alone."

The young shinobi straightened, shock apparent on his face.

"I need to spend the afternoon preparing a report for the Koga ryu." Fuyu walked to the door. "I want to record the events of this visit before my memory fades."

As Hiro nodded, footsteps pattered on the path behind him.

He turned as Tane came to an awkward halt several steps away. Her features froze, and her hands drew back against her body as she noticed the Koga men on the porch.

Hiro thought the girl might flee, but after a brief hesitation she bobbed a hasty bow.

"Good afternoon, Tane," Hiro said. "What brings you here?"

She tipped her head to the side, looking over Hiro's shoulder as if to avoid meeting his gaze. Her hands fluttered through a series of gestures that, although meaningful, shifted far too rapidly for him to comprehend.

He raised a hand, and she drew back, her fingers curling into fists.

"Slow down," he said. "Repeat yourself."

Her eyes went wide, and she raised her hands to hide an unexpected smile. A moment later, she bowed again and touched her fingertips to her forehead.

Hiro nodded. "I accept your apology."

Tane's hands dropped to her sides. Her mouth fell open.

"If you move slowly, we will try to understand." Hiro raised his hand to touch his forehead. "This means you are sorry. Tell me the rest at that same speed."

Tane glanced over his shoulder at the porch. Her breathing grew shallow, and once again she drew her hands in close, across her stomach.

"She's nervous." Father Mateo stepped off the porch and came to stand at Hiro's side. "We should try to guess what she came to say."

"The girl can tell us," Hiro said. "Just give her time."

CHAPTER 29

"This is ridiculous," Fuyu sneered. "Who sends a worthless mute to deliver a message?"

Father Mateo raised a hand. "No life is worthless in the eyes of God."

"Her parents should have sold her to a brothel. There, at least, it doesn't matter if the girl can talk." Fuyu looked at Hiro. "That is a statement of fact, not an insult."

Tane's cheeks flushed scarlet, and she raised her hands as if to hide her shame, but just before they touched her cheeks she clenched them into fists and lowered them carefully to her sides. She drew a breath and slowly tamed her emotions.

Hiro's opinion of the girl went up a notch.

Father Mateo caught Fuyu's eye. "Don't you have a report to prepare? We would hate to delay you any longer."

Few samurai could have accomplished the dismissal with greater skill.

Fuyu scowled but slipped off his sandals and entered Midori's house without a word.

"Now," Hiro said to Tane, "repeat your message."

Her forehead wrinkled as if in thought. Looking down at her hands, she moved her fingers through some smaller gestures, as if working out a better way to get her point across. Finally, she gave him a helpless look and pointed back the way she came.

Hiro decided to help her. "Did someone send you?"

Tane knelt and scratched an image in the dirt with her index finger.

Hiro recognized the crest before she finished. "Hanzō sent you."

The girl stood up and pointed to the sun.

"The sun," Hiro said.

Tane nodded and rested her left elbow in the palm of her right hand. Pointing her left index finger toward the sun, she slowly lowered her hand and upper arm halfway down to the right one.

Seeing no comprehension in Hiro's eyes, she raised her left hand toward the sun again and repeated the gesture. When it failed to produce a response, she frowned.

"She cannot tell us," Toshi said.

The words made Tane scowl. She glanced at Hiro once again, pointed to the sun, and slowly traced an arc from its current position toward the Western horizon, stopping just above the tree line.

Hiro understood. "Sunset."

Tane shook her head and repeated the gesture, once again pausing when her hand had barely reached the trees.

"When the sun sits atop the trees?" Hiro asked. "An hour *before* sunset?"

Looking shocked that he had understood her, Tane nodded. With one hand, she made an expansive gesture that included Hiro, Father Mateo, and also Toshi. With the other, she pointed first to the symbol in the dirt, then to the sun, and finally down the arc to the horizon.

"Hanzō wants to meet with us an hour before sunset." Hiro calculated; this late in the year, the days were growing short. "About two hours from now."

Tane's face lit up with joy.

"The first time, you used different gestures," Hiro said. "Show me those again."

Tane repeated the smaller, faster gestures she had used the first time through. Hiro recognized the message now; he would not have understood had he not already known her meaning, but the gestures made him realize Akiko had judged the girl correctly. Although mute, Tane was definitely smart.

"Did your parents teach you to speak with your hands?" Father Mateo asked.

Tane paled and gripped her kimono. She bowed deeply before the priest, turned, and raced away into the trees.

The Jesuit looked deeply disappointed.

"Can you finish your prayers in time for the meeting?" Hiro asked.

Father Mateo switched to Portuguese. "Time is no issue. I am only doing this to keep them here another night."

"I thought so," Hiro replied in the Jesuit's language, "but your motive escapes me."

Father Mateo switched to Japanese. "Toshi-*san*, our time grows short. We should proceed at once."

Hiro couldn't remember the Jesuit ever cutting him off before. "Shall I come with you and stand guard?"

"No need." Father Mateo switched to Portuguese. "Continue the hunt for the killer, while there's time." He started off along the path, and Toshi hurried to catch up.

Hiro wanted to follow them, but realized the Jesuit spoke the truth. Their time was up; he had to find the killer now.

As Father Mateo's footsteps faded, Hiro stared at the wooden porch, worn smooth by use and time. A fraying cypress broom stood near the door. Midori made a new one every winter, burning the old broom in the hearth as winter snows gave way to spring. She did it not from superstition, but because an aging broom left bits of twig on her otherwise spotless porch. Unless he found Yajiro's killer before sunset burned the sky, this could be his mother's final broom.

He pushed the maudlin thought aside. Midori would not join his father and his elder brother on the list of people Hiro grieved. Hopefully, she had not killed Yajiro. If she had, he only hoped that Father Mateo would forgive whatever Hiro had to do to save his mother's life.

The door to Midori's house swung open. Kiku appeared with a folded towel in her hands.

Hiro bowed.

She bowed in return and raised her towel. "Midori mentioned the bathhouse in Iga is open for women this afternoon. Would you mind showing me the way?"

Neither her tone nor her bearing seemed suggestive, so Hiro took the question at face value. "Wouldn't you prefer a female escort?"

She looked him up and down. "Do you plan to assault me?"

"No, but . . ." Hiro trailed off as his cheeks grew warm.

Kiku slipped on her sandals. "No one else in Iga is likely to bother me either, with an escort, and I trust you more than I trust your mother or your former lover."

Hiro wanted to deny the allegation about Neko, but protest would only make it seem more true. "The shortest route to the bathhouse runs directly through the forest, but the path is less secluded."

She glanced at the dagger hanging from her obi. "The shorter route is fine with me."

Hiro started north into the forest. Kiku fell in step beside him, stride and bearing suggesting a woman unafraid. He resisted the urge to talk, hoping the kunoichi would break the silence with useful or revealing information.

After several minutes, Hiro realized—to his discomfort—that he found her presence strangely pleasant. To many people, silence felt oppressive, a void that needed filling. Kiku seemed to feel no such concern.

Deep in the forest, Hiro heard a crackling noise and stopped to identify the sound. Kiku crouched and scanned the trees, as if prepared for an attack.

Hiro pointed to the base of a nearby maple. "There," he whispered, "do you see it?"

Kiku nodded as a smile drained the tension from her face. "*Tanuki*."

The knee-high, doglike animal watched them cautiously, glittering eyes surrounded by a mask of charcoal-colored fur. Its fuzzy ears pricked forward as it hesitated, wary of the humans. Slowly, the creature raised its muzzle and sniffed the air in their direction. Smelling nothing noteworthy, it waddled off through the fallen leaves.

Hiro watched it go. Only after the animal disappeared into the forest did he realize that Kiku made no move to hurry him along.

"You like them, too?" he asked.

"My grandfather called them 'hairy gods of the forest,'" she replied. "He said the tanuki would bring us luck as long as we let it go its way in peace."

"And if you didn't?"

She laughed. "Complete disaster—isn't that how all old stories end for a foolish man?"

"Not just the old ones." Hiro started walking.

Once again, she matched his pace. "It is Fuyu and Toshi who insist that we leave for Koga in the morning. I wanted to keep my word and give you the full three days to investigate, but they overruled me."

"Hattori Hanzō has agreed to meet with your delegation tonight, an hour before sunset."

"I knew he would," she said. "By custom, he could not refuse. That's why I decided to risk the bath. I assumed our meeting would occur tonight, and I have no intention of attending a formal meeting smelling of archery practice and filthy socks."

Hiro found that curious. "Then you consider this meeting more important than the feast?"

Her levity faded. "I hope you plan to identify Yajiro's killer at the meeting. I would rather not return to Koga without an adequate explanation."

"Will his death create unrest within the Koga ryu?" Hiro asked.

She gave him a sidelong look. "That's not the answer I expected." After a moment, she continued, "I cannot guess the impact Yajiro's death will have on the ryu. But you know I would not tell you, even if I could. Which begs another question: what do you hope to learn from me?"

Hiro opted for the truth. "Anything to help me find the killer."

"If I knew who killed Yajiro, that man—or woman—would be dead already." She hugged the towel to her chest.

"You thought of him as more than just a friend." Hiro studied her closely.

She stared ahead into the trees. "He was to me as Neko is to you."

Hiro thought of the scars beneath his kimono. "Please forgive me, but I doubt that."

"Yajiro and I had not been close for several years," she said. "We were close, once, but our relationship became . . . impossible. He changed, and we could not continue as we were before. At the time of his death, he was a friend, but nothing more. He asked me to join this delegation because he trusted me."

And that, Hiro thought, *is precisely why your relationship was nothing like mine with Neko.*

"Why did Koga send emissaries who disagreed with the alliance?"

"To ensure all opinions were represented. The clans agreed to abide by whatever decision the delegation reached."

"Did Koga truly think you'd reach a unanimous decision?"

"We would have," Kiku said, "had Fuyu's clan not tried to subvert the outcome."

CHAPTER 30

"Fuyu's clan?" Hiro wondered if Kiku told the truth, or if her openness was merely a deception. "What did they do?"

"They insisted on sending Toshi."

"Two men from a single clan?" Hiro asked.

"Fuyu and Toshi come from separate clans, although they are related. My clan objected, as did the Koga, but Fuyu's father persuaded several smaller clans to take his side. In the end we had to agree, or they would have blocked the delegation altogether."

"Toshi clearly lacks experience." From the beginning, Hiro had thought it strange that the Koga leadership would send him, even with politics in play.

"He just completed an assignment in Mikawa Province, where he helped assassinate an important target. He survived, although his mentor died, which proves he has some skills. The problem is he lacks the age and fortitude to hold his ground against Fuyu. I fear, with Yajiro dead, the proposed alliance will not prevail."

She sounded sorry, but Hiro suspected otherwise. Fortunately, her comments also gave him the chance to test her.

"Yajiro's death made Toshi change his mind about the alliance," Hiro lied. "He told the priest, in confidence, that he intends to vote in favor of it."

Kiku stopped walking. "Are you certain?"

"He believes Hattori Hanzō is not responsible for Yajiro's death."

"As it happens, I agree with him about Hattori-*sama*," Kiku said.

"You do?" Hiro hadn't expected that.

"Hanzō would have killed us all, not just Yajiro. Only a fool would murder one and leave the rest of us alive, and Hattori-*sama* is no fool." Kiku stepped around a stone that jutted upward through the fallen leaves. "If he wanted us dead, he would have arranged an ambush on the road, near the border, and blamed our deaths on the daimyō he wants to lose in the coming war. That way he would obtain his alliance and also ensure that Koga attacks the samurai lord he wants eliminated."

As he listened, Hiro realized she was correct. That was precisely what Hanzō would have done. "So, if not him, who killed Yajiro?"

"I already told you, I don't know."

They crossed over a well-worn footpath. "Make a guess."

"You will not like it," Kiku said. "The welcome tea Neko brought us was sencha, of the type and grade that almost poisoned us this morning."

"You didn't say so earlier." Hiro realized where this was headed.

"I wanted to be certain before making such a serious accusation. After you left, I inspected the remains of the poisoned tea in your mother's home. It is the same."

"Sencha is a common tea."

"Poisoned sencha is far less common."

They emerged from the trees and entered the clearing where the wooden bathhouse sat adjacent to the river. Today, an indigo *noren* hung in the doorway. Large white characters reading "BATHHOUSE" ran down the left-hand panel, while the one on the right bore a single character: "WOMEN."

As he read the panels, Hiro realized with disappointment that he'd missed his chance for a bath. It hadn't occurred to him on the way, but since the bathhouse alternated between the genders at different times, one in the morning, the other at afternoon, the time for men to take a bath was over for the day.

Kiku's voice snapped Hiro back to the moment. "I trust your emotional bond with Neko will not interfere with your duty to reveal Yajiro's murderer."

"I assure you," he replied, "that bond was broken long ago. I will catch the killer before you leave for Koga."

"Good luck with that." She started toward the bathhouse. "You may leave. I'll find my own way back."

A few minutes later, Hiro knocked at the entrance to Hanzō's mansion.

As he hoped, Akiko answered the door.

"Good afternoon, Grandmother." Hiro bowed.

"It would have been nicer without a hostile kunoichi stalking through my kitchen," she replied, "but not even an elderly woman gets any peace when strangers come to town."

"Which kunoichi?" Hiro asked.

"The Koga woman." Akiko sniffed in disapproval. "She showed up right after you left this morning, demanding to see where I stored the tea we sent to the guesthouse yesterday."

"Hanzō allowed it?" Hiro found that difficult to believe.

Akiko's wrinkles deepened into a frown that almost hid her eyes. "His grandfather would not have approved, but Hanzō-*kun* will do things his own way."

"Will you show me what Kiku looked at?"

"The two of you are on a first-name basis?" Akiko's wrinkles parted in a grin. "Does Neko know?"

"That isn't funny, Grandmother."

"Not to you, perhaps." She led him through the house, still grinning.

Hiro followed her through the maze of passages and covered walks until they reached the kitchen. Unlike the rest of the mansion, the cooking area sat directly on the ground, where earthen floors reduced the risk of fire and helped with cleaning. A pair of wide, wooden steps led down to the ground, where several pairs of braided sandals waited.

A large brick fireplace and oven dominated the center of the kitchen; circular openings on top allowed the pots to rest above the flames. Across the room, against the wall, a waist-high water barrel sat beside a wooden basin and a platform where a cook could sit or kneel to prepare a meal.

Hiro started down the stairs, but hesitated as he noticed the narrow, parallel lines that marked the ground. "You've swept the room since Kiku left?"

"I haven't swept this floor in weeks." Akiko passed him on the stairs and slipped on a pair of sandals. "I haven't had to. Tane would sweep all day if I allowed it. Sweep and fish and swim. That's all she wants to do."

"She likes to clean?"

"I would not say she likes it, exactly. The child gets agitated in a dirty room, or when she notices something out of place. She cleans with more skill than women twice her age."

Akiko started across the room. "I keep the tea through here."

Hiro put on a pair of kitchen sandals and followed his grandmother to the door of a narrow storage room on the opposite side of the kitchen.

A barrel of rice sat against the storeroom wall, but close enough to the entrance for a cook to reach it through the door. Shelves along the far wall of the storage room held jars of pickled vegetables, dried mushrooms, and assorted spices. On the highest shelf, a set of cylindrical, wooden canisters rested in a line.

Akiko stepped out of her sandals and onto the raised wooden floor of the storeroom.

Hiro remained in the doorway. "Who prepared the welcome cakes for the Koga emissaries?"

"I baked them myself, and Neko plated." Akiko reached for a three-legged stool that sat in the corner.

"Neko prepared the welcome tray?"

"She does have skills aside from killing people." Lifting the stool, Akiko asked, "What does all this have to do with the Koga woman's interest in my tea?"

CHAPTER 31

"Where is Tane?" Hiro looked around.

"Why?" Akiko asked. "Do you suspect the child of something?"

"Only possessing functional ears."

"She's guilty of that, for certain." Akiko set the step stool on the ground in front of the shelves. "I haven't seen her in over an hour, but if her past behavior counts for anything, the child will be back at sunset with a brace of fish on a bamboo stake."

Hiro didn't think of Tane as a child, but then, Akiko still referred to him as Hiro-*kun*—a nickname no one else had used since he was nine.

"Tell me," Akiko asked, "what made the Koga woman decide to inspect my tea this morning? If she thought I poisoned the welcome tea, she would have asked to inspect my kitchen sooner."

Hiro opted for the truth. The evidence did not point to Akiko—at least, not as strongly as it did to the other suspects. More importantly, he doubted she would hide her guilt. If his grandmother murdered Yajiro—or anyone else—she would also be the first to claim the kill. "Someone poisoned Mother's tea this morning. It almost killed the other Koga emissaries."

"That explains why the Koga woman got so angry when I wouldn't let her touch my tea. I showed her the canisters, and their contents, but she wanted to root around inside, and I refused."

"And she grew angry when you wouldn't let her?"

"Accused me of hiding something. Lucky for her, she didn't push the issue." Akiko smiled. "Hanzō-*kun* would not be happy if I stabbed his guest."

She stepped up onto the stool and reached for a canister at the left end of the row. Clutching it carefully, she removed the lid.

The scent of summer grass wafted up from the canister, filling the tiny room. Hiro inhaled deeply as his grandmother tilted the tea container toward him.

"This is the tea we sent the Koga emissaries," Akiko said.

"Sencha," Hiro noted, "the same grade as Mother drinks."

"It was your father's favorite also, in the autumn." Akiko lowered the canister until the light from the kitchen reached the leaves.

Hiro saw no dust or foreign material in the tea. "Has anyone touched the canister since yesterday?"

"The Koga woman asked that question too." Akiko replaced the lid and set the container in its place atop the shelf. "You do not burn an entire forest to kill the fox that raids your hens, and no one ruins a month's supply of tea to assassinate one man."

She fixed her stare on Hiro. "Surely you don't think me such a fool."

"The killer ruined Mother's whole supply," Hiro said.

Akiko snorted. "Proving Midori's innocence." She stepped lightly off the stool. "Your mother would not waste good tea."

Unless she wanted to avoid suspicion. Hiro wished the thought had not occurred to him.

"Did Neko help Mother prepare the welcome dinner, or just the tea and cakes?"

"Neko *delivered* the tea and cakes—and nothing more." Akiko crossed her arms. "The woman's a good assassin, but not even a starving dog would eat her cooking."

"Mother mentioned that Neko didn't want to carry the tray."

"Tane went missing, or I'd have made her do it," Akiko said. "But at least, when she returned, she brought that lovely fish we served at dinner—and I made her retrieve the tray from the guesthouse before she helped me serve the feast."

"Tane was alone with the fish you served?"

"She caught the fish," Akiko corrected, "and before you ask, she didn't poison it. We tested her skills when she arrived in Iga. She didn't recognize even the simplest toxins in any form, and though we have begun to teach her, the child could never have poisoned a single target in a group of eight. If she were responsible, everyone in that room would now be dead."

She frowned. "Your mother is the only assassin in Iga capable of poisoning with such accuracy."

"Tane's lack of knowledge could be faked."

"True," Akiko admitted, "and we all suspected as much, at first, because she arrived so shortly after the last attempt on Hanzō's life. However, we tested her thoroughly, and I've trained enough kunoichi, and known enough liars, to recognize innocence when I see it. I will turn Tane into a skilled assassin, given time, but at the moment she is every bit the frightened child she seems."

"Was anyone else alone with the welcome cakes or the food for the feast?"

"Every one of us was alone with the food at one time or another." Akiko stepped out of the storeroom and into her sandals. "Neko prepared the welcome tray. Tane caught the fish. Midori prepared the dishes while I fetched the water, and I'm always here alone."

"I thought you said Midori planned the menu in advance. How could Tane have caught the fish that very afternoon?"

"We planned to serve the catch from the day before. When Tane brought in fresh ones, it made sense to use the best we had available."

"One last question. Would you tell me who killed Yajiro, if you knew?"

Her expression revealed nothing. "What do you think?"

"I believe you would tell me if you killed him," Hiro replied. "If someone else was responsible, I suspect that you would not."

She smiled. "That is why you are my favorite grandson."

"Will you tell me, at least, if you know who did it?"

"No." After a silence long enough to taunt him, she continued, "Meaning, I do not know who poisoned either the Koga emissary or Midori's tea."

"Thank you, Grandmother." Hiro bowed and started toward the door. "I won't disturb you any longer."

"Not so fast. Hanzō-*kun* left clear instructions. If you showed up here, he wants to see you."

Hattori Hanzō looked up as the door to his private study slid open. "Good afternoon, Hiro." He shifted his gaze to Akiko. "Thank you, Grandmother."

A ripple of frustration ran up Hiro's spine at his cousin's dismissive tone. Akiko merely nodded, backed away, and closed the door without a sound.

Hanzō made a gesture. "Please, be seated."

Hiro knelt across from the Iga commander, noting the odors of cedar and parchment that perfumed the air. As always, he found it ironic that Hanzō's private quarters lacked the scent of the blood that paid to build them. Of course, the same was also true of many other homes in Iga.

Hanzō nodded, granting Hiro permission to speak.

Instead, Hiro folded his hands in his lap and gazed at the scroll in the tokonoma, wondering how long his cousin would once again tolerate his silence. As he waited, Hiro tried to decide what he hoped to achieve in the conversation, thoughts unfurling and straightening like the ferns that grew beneath the massive cedars.

He suspected his cousin knew more about Yajiro's death than he chose to reveal. However, Hiro was not certain how to force a revelation. Hanzō had perfected the arts of secrets and misdirection.

A samurai lord would have already insisted that Hiro speak, but the Iga commander merely waited. Hiro decided on his objective and opened the conversation. "It appears the weather has grown cold."

Hanzō's eyebrows lowered slightly. "Did you come here to report what I already know?"

"Knowledge without wisdom is a load of books on the back of an ox."

Hanzō sighed. "Just once, could we have a normal conversation? I understand your love of games, but I am not your adversary. You would do well to remember who the enemy truly is."

"Have we enemies in Iga?" Hiro asked. "I thought the Koga came in peace."

Hanzō clenched his jaw and did not answer. After a silence long enough to show displeasure, but not weakness, he continued, "The Koga emissaries have requested a formal meeting, at which I believe they intend to announce their departure. They will also demand the killer's name."

"As I recall, you have a name to give them." Hiro took special care to keep his tone entirely neutral, but anxiety rose in his chest at the thought of his mother taking the blame.

"I do not wish Midori's death any more than you do," Hanzō said. "She would be . . . difficult to replace."

"On that, we agree."

"Then give me another name," Hanzō pressed.

Hiro stood. "Hattori Hiro. I will take the blame."

CHAPTER 32

Hanzō gave a mirthless laugh. "A noble gesture, but no one will believe it. You arrived in Iga too late in the day to have killed Yajiro."

"On the contrary," Hiro said, "I could have slipped into the kitchen and poisoned the food before I joined the feast. The priest and I were late, if you recall."

"And the tea at Midori's house? You discovered the poison."

Hiro shrugged. "Who better to reveal it than the one who put it there?"

"No one will believe that tale. I need a different name."

"Until I discover the real killer, mine is the only name you will receive."

"You disappoint me." Hanzō frowned. "My reports from Kyoto say you had no problem finding a name on a deadline there."

"Because I learned the truth in time."

"Your time is up. I need a name." Hanzō crossed his arms.

"You have one. Mine." Hiro met his cousin's stare.

After a long, uncomfortable silence, Hanzō said, "If you will not be reasonable, at least report the facts you know thus far."

Hiro knelt again before he answered. "We believe Yajiro died from a fatal dose of torikabuto. The symptoms match, and given its presence in Mother's tea, it seems the likely choice. However, the toxin acts too slowly for him to have consumed it at the feast."

"You suspect the welcome cakes I sent to the guesthouse."

Hiro nodded. "Or the tea. Sencha can mask a poison, as you know."

"The female Koga emissary, Kiku, had the same idea." Hanzō uncrossed his arms and rested his hands on his thighs. "She came here earlier, asking questions about the kitchen and the tea."

"Reasonable," Hiro said. "The welcome cakes and tea originated in your home."

"Which proves precisely nothing." Hanzō's voice revealed a hint of anger. "Any of the emissaries could have added poison after the tray arrived. Did you know they refused to let Neko brew the tea?"

"It sounds as if you have a name in mind already." Hiro wondered why his cousin continued to threaten Midori—at least by implication—if he suspected the Koga emissaries committed the crime.

"I do not know which one of them did it." Hanzō glared at Hiro. "I need evidence that you have failed to deliver. Have you nothing else of relevance to share?"

"Only a strange coincidence."

Hanzō leaned forward. "Tell me."

"Many times, a killer tries to 'help' an investigation by suggesting the name of a person who might be guilty."

"To divert attention from the truth. A standard tactic," Hanzō said. "Has that happened here?"

You did it yourself, two minutes ago. Aloud, Hiro answered, "Neko claims that Kiku is the killer."

For the moment, he omitted Kiku's counteraccusation.

"Neko follows my orders without question," Hanzō said. "No one in Iga is more loyal."

"You know she disapproves of your alliance."

"Do not allow emotion to cloud your judgment," Hanzō warned. "Last time, it cost you dearly—"

"This is not a case of clouded judgment. Neko has accused the other woman twice, and seems unusually eager to ensure that Kiku takes the blame."

"Perhaps because the Koga woman did it!" Hanzō raised his hands. "It fits the evidence, and it would save Midori's life. In fact, it seems that everyone would benefit from this solution."

"Everyone but Kiku." Hiro found himself at odds internally. He recognized the truth of Hanzō's argument. The evidence implicated Kiku enough to persuade the others of her guilt and save his mother. Yet, as tempting as that answer was, he found himself unable to accept it.

Hanzō lowered his hands to his knees. "I am not your enemy, Hiro. Do not fight me when we have no argument. The evidence now suggests a way to implicate the Koga woman rather than a member of our clan. Why sacrifice your mother's life unnecessarily?"

The words should have brought relief, but Hiro felt only anger. "Justice requires more than merely trading one innocent life for another."

"You are shinobi," Hanzō said. "Lies and violence are your trade. You have until sunset to find or arrange the evidence we need to blame Koga Kiku."

"At the cost of my honor."

"Your honor depends entirely on faithful service to this clan." Hanzō paused. "Perhaps what you truly fear is that the Koga emissaries won't believe the evidence you offer."

"Arranging evidence is not the problem."

"If you say so. . . ." Hanzō's tone suggested otherwise.

"You cannot goad me into compliance with your wish to condemn the innocent." As he spoke, Hiro realized the words were not only true but the source of his fury. Years of training had taught him success would justify any action taken to ensure it; suddenly, he found himself unable to accept that premise.

Life had been much easier before he met Father Mateo and grew a conscience.

"Neko told me about the emissaries' argument," Hanzō said, "and also that Kiku brewed the welcome tea. Given that evidence, how can you defend her?"

Hiro wondered if his cousin's quick adoption of Kiku's guilt was planned, or merely coincidental. Either way, he refused to accept it.

"I am not defending anyone." Hiro rose. "I merely wish to complete my investigation and find the truth."

"Your investigation is over. At sunset, the Koga emissaries will arrive for our final meeting, which cannot end with the murder still unsolved."

"Then I will solve it," Hiro said, "before your meeting."

"Why do you still refuse to cooperate?" Anger heated Hanzō's voice. "The truth is no longer relevant!"

"The truth is always relevant."

"You sound exactly like the foreign priest."

Hiro bowed. "Thank you. I consider that a compliment."

"It was not." Hanzō brushed invisible dust from his kimono. "Tonight, at the meeting, you will announce that Kiku killed Yajiro."

"I will not," Hiro declared. "And it has not escaped my notice that you, like Neko, attempt to offer a name besides your own."

"Cousin or not, you go too far." Hanzō sprang to his feet. "Do not force me to give an order we will both regret."

"Do not force me to choose between your orders and my conscience. We both already know how that will end."

Hiro bowed and left the room without awaiting permission, uncomfortably aware that he was out of time and no closer to finding Yajiro's killer.

CHAPTER 33

As Hiro left Hanzō's study, he caught a glimpse of a foot disappearing around the corner at the far end of the passage.

He hurried after it, taking care to ensure his footsteps made no sound. At the end of the passage he whispered, "Tane, do not run. I mean no harm."

The girl's face appeared around the corner.

"Why were you listening at Hanzō's door?" Hiro whispered.

She cupped a hand to her ear and shook her head.

"Don't lie to me. I saw you run away as I left the room."

She looked past him toward the study door. Returning her gaze to Hiro, she shook her head again and pointed to his chest. A flush spread through her cheeks.

"Were you waiting for me?" he asked.

She nodded slowly.

"Have you something to tell me?"

Tane looked over her shoulder, as if to ensure they were alone, then nodded.

"Come with me." Hiro started toward the front of the mansion, wondering what the girl could possibly have to communicate and also nervous about what she might reveal. He suspected she knew something about the murder. Nothing else would make her set aside her fear of strangers. However, her choice to reveal her knowledge to Hiro implied Akiko's involvement in the killing. His stomach shifted uncomfortably. It seemed there was no longer anyone in Iga he could trust.

At the front of the mansion, Hiro opened the door and stepped out onto the wide veranda. Tane stopped on the threshold as if restrained by invisible bonds. She shook her head.

"We won't go far." Hiro slipped on his sandals. "Just to the other side of the walls, where no one can see us talking."

Tane made a helpless gesture, as if wishing to explain but aware she could not make him understand.

Hiro stepped back inside the entry. "Can you tell me here?"

She nodded but still looked nervous.

"Does Akiko know what you're about to tell me?" Hiro asked.

Tane bit her lower lip and looked away, refusing to meet his eyes.

"It's all right." Hiro tried to infuse his voice with as much encouragement as possible. "I won't tell anyone what you reveal."

She glanced up but would not hold his gaze. She tapped her right hand to her chest, then tapped her mouth, and flicked her hand away, exasperated. Clenching her fists, she struck them together, as if annoyed by their inability to convey her thoughts.

Tane's reaction impressed upon Hiro just how difficult her life must be, especially when questions required more than just a nod of response. "Did you *try* to tell Akiko what you wish to tell me now?"

She nodded.

"Did Akiko understand you?"

As Tane shook her head, Hiro's stomach settled. That, at least, explained her choice to tell him. He and the priest had shown her patience, probably more than she received from anyone other than Akiko.

He hated putting words in her mouth, but in this case he had no other option. "Does your message relate to the Koga man who was murdered here last night?"

Tane nodded.

"I cannot guarantee that I will understand you," he said, "but I will try."

She made the sign of the cross and laid her palms together, fingers straight, in the gestures Father Mateo used in prayer.

"The priest?" Hiro asked. "How did you learn his holy sign?"

She scowled in frustration, and he realized the futility of asking indefinite questions without context.

"Have you seen a foreigner before?"

When Tane nodded, Hiro continued, "In your village?"

Another nod, and the girl repeated the sign of the cross, looking out the door with a hopeful expression that made him realize he might not have been the one the girl had hoped to speak with, after all.

"Did you want to"—Hiro barely stopped himself from saying "speak to"—"see the priest?"

When she nodded, he said, "He cannot see you now, but I will take your message to him if you wish."

She bit her lip and looked at the ceiling, fingers clenching and unclenching. Just when Hiro thought she would refuse, she exhaled heavily and nodded.

Tane raised her hands to chest level and held them there, palms up. When Hiro did not respond, she shook her hands as if to call attention to them.

"I do not understand you," Hiro said. "You need to start with something clear."

Tane lowered her hands and bit her lip again. Suddenly, she pointed to Hiro's kimono.

"Me?"

She shook her head and pointed more distinctly, to his sleeve.

"My sleeve?" He raised his arm to look more closely.

Tane's hand snaked toward the cuff as if to reach inside.

Hiro jerked his hand away, but the girl pointed insistently at the sleeve. Cautiously, he moved his arm back toward her.

Tane reached inside his sleeve and tapped the hidden pocket where he stored his shuriken. When her finger touched the metal stars, she pulled away as if burned and backed against the wall.

"They're only shuriken." Hiro took one out to show her.

Tane waved her hands as if by doing so she could make the weapon disappear. Once again, she pointed to his sleeve.

"Not the weapons, then. The pocket?" Hiro asked. "Something about my kimono pocket?"

Tane nodded enthusiastically. She clasped her left hand into a loose fist, leaving a circular opening between her thumb and forefinger, turning the fist into a kind of pocket. Holding it toward him, she used her right hand to pantomime putting something inside it.

"You want to put something in my kimono pocket?" The question made Hiro highly uncomfortable.

Fortunately, Tane shook her head.

Hiro tried to figure out what else the girl might mean. "Did you put something in another kimono pocket?"

Her face lit up. Once again, she made the sign of the cross and bowed her head as if in prayer.

Hiro wondered what Father Mateo had to do with kimono sleeves—and then, in a flash, he understood. "You put something in the sleeve of the kimono you delivered to the foreigner this morning."

Tane hugged herself in delight, gripping her own kimono sleeves and shivering with joy.

"Can you tell me what it is? Will it help us find the person who killed the emissary?" In his excitement, Hiro almost forgot the girl couldn't answer him in speech.

Frustration passed across Tane's face, but it disappeared quickly. Releasing her sleeves, she raised a hand and tapped her temple hesitantly.

"Tane?" Akiko's voice preceded her presence only by an instant, but in that time the girl's face and bearing changed completely.

By the time Hiro's grandmother rounded the corner, Tane was swaying from side to side, arms crossed over her chest as she stared at the floor.

"Hiro-*kun*, I thought you'd left already." Akiko's expression shifted to concern at the sight of Tane. "What happened?" She looked at Hiro. "What have you done?"

"I . . . nothing." With no other options, he gambled on a version of the truth. "I simply asked if she knew anything about Yajiro's murder."

Tane's hands flew up to cover her ears. She closed her eyes and shook her head.

"Do not discuss it in front of her." Akiko grabbed Hiro by the arm and escorted him out to the veranda. "I told you the child is frightened of strangers. If you wanted to speak with her, you should have gone through me. You can't just speak to her of death. It upsets her . . . as you see."

"I'm sorry. I didn't mean to . . ." Hiro wondered if Tane's fright was real, or an act to prevent Akiko from learning about their conversation.

"She will be fine." Akiko's tone softened. "But do not do that again."

CHAPTER 34

Hiro started down the hill, wondering what Tane hid in Father Mateo's kimono sleeve and how the Jesuit could have missed its presence. He suspected the girl had lied about attempting to share the evidence with Akiko. More likely, the object implicated someone from Iga in the murder, and Tane feared revealing it to anyone connected with the kitchen—or, potentially, the crime.

Her choice of the priest did not seem strange. Father Mateo inspired trust in those he met. The Jesuits Tane encountered in her village must have behaved in a similar manner.

Hiro wished Akiko had not arrived so prematurely, but hoped the evidence in Father Mateo's pocket would speak with the voice the girl had now been twice denied.

At the base of the hill he took a right and began to construct a plausible excuse for interrupting a funeral prayer. He had no intention of waiting to discover what lurked in the Jesuit's sleeve.

"Hiro!"

Father Mateo was walking toward him on the path. Surprisingly, the priest was alone.

"I didn't expect to see you here." Father Mateo looked up the hill. "Did you try to persuade Hattori Hanzō not to blame Midori?"

Hiro looked past the Jesuit. "Where is Toshi?"

"When I finished praying, he asked to spend some time alone with Yajiro's body—to ask forgiveness?" The Jesuit's voice rose uncertainly, turning the statement into a question.

"Not surprising. Yajiro led the delegation, and his death brings shame upon them all. I need to ask you—"

"Hiro!" Neko emerged from the trees on the northern side of the road and hurried toward them.

Hiro lowered his voice to a whisper. "Guard your words. Don't trust her."

Father Mateo gave him a curious glance and bowed to the approaching woman.

She gave them a genuine smile—the first one Hiro had seen since his return. He wondered whether the show of emotion was yet another attempt to gain his trust, and was irritated at the unwanted delay in discovering Tane's evidence.

Outwardly, he forced a smile, and Neko brightened even more.

"I'm glad I found you," she said. "I have the evidence you need to prove that Kiku murdered Koga Yajiro."

She nodded to indicate Father Mateo. "How much does he know?"

"We have no secrets," Hiro answered.

"None?"

Her feigned surprise irritated Hiro like sand in a loincloth. "Not where Yajiro's murder is concerned."

She nodded, instantly serious. "When Kiku returned from the bathhouse, she had an argument with Fuyu."

"How did you know she went for a bath?" Hiro asked.

"I saw you in the woods and followed you to keep you safe. After you left her, I hid in the forest and trailed her back to Midori's house." Neko paused. "I warned you not to trust her."

Hiro began to deny that he trusted anyone, but the priest spoke first. "What happened at Midori's?"

"I missed the start of the conversation, but they were fighting about Yajiro's funeral rites." She looked at Hiro. "Fuyu called Kiku a murderous whore and said she had no right to make demands."

It was Hiro's turn to feign surprise. "Fuyu accused her of having an affair with Yajiro in order to assassinate him?"

"More than an accusation," Neko said, "he seemed to have evidence. She apparently walked in on him while he was searching her poisons box. He was furious, and swore to expose the truth upon their return to the Koga ryu, about her affair and about her pretending to favor the alliance in order to murder Yajiro when his guard was down."

"How does that prove she murdered Yajiro?" Father Mateo asked. "Maybe she caught Fuyu stealing poison from her box, and he accused her to divert attention from his own misdeeds. He doesn't want the alliance, either, and he was the only one not present when we discovered the poisoned tea this morning."

Hiro wished the Jesuit hadn't—

"Poisoned tea?" Neko glared at Hiro like a judge inspecting a criminal. "What poisoned tea?"

"Besides," Father Mateo continued, "why would Kiku murder a man she loved?"

Hiro snorted. "Plenty of women have affairs with men they do not love."

A flicker of emotion passed through Neko's eyes, but she hid it quickly. "Fuyu made his accusations when he thought they were alone. That's not the time to lie."

"Unless he murdered Yajiro himself and took the offensive so Kiku would not accuse him," Hiro countered.

Neko made a derisive noise. "No kunoichi risks a personal indiscretion on a mission this important. That is, unless the affair is part of the mission. Clearly, someone wanted her to stop the alliance—by persuasion if possible and, if not, by any means necessary."

"You have an unusual definition of 'clearly,'" Hiro said.

"Why would she kill him the night they arrived?" Father Mateo's tone conveyed his disbelief. "Negotiations hadn't even started."

"Most likely, she measured his fortitude on the journey," Neko replied, "and knew he would not change his mind."

Hiro couldn't help but remember Kiku's words: *"He asked me to join this delegation because he trusted me."*

He hated to agree with Neko, but also knew—only too well—how quickly a woman could turn a man's trust against him.

CHAPTER 35

"You believe that Kiku got close to Yajiro in order to murder him?" Father Mateo asked.

"She seduced him in order to kill him," Neko corrected. "Most likely, on someone else's orders."

"Who would order such a thing, and why?"

Neko shrugged. "The motive doesn't matter."

Hiro straightened. "Motives always matter."

"Where did you discover poisoned tea this morning?" Neko asked the priest.

"At Midori-*san*'s. Hiro and I had tea with Kiku and Toshi—that is, we began to, but discovered that someone had poisoned the tea with . . . ah, with poison."

Hiro noted the priest's unwillingness to risk another linguistic gaffe with *torikabuto*.

"Kiku must have done it," Neko said. "With two of the emissaries dead, the Koga ryu would demand a war—a war her clan could offer to lead while the Koga mourned Yajiro."

The explanation fit the facts almost too well, and certainly too conveniently, for Hiro's liking.

"Did Kiku object to Fuyu's accusation?" Father Mateo asked.

"Of course," Neko scoffed. "She accused him of killing Yajiro himself, but that's no proof of innocence." She gave Hiro an urgent look. "As soon as I heard the evidence, I came in search of you."

Hiro didn't consider accusations reliable evidence, but let that pass in favor of a greater inconsistency. "Mother's house lies east of here, but you came out of the trees to the north."

"I've been hunting for you for over half an hour." She glanced at the sun. "You need to see Hanzō immediately. This evidence saves your mother."

"Midori is indeed quite fortunate," Hiro said drily. "What would we have done if Fuyu and Kiku had not engaged in such a revealing argument at such a convenient time?"

Neko stepped away. "Do you accuse me of a lie?"

"It would not be your first."

She narrowed her eyes. "You do not know as much as you think you do."

"Maybe not, but this much I know: if you have something to say to Hanzō, you know where to find him." Hiro crossed his arms.

Neko hesitated on the edge of speech. After a moment she shook her head and walked away into the trees.

"You're not going to stop her?" Father Mateo asked.

"She's trying to sway the investigation." Hiro recounted his recent conversation with Hanzō, ending with the Iga leader's stated desire to shift the blame to Kiku. "I don't know whether Neko is acting independently or following Hanzō's orders. Either way, we cannot trust her."

"That sounds like an assumption," Father Mateo said. "In fact, it sounds like several."

Hiro looked into the woods. "I will not be a piece in Hanzō's game. I intend to find the real killer."

"But he knows you don't trust Neko. Why would he believe she could deceive you?"

"She persuaded me to ignore my instincts once before," Hiro said. "He must think she can do it again."

"Or perhaps she told the truth, and Kiku is the killer," the Jesuit offered.

Hiro glanced at the sun, which hovered only a handsbreadth above the trees. "In either case, we're running out of time."

"I'm sorry I couldn't extend my prayers longer." Father Mateo raised a hand and rubbed the scar at the base of his neck. "I had hoped to delay the ambassadors past nightfall, but with Hanzō's meeting . . ."

"You did more than I expected." Hiro chose his next words carefully, knowing they tread on ground that his friend held sacred. "Once, you told me prayers for the dead were useless."

"That's not exactly what I said. Posthumous prayers cannot affect a man's eternal fate. At least, not as most Buddhists think they do. However, my prayers this afternoon made no attempt to save Yajiro's soul. Instead, I prayed that God would help us find his killer and prevent a war between the people of Iga and the Koga ryu."

"You led Fuyu to think otherwise," Hiro pointed out. "At least, you allowed the mistake."

"I told him only that I wished to offer appropriate prayers on Yajiro's behalf." Father Mateo shrugged. "If he and Toshi thought I meant a funeral, the mistake was theirs alone."

Hiro raised an eyebrow at the priest. "It seems we have contaminated one another's morals. You tell half-truths to those you serve, while I refuse to lie to save my mother."

"I serve only God." The Jesuit smiled. "And I am proud that you refuse to lie."

Suddenly, Hiro remembered Tane. "You need to look—"

"Good afternoon!" Toshi called from behind them. "Are you heading to the meeting?"

As the young shinobi approached from the direction of the guesthouse, Hiro covered his frustration with a bow. "Good afternoon, Toshi-*san*."

Toshi bowed. "Are you headed to the meeting? May I walk with you?"

Hiro desperately wanted to refuse, but etiquette made him force a smile. "Of course."

Together, they started back toward Hanzō's home.

"Thank you for giving me time alone with Yajiro-*san*," Toshi said. "Fu— That is, not everyone would understand my need to apologize and say good-bye."

"Of course," the priest replied.

The conversation died as Hiro followed the other men up the hill, trying to figure out how to talk with Father Mateo before the meeting.

Even though he doubted Hanzō planned to blame Midori, he still felt an urgent need to learn who truly killed Yajiro. It was the only way to know, for certain, who he could and could not trust. Also, he suspected Midori would still confess to the killing if Fuyu and Toshi did not accept Kiku's guilt.

Hiro slowed his pace as they passed the black-tiled gates of Hanzō's compound. "Forgive my rudeness, Toshi-*san*, but may I speak with the priest alone? I must instruct him on the proper etiquette for this meeting, to ensure he causes no offense."

Toshi bowed. "I understand. I will wait for you inside."

Hiro ignored the Jesuit's look of suspicion and waited as Toshi crossed the yard, stepped onto the porch, and knocked.

After Akiko let Toshi into the mansion and closed the door, Hiro said, "I need you to check the pocket inside your sleeve."

The Jesuit raised his arm and looked at the sleeve. "My pocket?" He started to reach inside, but Hiro seized his arm and hissed, "Not here."

Without releasing the Jesuit's sleeve, Hiro walked back through the gates and around the edge of the wall, where they were hidden from the mansion.

"Now." He released the priest. "The pocket."

Father Mateo reached inside the sleeve of his kimono. Hiro felt a surge of anticipation as the priest withdrew his hand and opened it, revealing an empty palm.

The Jesuit looked confused. "There's nothing there."

CHAPTER 36

"Try the other pocket," Hiro said, "the other sleeve."

The Jesuit reached into his kimono. "What am I looking *for*?"

His eyes grew wide. He pulled his hand back out of the sleeve, this time holding a folded paper the size and shape of the envelopes Hiro used to store his poisons.

"Where did this come from?" Father Mateo started to lift the flap at the top of the envelope.

"Wait!" Hiro raised a hand. "It could be dangerous."

The Jesuit looked at the envelope as if it might become a snake and bite him. Slowly, he extended it to Hiro. "As you say . . . assumptions kill."

"Some more quickly than others."

The paper felt lighter than Hiro expected. He angled the opening away from both himself and the priest as he raised the flap, half expecting to find it empty.

Carefully, he peered inside.

"What is it?" Father Mateo leaned forward. "Can you tell? Where did it come from?"

Hiro tilted the envelope toward the priest, revealing a few dried petals mixed with a pinch of fine-grained powder the color of dirt.

Father Mateo frowned. "That looks like . . ."—he struggled with the word—". . . torikabuto? How did it get in the sleeve of my kimono?"

"Tane put it there." Briefly, Hiro explained about his conversation with the girl, ending with Akiko's sudden appearance. "The child will not reveal what she knows with Grandmother present."

"Which means we need to meet with her alone. She knows who killed Yajiro!"

"Not necessarily," Hiro said, "and adult men do not request a confidential meeting with a child. Not without an excellent reason, anyway."

"Yet we cannot give our reason without risking the killer learning what we know." Father Mateo stared at the envelope. "Which, in turn, would place the girl in danger."

Hiro nodded.

"Even so, we have to find a way," the Jesuit said. "We cannot accept defeat with the answer so close at hand."

"I never accept defeat." Hiro folded the flap back into place, sealing the envelope, and slipped the paper into his sleeve. "The emissaries will not leave for Koga until morning, at the earliest. That gives us the rest of the night to speak with Tane and find the killer. However, I would prefer you not attend this meeting."

"If I don't, the Koga ambassadors will think that I betrayed them."

"I will explain that you felt ashamed because we failed to solve the crime. After the meeting, I will meet you back at Midori's house and we'll make a plan."

"I'm not leaving." Father Mateo crossed his arms. "Why are you so opposed to me attending?"

"The exact same reason I give you every time you ask that question," Hiro said. "To keep you safe. Also, your absence gives me freedom to manipulate the meeting."

Lowering his voice even more, Hiro continued, "More importantly, this meeting may end in violence, and if it does I do not want you there."

"I promised that I would find the person who murdered Koga Yajiro. You know I cannot turn away or allow an innocent person to take the blame."

"You cannot prevent it, if Hanzō wishes otherwise. Your status as a foreigner will not save you here."

"Hattori Hanzō wants peace with Koga, just as I do," Father Mateo said. "Attempting to find Yajiro's killer will not harm his plans."

"I thought so too, at first." Hiro shook his head. "I can no longer tell his truths from lies."

"Hiro-*kun*?" Akiko's voice called out from the other side of the wall. She emerged through the gates, confusion deepening the wrinkles on her face. "What are you doing out here?"

"He doesn't want me to attend this evening's meeting," Father Mateo said. "He thinks it might be dangerous."

"It is, but not for you." She glanced at Hiro. "Nor for you, unless you provoke your cousin, although I suspect you'll do it anyway."

"That isn't why I thought it might be dangerous," Hiro answered.

Akiko shrugged. "Are you coming inside or not?"

"We are." Father Mateo started toward the gates.

Hiro hurried after the Jesuit, wishing his grandmother didn't speak Portuguese.

Inside the mansion, Hiro and Father Mateo followed Akiko through the entry and along the passage to a formal reception room, where the dusty scent of withered chrysanthemums hovered in the air like the ghost of autumn.

Twelve tatami covered the floor, arranged in auspicious patterns to minimize the number of corners adjacent to one another. On the wall to the right of the entrance, a painting of a lifelike cedar rose from floor to ceiling, branches spreading across the panels like so many outstretched arms. Near the end of the longest branch, the artist had added a male falcon perched at rest, with features so detailed that the feathers seemed to rustle in the breeze.

Across from the entrance, the falcon's painted mate soared proudly, pinions rendered with exquisite care. Her central position on the wall would create the illusion that she circled over Hanzō's head when he knelt in the host's position to meet with guests.

At the moment, however, the falcon soared over empty space.

Toshi knelt to the right of the entrance. He bowed from a kneeling position as Hiro and Father Mateo entered the room.

After returning the young man's bow, Hiro knelt on the opposite side of the room, to the left of the door, leaving the area next to Toshi for the remaining Koga emissaries.

Father Mateo knelt beside Hiro, gaze fixed on the wall. "These paintings . . . I have never seen their equal."

"Nor will you again," Hiro said. "The artist died the same year they were painted."

"I am sorry to hear it," the Jesuit replied. "Why paint directly on the wall? Normally, artists paint on wood or canvas, so the image can be moved."

"Moveable paintings can be stolen," Toshi said.

"Or saved from fire." Father Mateo stared at the soaring falcon. "You know, I'm not an expert, but I think I've seen this artist's work before."

"How could you?" Suspicion rang in Toshi's voice. "I thought you had never been to Iga."

"The brushstrokes . . ." Father Mateo trailed off. "On second thought, no, it merely reminds me of art I've seen in Kyoto."

A subtle shift in the Jesuit's posture betrayed the lie. Fortunately, Toshi was looking at the painted falcons, not the priest.

"Don't feel badly," the young shinobi said. "Many Japanese artists imitate the styles of other, far more famous men. Sometimes even experts cannot tell their work apart."

"Indeed." Father Mateo gave an embarrassed smile. "I have made a foreigner's mistake."

Hiro had no doubt the priest had recognized the artist. Other works by Hiro's father hung in Hanzō's study and in the room they shared at Midori's home. The brushwork was, indeed, distinctive, and the Jesuit had an eye for art.

However, Hiro approved of the decision to conceal that knowledge. Familiarity with Iga would make Toshi and the others question Father Mateo's honesty.

Behind them, the floorboards gave a barely audible creak.

Hiro bowed his head, but did not turn. "Good evening, Hattori-*sama*."

CHAPTER 37

Hanzō crossed the room without a word. He wore a black kimono of patterned silk over dark pleated trousers. His hair was bound in a samurai knot, his cheeks looked freshly shaven, and his mustache gleamed with oil. His choice of ceremonial dress displayed respect for the emissaries, but the swords thrust through his obi also made a lethal promise: should the need arise, the Iga ryu was prepared to fight.

When Hanzō reached the wall, he faced the visitors and knelt beneath the image of the flying falcon.

Father Mateo bowed from a kneeling position, touching his forehead to the floor and holding the obeisance before straightening. Toshi bowed as well, though not as deeply or as long.

Hiro lowered his face and bent his shoulders in the smallest bow required to avoid a reprimand. Raising his head, he met his cousin's gaze, daring Hanzō to mention the stingy bow. As usual, Hanzō's face remained unreadable.

"Good evening, Hattori-*sama*." Father Mateo unknowingly broke the stalemate.

Hanzō regarded the priest. "Have you learned who murdered Koga Yajiro?"

"Regrettably, no," the Jesuit said. "Perhaps by morning—"

"Most unfortunate." Hanzō spoke over him. "My captain, Kotani Neko, will join us soon. Perhaps she has discovered the truth instead."

"I hope so." Father Mateo sounded at ease. "It would be . . . unfortunate . . . to blame an innocent person by mistake."

"Indeed." Despite Hanzō's neutral expression, Hiro heard the warning in his voice.

"I hope your captain will provide sufficient evidence of her theory," Father Mateo added. "God protects the innocent, condemning those who make false accusations."

Toshi stared at the priest in shock.

Hiro knew exactly how the young shinobi felt.

Behind them, the door slid open.

Kiku entered the room in formal fashion, on her knees. She wore a kimono of patterned silk in shades of gray and blue.

Hanzō nodded. "Welcome, Koga-*san*."

"Where is Fuyu?" Toshi looked confused.

"He said he wished to walk alone." Kiku settled beside the younger man. "Doubtless, he will join us when he's ready."

"May I offer you tea while we wait?" Hanzō asked.

"Thank you, but . . ." Kiku trailed off.

Hiro admired her deft refusal, which also managed to avoid offense.

"We appreciate you granting our request for a meeting on short notice," Kiku said. "As you know, we have come to take our leave and to hear the Iga ryu's official statement regarding Yajiro's death."

"Yajiro's murder," Toshi corrected.

Kiku shot the younger man a disapproving glance.

"Surely you do not intend to leave so prematurely." Hanzō's pretended ignorance fooled no one, and wasn't intended to. "We have not yet begun negotiations for a treaty."

"Negotiations began and ended with Yajiro's assassination," Kiku said. "Only a fool would grasp the hand that holds a blade."

"You accuse me of murder?" Hanzō slid his hand along his thigh until the heel of his palm rested against the hilt of his sword.

"Do you not lead the Iga ryu?" Kiku's voice remained polite, a smile frozen on her face. "Is a leader not responsible for everything that happens in his village, and within his home?"

"You may not have touched the poison," Toshi said, "but you killed Yajiro all the same."

"Dangerous words from a man not old enough to grow a beard." Hanzō gripped the sword more firmly. "Are you prepared to back them up with steel?"

Toshi jumped to his feet. "Is that a challenge?"

Hanzō laughed, loud and long, as if the younger man had told a joke.

Toshi's cheeks flushed red. His expression wavered as anxiety took hold, and he looked around as if for support.

The second his gaze left Hanzō, the Iga leader sprang to his feet, drew Toshi's own katana from its scabbard, and pressed the blade against the young man's throat.

"See the candle challenging a bonfire." Hanzō's mirth had vanished. "You will live, but only because I choose to overlook your insult for the cause of peace."

He withdrew the sword and stepped away. After a moment long enough to increase the younger man's humiliation, he spun the sword around and offered the hilt to Toshi.

The young shinobi watched the blade, but seemed afraid to move.

"Take it," Kiku hissed.

Toshi accepted the katana, returned it to its sheath, and knelt, cheeks the color of pickled plums.

Hanzō returned to his place at the head of the room. "Need you additional proof of my intentions, Kiku-*san*? You know as well as I that I had every right to kill him."

"Even a tiger may show mercy once his belly's filled," she said. "Still, Koga thanks you for your mercy to a foolish child."

Who you made no attempt to save, Hiro noted silently.

Facts and accusations swirled in his thoughts like leaves in a river. Unreliable witnesses and shifting evidence made him question who and what he chose to trust as true. He longed for Kyoto—and almost laughed at the thought's absurdity.

Once again, the door at the back of the room slid open.

Hiro turned, expecting Fuyu. Instead, Midori knelt in the doorway, wearing a cream-colored silk kimono and a dark blue obi striped with silver. Embroidered chrysanthemums spilled across the side of her robe, a waterfall of silver, brown, and orange.

Chrysanthemums were symbols of the emperor, and autumn, but in pale shades they also stood for death. Midori's clothing indicated Hanzō had not told her of the change in plan.

As she bowed, Midori caught Hiro's eye. The silent exchange lasted only a moment, but Hiro understood her warning: *do not intervene*.

Whether he would obey remained in question.

The moment Midori crossed the threshold, Neko appeared in the doorway and bowed her forehead to the floor.

In sharp contrast to the other women's formal attire, Neko wore the familiar blue practice tunic and trousers she had worn all day. A dagger hung at her waist, along with a sword.

As she followed Midori into the room, Hanzō said, "We are waiting for Koga Fuyu."

Neko and Midori knelt directly behind Hiro and Father Mateo. Uncomfortable prickling ran up Hiro's spine. Custom required lower-ranking guests to sit at the back of the room, but Hiro's mother ranked higher than he did within the Iga ryu, and even Neko was his equal. He struggled against the nearly overwhelming urge to ask them to move forward.

Kiku stared at the other women, visibly tense. "What are they doing here?"

"Kotani Neko serves as my personal bodyguard," Hanzō replied. "I asked her to attend in that capacity. As for my aunt, I will gladly explain her presence after Fuyu-*san* arrives. I see no reason to explain it twice."

"Move them forward," Kiku said. "I want them sitting where I can see them."

When Hanzō did not answer, Kiku reached a hand into her obi. "I said, move them forward now."

This time, Hanzō nodded.

Midori and Neko moved up to kneel beside Father Mateo, and silence fell as the wait resumed. Father Mateo closed his eyes, but not in sleep. The movements of his lips and downward cast of his face suggested prayer.

Kiku rested her hands in her lap and studied the painted falcons with a patient expression that revealed nothing, though her posture indicated readiness, should an attack occur. Toshi alternated between staring at Hanzō and fidgeting with the hem of his kimono. Looking up, he noticed Hiro watching. Color rose in his cheeks, and he folded his hands together to keep them still.

Hiro, too, remained alert. The longer Fuyu delayed his appearance, the greater the chance his arrival would trigger violence.

CHAPTER 38

"Where is Fuyu?" Hanzō's sudden question made Toshi jump.

Father Mateo raised his head, eyes open once again.

Kiku returned the Iga commander's stare. "Fuyu-*san* is not my commander, my father, or my husband. His whereabouts are not my obligation."

"Perhaps he lost track of the time," Toshi offered.

"More likely, he insults us all by forcing us to wait." Hanzō's voice revealed his disapproval. "Hiro, find him and escort him here. Take the foreigner with you."

"We cannot leave," Father Mateo murmured in Portuguese. "He will discuss the killing once we've gone."

"We cannot stop him, even if we stay," Hiro replied in the Jesuit's language. "And he won't blame anyone without the final emissary here."

Rising, Hiro switched to Japanese. "Forgive me, Hattori-*sama*. Father Mateo did not understand your words."

"I trust he understands them now."

To Hiro's relief, Father Mateo stood and left the room without an argument.

"We shouldn't have left," the Jesuit repeated as they crossed the yard. "Hattori Hanzō will resolve the murder while we're gone."

"Not without the entire Koga delegation present," Hiro replied.

"Do you believe that firmly enough to risk your mother's life?"

Hiro clenched his jaw and did not answer.

At the base of the hill, they started along the road to Midori's house.

"Do you think Fuyu's tardiness is accidental?" Father Mateo asked.

"Unlikely."

The sun had dipped beneath the trees, lighting the clouds with an orange glow. As they walked, the sunset's fire faded. Twilight washed the world in ever-deeper shades of blue.

Hiro wished he had thought to bring a lantern. Not for himself—he knew the paths of Iga far too well to lose his way—but Father Mateo could easily stumble if he wandered off the path.

By the time they reached Midori's house, he could barely distinguish the pale shapes of Fuyu's sandals by the door. Hiro crossed the porch, slipped off his shoes, and opened the door. "Koga-*san*, we have come—"

He froze on the darkened threshold.

No fire burned inside the house, and the air contained the faint but unmistakable scent of iron mixed with earth and fecal matter—the smell of a recent, violent death.

"Get back." Hiro stepped away from the door and shoved the Jesuit off the porch.

Father Mateo stumbled backward into the gloom.

Hiro drew his katana and shouted, "Show yourself at once!"

He faced the doorway, ready for a fight, but nothing moved inside the darkened room.

"What happened?" Father Mateo asked. "What did you see?"

Hiro continued to watch the door. "There's a body in that house."

"A dead one? How do you know?"

"I smelled it." Hiro stepped backward off the porch to join the priest.

"Is it Fuyu-*san*?" Father Mateo started toward the door. "He might need help!"

Hiro grabbed the Jesuit's arm and held him back. "If it is, you cannot help him now."

"We must go inside and confirm what happened." Father Mateo tried to free his arm but failed. The Jesuit gasped. "The body might be Ana!"

"Ana should be at the guesthouse. . . ." Hiro trailed off.

"She would have returned to cook our dinner." Father Mateo cupped his hands to his mouth and shouted, "*Ana!*"

"Stop that!" Hiro hissed. "The killer could still be in there."

"*Ana* might be in there." Father Mateo yanked his arm from Hiro's grip. "I'm going in."

Hiro lowered his voice to a whisper. "Through the kitchen door. The coals in the oven will give us light to see."

Father Mateo nodded assent, and they hurried around the house to the kitchen entrance.

Hiro motioned for the priest to step away, pushed the door open slowly, and peered inside. As he hoped, a fire glowed in the oven, faint but enough to confirm the room was empty. Turning his face to the Jesuit, he whispered, "Ana isn't here."

"She could be in the common room," Father Mateo countered. "Fuyu could have killed her and escaped into the forest!"

"Unlikely." Hiro opened the door, allowing the priest to see inside. "If she was here, she would have started dinner. Given the lack of pots on the stove, and the state of the fire, she's probably at the guesthouse."

"We still need to check the common room."

He thought about asking the priest to wait outside, but decided against it. Father Mateo was safer at his side and wouldn't agree to anything different anyway. "Stay no more than a step behind me. If we get attacked, stay clear, but do not let the attacker get between us."

When the Jesuit nodded, Hiro stepped inside.

They crossed the kitchen to the large brick oven. Hiro fed the fire with kindling from a bucket on the floor until a flickering light spread through the room.

Father Mateo indicated the paneled door that led to the common room and whispered, "Do you think the killer is still in there?"

"No." Hiro retrieved a lantern from a line of hooks beside the door, lit it, and handed it to the priest. "But if there's a fight, make sure that I can see."

The Jesuit held the lantern high as Hiro raised his sword, approached the door, and slid it open.

CHAPTER 39

Father Mateo's lantern sent a shaft of light through the common room, illuminating Fuyu's body lying by the hearth in a pool of blood.

Aside from the corpse, the room was empty.

"Stay close." Hiro stepped up onto the floor without removing his sandals. After a death, Midori would have to replace the tatami anyway.

With Father Mateo at his side, he approached the body.

Fuyu lay facedown, but the amount of blood around him—and the dagger poking upward through his neck—confirmed that he was dead. His body was naked to the waist, with his hands tucked underneath his chin, most likely clutching the dagger's hilt. His elbows rested close to his sides, as if he had clutched them to his body after delivering the fatal strike.

"Is he dead?" Father Mateo leaned down toward the body.

"He isn't sleeping." Hiro glanced at the doors that led to Midori's chamber and the room he shared with the Jesuit. Both were closed. The front door still stood open.

"Should I light the braziers?" Father Mateo asked. "So we can see?"

Hiro nodded. "Do not step in the blood."

He looked at the dark, still pool encircling the upper half of Fuyu's body. It soaked the tatami from the corpse's forehead to his waist, suggesting the dagger in his neck was not his only wound.

As the braziers came to life, Hiro said, "Stay here," and quickly checked Midori's room as well as the one he shared with the priest.

After finding them empty, he rejoined the Jesuit at the hearth.

Hiro bent and laid a finger on Fuyu's neck. "He hasn't cooled much. He died an hour ago, two hours at most."

"He must have committed *seppuku* right after Kiku left for the meeting with Hanzō," Father Mateo said. "She knew he killed Yajiro, so he chose death over shame."

"Incorrect," Hiro said. "Fuyu did not kill himself, though someone took great pains to make it look as if he did."

"He died from a self-inflicted wound, while kneeling on the floor with his chest stripped bare. What about that says murder instead of seppuku?" Father Mateo walked around the body. "Maybe he left a suicide poem, telling us what happened."

"Even if he left one, it won't help us," Hiro said. "*Jisei* contain only last reflections on the writer's life. They don't explain the reason for his death. Not as you mean it, anyway. And you will find no poem here. Fuyu did not kill himself."

"It certainly looks like suicide to me."

"Disembowelment takes time to kill, especially without a *kaishakunin* to finish the job with a swift decapitation."

"Isn't that why he stabbed himself in the neck?" Father Mateo looked meaningfully at the bloody blade that pointed toward the ceiling. "To end it quickly?"

"The pattern of the blood is wrong." Hiro shook his head. "Had Fuyu stabbed himself in the neck before his heart stopped beating, spurts of blood would have spattered the floor in front of the place where his body fell.

"There's nothing on this floor except a pool. No spray, no droplets. He was dead before his neck was punctured."

"How is there a pool around his body, then?" the Jesuit asked. "You've told me often, dead men do not bleed."

"They don't bleed *properly*," Hiro corrected. "Blood no longer flows in the veins after the heart stops beating, but it will run toward the ground, and out through any open wound, for several minutes after death."

"Then how did he die?"

"Disembowelment," Hiro said, "but staged to look like suicide. I doubt the killer was here when we arrived. He, or she, is probably at Hanzō's mansion, waiting for us to return with this unfortunate news."

"Should we examine the body, in case the killer left a clue?"

"Not yet." Hiro raised an arm to prevent the priest from moving closer. "If we touch him, the Koga emissaries will claim we altered the evidence."

"Are you certain it's not suicide?" Father Mateo spoke slowly. "Fuyu was the first one to accuse Hattori Hanzō of Yajiro's murder, and the only one not here when we discovered the poisoned tea. According to Neko, Kiku caught him rifling through her poisons box this afternoon. He might be the murderer after all. He could have killed himself because he knew Kiku would expose the truth tonight."

"An interesting theory, but Fuyu would not have chosen a private suicide to atone for Yajiro's death. He would have needed at least one witness to verify that he died with honor. Also, he would have committed the act outside, to avoid defiling Midori's floor."

Father Mateo regarded the body. "The blood may be wrong for suicide, but it doesn't match murder either. Fuyu would have struggled, but that puddle looks as if he didn't move."

"Agreed," Hiro said, "suggesting the killer overpowered him almost instantly, before his blood could spatter the floor too much to hide by placing the body over it."

He started toward the door. "We will not find the answers here."

In the entry, he froze at the sight of a lantern bobbing toward the house.

"Father Mateo?" Ana's question carried toward them through the darkness. "Is that you?"

"Ana!" The Jesuit hurried past Hiro and onto the porch. "Where have you been? What are you doing out so late?"

Hiro retrieved their lantern, which the priest had left beside the brazier, and joined the Jesuit on the porch. As he stepped outside, he closed the door behind him.

Ana stood at the edge of the veranda with a lantern in one hand

and a carefully folded towel in the other. "I wanted to bathe before I prepared your dinner." She bowed. "I apologize. I did not think your meeting with Hattori-*sama* would end so quickly."

"It hasn't ended." Hiro hoped the Jesuit would not mention the dead man in the common room. "We returned for something I'd forgotten."

"Y-yes," Father Mateo stammered. "We came back, but just for a moment. We won't need any dinner here tonight."

"Can you find your way back to the guesthouse in the dark?" Hiro asked.

"I'm old, not stupid." Ana stepped onto the porch. "I'll just lay out your beds before I go."

"Not necessary," Father Mateo said quickly. "We can manage . . . can't we, Hiro?"

Ana frowned at the priest. "What's going on?"

"Nothing." Once again, the Jesuit answered far too quickly.

"Hm." Ana stepped back off the porch. "If you expect me to believe that, next time shut the door more quickly, so I do not see the dead man lying by the hearth."

She walked away along the path, leaving Hiro and Father Mateo stunned.

CHAPTER 40

"I can't believe she wasn't more upset." Father Mateo recovered his voice as Ana's lantern bobbed away into the darkness.

"She would have made a good assassin." Hiro left the porch and started walking.

"Did the same person murder Fuyu and Yajiro," the Jesuit asked, "or do you think we have a second killer?"

"For the moment, logic suggests just one, and Kiku and Neko are now our leading suspects," Hiro said. "Did Toshi stay in the guesthouse the entire time while you were praying?"

"Yes. I left him alone at the end, when he asked to say good-bye to Yajiro, but you were there when he met us on the road, just a few minutes later. He wasn't alone long enough to come all the way back here, commit a murder, and return. Not even if he ran."

"Which brings us back to Kiku and Neko," Hiro said, "both of whom had the skills and training to make a killing look like suicide."

"I hate to ask. . . ." Father Mateo hesitated. "Couldn't Midori or Akiko have murdered him just as easily?"

"Mother would have poisoned him, if not with food or drink, with a tainted dagger and a single strike." Hiro thought of Tane's reaction to Akiko and the girl's decision to place the clue in the Jesuit's sleeve. "Grandmother might have used a blade, but I don't think she would have staged a suicide. She doesn't hide her kills."

"All right, then, Neko and Kiku—but which one?"

"I do not know." Hiro exhaled heavily. "The facts suggest them both. Neko delivered the tea and cakes to the Koga guesthouse, and she has been trying to distract me since the night Yajiro died, when she came to Midori's and—"

"Neko came to Midori's house that night? You didn't tell me. . . ."

"It didn't seem relevant," Hiro admitted. "She wanted to talk about our past—though I realize now, she's been trying to distract me ever since I arrived in Iga. Also, she's been trying to blame Yajiro's murder on Kiku from the start."

"Suggesting guilt," the Jesuit added.

"Now, she conveniently overhears an argument between Kiku and Fuyu shortly before he ends up dead."

"Making the truth an issue of her word against Kiku's." Father Mateo sighed. "I'm sorry, but it does make Neko look guilty."

"Not so fast." Hiro started up the hill toward Hanzō's mansion. "Kiku brewed the welcome tea Yajiro drank before he died. She is familiar with torikabuto, and brought a medicine box from Koga, which certainly contains a selection of poisons along with the healing herbs."

"She wouldn't poison Midori's tea and then agree to drink it," the priest protested. "Also, she supports the alliance. Why would she murder the other emissaries?"

"She *claims* to support the alliance," Hiro corrected, "but once again, we have only her word to rely on. I will point out, also, that Kiku tried to trick Hanzō into killing Toshi less than an hour ago."

"How so? Toshi insulted Hanzō on his own."

"But Kiku made the initial accusation," Hiro said. "Toshi is young and wants to prove himself in order to emerge from Fuyu's shadow. Kiku set him up. If Hanzō had killed him, she would have returned to Koga alone—"

"—with no one to contradict her version of events in Iga." Father Mateo shook his head. "She looks as guilty as Neko does. How will we ever choose between them?"

"At the risk of multiplying the complications," Hiro said, "Akiko mentioned that Tane can throw a dagger with the accuracy required to kill a man in a single strike. We may not know until we turn him over, but if his injuries suggest a ranged attack, the girl may join the suspect list as well."

"At least that means we only have three people to investigate—and we have the envelope Tane gave us. Speaking of which, doesn't that suggest the girl is innocent?"

"Innocent or unusually devious," Hiro said. "We don't yet know."

"The envelope. . . ." Father Mateo trailed off. "Couldn't we check the medicine boxes and see which one is missing torikabuto?"

"Not likely. The killer will have left some in her box, to avoid that problem."

"Unless Tane stole it," the Jesuit offered.

"In which case, she'd also know better than to take the whole supply."

"Good point," the Jesuit said as they entered Hanzō's yard. "Now what?"

"We deliver the news, return to examine the body with Hanzō and the others, and hope the killer makes a mistake."

"That doesn't sound like much of a plan."

Hiro paused, torn between pride and honesty. "I have nothing better to offer. You were right. I'm compromised. I cannot let my mother die, and cannot tell if my suspicions stem from real facts or from emotions. When it comes to Mother, and to Neko, I can no longer tell the truth from lies."

The Jesuit's forehead wrinkled in concern. "I hope you're wrong."

Hiro continued toward the mansion. "You don't hope it half as much as I do."

CHAPTER 41

"Where is Koga Fuyu?" Hanzō demanded as Hiro and Father Mateo entered the room without the missing emissary.

Hiro bowed. "It is my unfortunate duty to inform you that Fuyu-*san* is dead."

Toshi sprang to his feet, triggering Neko to do the same.

Kiku rose more slowly, with suspicion in her eyes. "How did this happen?"

"It appears he committed suicide," Father Mateo said.

Hiro noted how deftly the Jesuit navigated the line between truth and honesty.

"He would not do that!" Toshi exclaimed. "I don't believe you!"

"I also find this difficult to believe." Hanzō stood up. "We will go, together, and see what happened."

Kiku gave Hiro an accusatory look. "Assuming the body has not been moved, or the evidence destroyed."

"We did not move him," Hiro said. "We lit the braziers in the room but otherwise touched nothing."

"This happened in my home?" Midori asked.

Hiro nodded.

She rose. "Then I wish to accompany you also."

The group left Hanzō's house, equipped with lanterns against the darkness. Kiku set off at a rapid pace, while Toshi scurried along behind her like a wolf pup trailing its mother.

Hiro increased his stride to catch them.

"Let them go." At Hanzō's order, Hiro slowed to match his cousin's pace.

Hiro expected Hanzō to have questions about Fuyu's death, but the Iga leader did not speak again. Father Mateo caught Hiro's eye and nodded to Hanzō. Hiro shrugged. He had no intention of giving away information that might help them solve the crime. From that perspective, Hanzō's silence was a welcome, if suspicious, situation.

Neko and Midori walked together at the back of the group, the first time Hiro could remember either woman choosing not to walk with men. Admittedly, the path lacked room for more than three people to walk abreast with ease, but Hiro felt uneasy with Neko at his back.

As they approached Midori's home, Hanzō increased his pace, ensuring they all reached the porch before Kiku and Toshi entered the house.

Without speaking, Kiku left her sandals by the door and went inside.

Behind her, Toshi froze on the threshold, blocking the entry. A sound emerged from the young man's throat, half gasp, half sob. Quickly, he recovered his composure and entered the house, clearing the way for the others to follow.

Kiku gave Hiro a curious look as he joined her beside the corpse. "You told us he committed suicide."

"That was me," Father Mateo said, "not him."

"Do you think otherwise, Kiku-*san*?" Neko stood just inside the door. "Obviously you would know, as you were the last to see him before he died."

Kiku turned. "Is that an accusation?"

"Should it be?"

Kiku's expression hardened. "As it happens, I probably was the last to see him—or, more accurately, second to the last. I argued with Fuyu before I left to attend this evening's meeting. During that argument, I accused him of murdering Yajiro. He refused to admit his guilt. I dressed and left to walk my anger off before the meeting." She frowned at the corpse. "I assure you, he was very much alive when I departed."

"*He* murdered Yajiro-*san*?" Toshi sounded incredulous. "Are you certain?"

"He wanted to sabotage the alliance with Iga at any cost," Kiku said. "I returned from the bathhouse and caught him going through my medicine box. He claimed he was looking for torikabuto, but that was a lie. He planned to steal my poison and blame everything on me!"

"So you killed him." Neko nodded in approval.

"If I had, why make it look like seppuku?" Kiku looked down her nose at the other woman. "Fuyu did not deserve the honor of self-determination. I planned to accuse him tonight, at the meeting."

Hiro wondered what more Kiku wasn't telling them. Fuyu's invasion of her privacy, though offensive, hardly seemed enough to change her mind about Neko's guilt. On the other hand, if Kiku was the killer, she might have shifted her story—and murdered Fuyu—to ensure her safe escape.

"Clearly, Fuyu-*san* opted for suicide over shame." Hanzō gestured to the corpse. "The crime is resolved. Yajiro-*san*'s murderer has confessed, in blood."

Hiro looked at the stained tatami around the corpse and wondered why no one mentioned the lack of spatter. Hanzō had witnessed plenty of ritual suicides and should have recognized the problem instantly. However, the Iga commander cared far less for truth than he did for resolving the situation in a way that matched his plans.

Hiro wished he knew, with clarity, what those plans entailed.

Looking around the room, he grew increasingly chagrined by his inability to separate the innocent from the guilty. Worst of all, he could not risk revealing the evidence for Fuyu's murder with the killer in the room. And the murderer *was* in the room.

Of that, he had no doubt.

He stared at Kiku. Silent moments passed.

Hiro found it interesting that, despite her statement that Fuyu was murdered, neither she nor anyone else objected again to Hanzō's characterization of the death as self-inflicted. However, Hanzō's theory fit the evidence well enough to let the shinobi clans avoid a war—provided the killer did not strike again—a fact that also escaped no one in the room.

Even Hiro found himself torn between the truth and the tenuous safety of Hanzō's lie.

"We cannot leave him here like this." Toshi joined them by the body. "We must lay him properly before his muscles freeze."

Kiku stepped away from the corpse with a look that indicated she did not care.

"I will help you move him." Father Mateo walked around to the far side of the body.

Toshi grasped Fuyu's left arm as the priest took hold of the right. They began to raise him.

"Wait!" Toshi lowered the corpse to the floor without releasing his hold on Fuyu's arm. He pointed to the dead man's side. "What's that?"

A two-inch wound marked Fuyu's skin between his ribs. While he lay on the floor, it had been hidden by his upper arm. The size and shape suggested a dagger—likely, the one projecting from his neck—and the angle of entry between his ribs revealed that someone else's hand had caused it.

Kiku returned and examined the wound. She turned to Hanzō. "As I suspected, Fuyu-*san* was murdered."

CHAPTER 42

An accusatory silence fell. Hiro looked around, but every face seemed carved from stone.

"Iga has now murdered *two* of Koga's emissaries." Kiku drew a dagger from her obi. "Your insult will not go unanswered."

"Please, there is no need for violence." Father Mateo raised his hands. "Allow us to examine the body. We will learn what happened here."

"We already know what happened here," Toshi protested. "The puncture wound between his ribs proves murder."

"But not who did it," the priest replied.

Kiku considered the Jesuit's words. "I will allow an examination, but not until those women leave." She gestured to Midori and Neko.

"Yes, this matter does not concern them," Toshi agreed.

"This has nothing to do with politics." Kiku gave the younger man a disapproving look. "We are outnumbered. Also, I will not have the killer gloating over Fuyu's body."

"Then you had better leave as well," Neko retorted.

"Enough!" Hanzō gestured to the door. "Midori, Neko, you may go."

"Please accept my condolences on the unfortunate death of Koga Fuyu." Midori bowed and left the house, with a scowling Neko on her heels.

"I trust you've no objections to my presence," Hanzō said, "since I do not intend to leave."

"I prefer that you remain, to answer for the actions of your clan." Kiku sheathed her weapon and reached for the dead man's arm, forcing Toshi to step away. "Let us see what Fuyu's corpse reveals."

Hiro found her reaction intriguing. Curiosity about the dead was rare, even among assassins.

Father Mateo reached for Fuyu's other arm. Together, he and Kiku raised the body from the floor. The dagger slipped out of Fuyu's neck and hit the tatami with a sticky thump.

Hiro's sensitive nose rebelled at the stronger odors of blood and excrement wafting up from the moving corpse. Hiding his disgust, he leaned in for a closer look.

Patchy bloodstains marked the spots where Fuyu's forehead, nose, and chin had rested on the floor. The skin beneath already showed the purple flush that appeared a short time after death on the parts of a corpse that rested on the ground.

A river of congealing blood flowed down Fuyu's neck and chest, while several feet of intestine dangled from enormous gashes carved both vertically and horizontally across the dead man's stomach.

Father Mateo and Kiku lowered the body onto its back, facing the ceiling, as Toshi stepped away with a grunt of disgust.

"Do you see anything unusual?" Hanzō asked.

"That depends," the Jesuit said. "Is disembowelment unusual?"

"Completion of both cuts is unusual," Kiku replied. "Few men remain conscious long enough to disembowel themselves completely. As I indicated, this is murder, not a suicide."

"Agreed," Hiro said.

"Clearly the killer did not know Fuyu well," Kiku continued. "No one who did would believe he had the fortitude to finish the cuts, let alone finish the ritual by plunging the dagger into his own neck."

"Do not insult my cousin in front of strangers!" Toshi's lips quivered.

"I show him no less respect than he showed others during life," Kiku retorted.

"The judges of the dead hear everything." Toshi sounded scared.

"The judges of the dead are nothing but a myth to frighten children," Kiku said.

Hiro believed the same, but was impressed that she would speak the thought aloud.

"Fuyu-*san* was dead before the cuts were made?" Father Mateo directed his question to Kiku. "If so, why did they bleed?"

"Blood runs toward the ground for several minutes after death, and sometimes longer," Kiku answered. "Wounds to the heart, delivered through the ribs, kill almost instantly. If the murderer cut the body open within moments after death, and placed it on the floor, facedown, to mimic suicide, the blood would leak enough to make these stains."

"What kind of person would do such a thing?" Toshi struggled to hold a neutral tone.

"An assassin." Kiku gave him a sardonic look. "Of which, Iga has no small supply."

Toshi's expression slowly changed from sorrow to suspicion. "Where is your poison box? You accused my cousin of blaming you for a crime you did not commit . . . and now he dies? Show us your supply of torikabuto and prove your innocence."

"You have no right to question me." Anger rose in Kiku's voice. "Remember your place."

Toshi took a step toward her. "If you did not kill him, prove it. Show us your torikabuto remains untouched."

Steel flashed in Kiku's hand as she leaped across the corpse and landed at Father Mateo's side. "Forgive me, Father." She pressed the point of her dagger to the scar at the base of the Jesuit's neck. "I believe your god calls this a sin."

Hiro reached for his cuff.

"Don't do it," Kiku warned. "I'll kill the priest before your shuriken clears your sleeve."

Slowly, Hiro raised his hands, palms up. "Let the foreigner go, and we'll resolve this situation peacefully."

"I fear that is now impossible." Kiku seized the Jesuit's arm and backed him toward Midori's room, keeping the blade against his neck. "Someone paid the Iga ryu to escort this foreigner safely to Yokoseura. I know enough about foreign priests to know they wouldn't hire you themselves, so Iga's client must be Japanese—most likely, a daimyō—which means that someone important finds this foreigner exceptionally valuable."

"He is not as valuable as I am." Hiro took a small step forward, careful not to seem a threat. "I am Hattori Hanzō's cousin. I will take the foreigner's place."

"A valiant bluff," Kiku said, "but everyone knows Hattori-*sama* will lose more face if the foreigner dies. A cousin, he can sacrifice."

"Kiku . . . why did you kill Fuyu-*san*?" Toshi's voice held the quaver of unshed tears.

"I did not kill him," she replied. "Clearly, Iga wants to ensure that no one from our delegation lives to return to Koga."

"No one wants to keep you here." Hiro motioned to the exit. "Free the Jesuit and leave."

"She murdered Fuyu." Toshi turned to Hanzō with a pleading look. "She killed him."

"I didn't kill anyone, you fool. Someone from Iga did this, either with his approval"—Kiku nodded to Hanzō—"or to stop the alliance. Either way, our lives are in danger. You and I will wait here until dawn, with the priest as hostage, and leave for Koga as soon as there's light to travel."

"Don't believe her," Hanzō said. "If she killed Fuyu, she will kill you also."

"Toshi." Kiku's tone made the younger man turn. "You must believe me. I did not kill Fuyu. Or Yajiro."

Toshi bit his lip. "Show me the torikabuto."

"Will that convince you?" Kiku asked. "Wait here."

With the priest in tow, she entered Midori's room.

A moment later, they reappeared in the doorway. Father Mateo looked worried, and Kiku's knife remained at his neck, skin puckering from the pressure of the blade.

"Someone is trying to set me up." Kiku glared at Hanzō, then at Hiro. "My medicine box is gone."

CHAPTER 43

"Are you certain?" Hanzō asked. "You claimed that Fuyu had it—"

"And I hid it, after our confrontation," Kiku interrupted him. "Beneath a secret board in the bedroom floor."

"My mother showed you her hiding space?" Hiro found that difficult to believe.

"I searched and found it," Kiku said. "There's one—or more—in every shinobi house."

A weighted silence fell.

Hiro breathed deeply and slowly. He needed time to decide which facts were worthy of belief. Unfortunately, he did not possess the luxury of time.

Father Mateo raised his hands in a placating gesture. "Hiro, let me stay with her. It's only for the night."

"It isn't." Hiro spoke to the priest, but looked at Kiku. "Whether or not she murdered the others, she cannot afford to let you go. The moment she does, someone will kill her, if only because she threatened you."

"Not if you don't permit it," the priest said evenly. "Hiro . . . swear you won't."

"I do not speak for Iga, and she knows it."

"But I do," Hanzō intervened. "Kiku-*san*, I give my word that no one will hurt you, if you release the priest unharmed."

She nodded. "I give you my word that I will do so . . . at the border of Koga Province."

"I don't believe you," Hiro said.

"Fortunately for him"—Kiku nodded at Father Mateo—"your belief is not required."

"I will be fine." Father Mateo sounded completely at ease despite the dagger at his neck.

"He is correct," Kiku affirmed. "As long as he does not try to escape and you do nothing foolish."

"What about Fuyu-*san*?" Toshi asked. "We can't just leave him lying here."

"I will have his body moved to the guesthouse," Hanzō said.

"I want to carry him there myself." Toshi's nose began to redden as his eyes filled up with tears. "He was my cousin."

"Iga can move the body." Kiku's voice dripped disapproval. "Do not risk your life for the dead."

"He was my *cousin*," Toshi repeated. "I cannot live with the shame of allowing a stranger to wash his corpse."

"You cannot carry him alone, and only a fool would go out there in the dark with a killer stalking us."

Unless the killer is still here, with us, Hiro thought. "I will help Toshi-*san* move the body, and guarantee his safe return, if you will promise not to harm the priest."

"Thank you, Hattori-*san*." Toshi bowed and looked at Kiku as if for approval.

She shrugged. "I already gave my word. No harm will come to the foreigner, as long as I reach the Koga border safely. As for him"—she indicated Toshi—"only death will cure a fool."

Toshi straightened. "I am a man of honor, not a fool."

"You will need a cloth to wrap the body," Hanzō said. "Does Midori have one?"

"I will check." Hiro searched the house but found nothing suitable.

"Neko has one," Hanzō offered. "I can borrow it for you."

"And arrange an ambush in the process," Kiku said.

"If I go with him, he won't have a chance to plan an ambush," Toshi said.

Hiro found the young man's courage both surprising and impressive. "I will go as well."

"You will stay here," Kiku countered. "Toshi stands a chance against one man . . . especially if Hattori-*sama* leaves his swords behind."

Hanzō watched her for a long, tense moment. "As a show of good faith." The Iga commander slipped his swords from his obi, still in their scabbards, and handed them to Hiro—who barely managed to hide his surprise at his cousin's acquiescence.

Hanzō left, with Toshi on his heels.

Standing there, holding Hanzō's swords, Hiro wondered what he would do if the Iga commander returned alone or, worse, if he did not return at all.

Kiku's voice interrupted his thoughts. "You are wondering why I let him go."

Ignoring the ambiguous pronoun, Hiro replied, "Actually, I'm wondering why you want to stay the night in a place so dangerous you feel you need a hostage."

"As opposed to taking my chances in the dark, on unknown roads?" She paused. "I will release the priest when I reach Koga."

"Why not seal an alliance with Hanzō and secure your safety permanently, along with that of the Koga ryu?" Hiro asked. "Although, admittedly, that would require you to reverse your position on peace between the clans."

Her expression darkened.

"I first suspected it at the welcome feast, when you showed up in peasant clothes. Since then, you've offered several clues—most recently, taking a hostage."

"For clarity: it isn't peace I'm opposed to. Only alliance. Yajiro knew my true position, but asked me to keep an open mind, and to pretend I favored the treaty in order to balance the delegation."

"You humored him because of your past?" Hiro asked.

"He was my friend," Kiku said bitterly. "Now, I wish I had told the truth from the outset. Koga does not require Iga's help, and I have no intention of swearing fealty to Hattori Hanzō."

"Alliances do not equate to servitude," Hiro countered. "Hanzō intended for Iga and Koga to work together, as equals."

"Truly?" Kiku asked. "Which daimyō does Iga support for the shogunate?"

"I do not know, and it does not matter. We could reach consensus. " Hiro noted Father Mateo's unusual silence. "Are you all right?"

"Splendid," the Jesuit said, "except for the dagger at my throat."

Kiku glanced at the priest. "I apologize. It cannot be avoided."

Hiro would have argued that, but Father Mateo spoke before he could.

"You loved a man who wanted this alliance. Won't you support it, in honor of his memory?"

"Before his death, perhaps. But now?" She shook her head. "Also, Koga Yajiro was my friend, but I did not love him."

"Surely even a friend would not have wanted you to hold me hostage?"

"A fair attempt at persuasion," she replied, "but ineffective. I will release you, as promised, upon my safe return to Koga."

"Don't you mean, when you and Toshi return to Koga?" Hiro asked.

Kiku shrugged. "Assuming he doesn't get himself killed in the process."

"If I discover who murdered Yajiro and Fuyu before morning," Hiro said, "will you release the priest before you go?"

In the silence that followed Hiro wondered, if Kiku was the killer, whether she would gamble on his failure.

"I cannot," she said. "I need him to ensure my safety, and Toshi's, on the road. However, if you discover the murderer's identity by dawn, I will let you travel with us to the border of Koga Province and release the foreigner to you there."

"Acceptable." It wasn't, of course, but Hiro only needed to ensure the Jesuit's safety long enough to figure out another plan.

"I am sorry. I do not understand what is happening." Father Mateo switched to Portuguese. "Has it occurred to you that she might be the killer?"

"Obviously," Hiro replied in the Jesuit's language. "But I need the time to plan a rescue."

"For me?"

"Do you see someone else in need of rescue?"

Father Mateo smiled and switched to Japanese. "Thank you. Now I understand."

As he finished speaking, Toshi and Hanzō returned with a bolt of cloth. After handing back the commander's swords, Hiro helped the other men spread out the cloth and move the body onto it.

Toshi knelt and gently wrapped the cloth around the body.

When he finished, Kiku said, "Do what you must and come back quickly. Use the coded knock when you return."

The young man nodded.

Kiku looked at Hiro and then at Hanzō. "Anyone who enters this house without the proper knock will cost the foreigner his life and get a dagger through the eye. I recommend you do not test my patience . . . or my aim."

CHAPTER 44

Hanzō accompanied Toshi and Hiro along the path back through the village. He carried a lantern, but did not offer to help them with the corpse. At the base of the hill that led to his mansion, Hanzō asked, "Would you like to take the lantern?"

Hiro nodded toward the moon that glowed above the trees. "That will suffice."

Hanzō started up the hill as Hiro and Toshi continued along the path with Fuyu's body.

"I humbly apologize for shaming you." Toshi sounded both sorry and serious.

"Shaming me?" Hiro echoed.

"By asking you to defile yourself by carrying the body of your enemy."

"Fuyu was not my enemy," Hiro said, "and corpses cannot defile the living. The dead are merely dead and cannot hurt us. Even Father Mateo knows this truth."

"The foreigner believes this also?"

"More than most Japanese people do. According to his holy scriptures, only the evil inside a man can defile him."

In the moonlight, Toshi lowered his head to look at the body. "Fuyu-*san*'s insides did not make this happen."

Technically, they did, when they fell out of him. Wisely, Hiro kept the thought to himself. "I am sorry about his death. It was unfortunate."

When the younger man nodded, Hiro continued, "You said he was your cousin?"

"Through my mother's sister. When I was young, my father sent me to live and train with Fuyu's family. In many ways he seemed more like an older brother than a cousin." Toshi paused. "May I speak honestly?"

"An honorable man would do no differently."

Toshi did not answer for several seconds, as if struggling with the words. "I wish Fuyu-*san* had not died, but he was a difficult man to know, at times."

"Some men are like that," Hiro said.

"Some women too."

It was the opening Hiro hoped for. "You accused Kiku-*san* of killing him. . . ."

Toshi did not answer immediately, but Hiro let the silence hang.

At last, Toshi made an embarrassed sound. "It seemed safer than accusing Hattori Hanzō. When I realized Fuyu hadn't killed himself, I worried someone would start a fight, and that I might end up dead as well. Seeing Fuyu on the floor, I realized I didn't want to die. That sounds cowardly, but it's the truth."

"And now," Hiro continued, "do you believe she killed him?"

"I don't think so," Toshi replied, "mainly because I don't believe she murdered Yajiro-*san*, and it seems more likely that the same person killed them both."

"Have you any idea who that might be?"

"With no offense intended, I can tell you why I think it's someone from Iga and not Kiku-*san*," Toshi said. "The night we left Koga, I had an upset stomach, and I ran to the latrine all night. On one of the trips, I heard moaning coming from Yajiro's room. At first, I thought he was hurt, so I ran to help. . . ."

After an awkward silence, he continued, "I saw Kiku leaning over him. . . ."

Once more, the young man's voice faded away.

"I see," Hiro said.

"I wish I hadn't."

A twig cracked in the darkness north of the road. Hiro and Toshi froze on the path. Overhead, the waxing moon sent silver beams across the fields, but in the forest, shadows ruled. A chilly wind rustled through the trees.

"Who's there?" Toshi called.

They heard no answer. Hiro did not expect one. Only two people would follow them in secret: Neko and the killer. And if he was honest, he wasn't certain whether that was truly two people or only one.

"Keep moving," he said, "it's just the wind."

Toshi must have believed the lie, because he continued along the path and also continued talking. "The following morning, I told Fuyu about the affair. He flew into a rage and planned to confront Yajiro when we reached Iga. He also said that he and I would expose the truth to Koga when we returned."

"Are such affairs forbidden?" Hiro asked.

"They are when the participants are promised to someone else."

Once again, Hiro appreciated Fuyu's hesitance to leave the younger man unsupervised. Toshi trusted far too quickly, revealing information a more experienced spy would keep to himself.

Before Hiro could settle on a sufficiently innocuous follow-up question, Toshi continued, "Yajiro-*san*'s father hadn't announced the betrothal, but I overheard Yajiro-*san* discussing it with Kiku, the night I caught them together. Actually, they were arguing. She seemed angry that he wouldn't break it off with the other woman and agree to marry her instead."

"You are certain you heard correctly?" Hiro asked.

"Absolutely." Toshi's head bobbed up and down in the moonlight. "Kiku said, 'You promised me that you wouldn't allow this to happen.' Yajiro said he had tried to break it off, but wasn't strong enough to resist the woman's tears."

"Did either of them mention the woman by name?" Hiro asked.

"No, but Kiku said, 'No man should ever be a slave to tears.' I shouldn't say any more, but now you know why I believe that Iga is to blame."

Inside the guesthouse, Hiro and Toshi laid Fuyu's body gently beside the hearth.

Hiro stirred the coals to life. Someone had left a well-banked fire, presumably as a show of respect for Yajiro's body in the adjacent room.

"May I help you make arrangements?" Hiro asked, mostly out of politeness.

"No, but thank you," Toshi said. "I wish to wash his body, and arrange him properly, before he stiffens."

"Shall I bring you a bucket of water?"

"Thank you, but I must do this myself, so I can tell his father—and mine—that I handled everything personally." After a pause, he added, "If you do not mind . . . I would prefer to be alone."

"I gave my word that I would ensure your safety until you returned to Midori's house."

"With respect, I do not need a bodyguard to wash the dead. I will explain to Kiku and take full responsibility."

Hiro nodded and started toward the door.

Unexpectedly, Toshi asked, "If I persuaded Kiku-*san* to release the priest, would Hattori-*sama* still agree to a treaty with the Koga ryu?"

Hiro turned around. "He might."

Toshi looked down at Fuyu's empty eyes. "This death has made me realize, even more deeply, how much I stand to lose if Iga and Koga go to war." He looked up. "I wish to know if a chance for peace remains."

"I cannot speak for Hanzō," Hiro said, "but I will speak to him on your behalf, if you arrange the Jesuit's release."

"Thank you." Tears filled Toshi's eyes. "Perhaps these men will not have died in vain."

CHAPTER 45

After leaving the guesthouse, Hiro stood in the darkness beneath the trees and plotted his next move. He needed to rescue Father Mateo, but doubted he could manage it alone. Unfortunately, he didn't know who he could trust to help him.

He noticed a flickering glow from the oiled paper windows of the other Iga guesthouse, just a couple of minutes' walk through the trees. The light pierced the darkness like a beacon, in more ways than one.

Ana could create a diversion and help him free the priest.

He started toward her guesthouse, but abandoned the plan before he reached the door. Ana would help, and gladly, but Hiro would not put her life in danger.

He thought of other people he might ask.

Midori and Neko had the skills, but both had touched the tea and cakes that probably killed Yajiro, both had access to Midori's tea, and either could have murdered Fuyu before arriving at Hanzō's home. As far as he knew, only Neko opposed the alliance, but either would have killed at Hanzō's order. In the end, he couldn't trust either woman enough to ask for help, though it did occur to him that the killer might jump at the chance to murder Kiku too.

"Hiro? Is that you?" Ana appeared, carrying a lantern. "What are you doing out here in the dark alone?"

"I could ask the same of you."

"Hm. An elderly woman can't use a latrine without someone asking questions?" The lantern deepened the wrinkles on her face. "In any case, I'm glad you're here. That woman came by with a message for you, and now I don't have to deliver it to the other end of Iga in the dark."

"A woman?" Hiro asked. "Which woman?"

"Hm. The one you *didn't* name Gato for."

"I didn't name the cat for Neko. It's merely coincidental that they both mean . . ." He trailed off. The more he tried to explain the less persuasive it sounded, even to him.

Ana rested a hand on her hip.

"Neko came to see you?" Hiro hoped the question would put the conversation back on track.

"A little while ago. She said she has urgent information that can help you, and wants you to meet her at the bathhouse by the river. She said you must come alone and ensure that no one follows you. She'll be waiting in the tub, as a sign of good faith, because 'naked people can't hide weapons.'" Ana scowled. "This is not the time to rekindle old affairs."

Hiro suddenly felt even more defensive. "It's not what you're thinking."

Ana's eyebrows raised in unison. "It's exactly what I'm thinking." She looked around, suddenly confused. "Where's Father Mateo?"

"Sleeping." *Hopefully, at least.* "Did Neko tell you why it's so important that she meets with me alone?"

"Hm. I think that's obvious."

Something crackled behind them in the forest.

Ana raised the lantern and her voice. "Who's there? Come into the light!"

Hiro couldn't help but admire the lack of fear in the housekeeper's voice and posture.

When no one appeared, Ana lowered the lantern. "Probably an owl. I saw a huge one in a tree by the latrine."

Hiro lowered his voice and repeated, "Did Neko say anything more?"

"That you should trust her." The housekeeper frowned. "Nobody worth trusting has to say that you can trust them. Don't you put Father Mateo in danger, either."

"I promise not to take him with me." Hiro felt a rush of relief that Ana didn't seem to know about the Jesuit's current predicament.

She gave him a long, judgmental look. "Hm. You'd better be telling the truth."

"I give you my word."

Hiro escorted Ana back to the guesthouse and ensured that no one was hiding in or around the building. As he expected, the search revealed nothing.

"Thank you for delivering Neko's message," he said as the housekeeper went inside. "Secure the door, and open it only for Father Mateo or for me. We will not send a message to you by anyone else tonight."

Suspicion hardened the housekeeper's features, but she asked no questions. Instead, she merely nodded and closed the door.

After waiting to hear the bolt slide shut, Hiro returned to the path. He walked as silently as he could without sacrificing a normal pace, listening for any sign of another person in the trees. Slowly, his thoughts returned to the pressing problems: freeing the priest, identifying the killer, and whether or not to accept Neko's invitation.

Out of time and with no better options, he decided it was time to force the truth.

CHAPTER 46

Lanterns glowed in Hanzō's courtyard, setting the maple trees ablaze. Normally, Hiro would have paused to savor the contrast between the warm-colored foliage and the chilly air. Tonight, he passed without a second glance.

If he wanted to survive the next few minutes, he could not afford distractions.

He crossed the veranda, slipped off his sandals, and banged his fist on the heavy door. Moments later, it swung open, revealing Hattori Hanzō. The Iga commander seemed surprised to see Hiro, and looked past him as if expecting someone else.

Without bowing, Hiro stormed inside, bumping Hanzō's shoulder in the process.

"Hey!"

Ignoring Hanzō's angry comment, Hiro stalked through the entry and did not stop until he reached the audience chamber. He stopped in the center of the room and stared at the flying falcon rendered by his father's hand. In the flickering light from the braziers, she almost seemed to breathe.

For an instant, Hiro wished he believed in gods, or even ghosts. At least, if they existed, he would not have to face this fight alone.

The unfamiliar chill of fear sent icy fingers down his spine, where they grasped the surge of adrenaline that flooded outward through his limbs.

Inhaling deeply, he stilled his thoughts and slipped his hand into his sleeve. His fingers brushed the envelope of torikabuto as they closed around his shuriken. He gripped the metal star in his fist, allowing the pointed edges to poke out between his fingers.

Footsteps entered the room behind him.

"What is the meaning of this!" Hanzō demanded. "Have you lost your mind?"

Hiro did not turn around.

"You will answer when I speak!" Hanzō approached with heavy, angry steps.

Just before the commander reached him, Hiro pulled his hand from his sleeve. He spun around, swinging his loaded fist at Hanzō's neck.

The Iga commander sprang away, angry scowl replaced by disbelief as a line of bloody droplets rose across the base of his neck.

Hanzō raised a hand to the spot. His fingers smeared the droplets. As he drew his hand away, he glanced at his bloodstained fingers and then at Hiro. His eyes narrowed.

A dagger appeared in Hanzō's hand.

Hiro ducked the initial strike and somersaulted backward out of range.

He sprang to his feet as Hanzō lunged again. The blade fell short, and Hiro slashed with the shuriken, forcing his cousin to back away.

They circled one another, feinting.

Hiro focused on the commander's eyes, trusting them to indicate a strike before it came.

"What's wrong with you?" Hanzō snapped.

"If you can't tell, I'm doing it wrong." Hiro swung his shuriken-loaded fist at Hanzō's face and backed away—but not quite fast enough.

Hanzō's dagger slashed through Hiro's kimono and opened a gash in his arm just above the wrist.

Hiro frowned at the gaping rip in the silk and the crimson blood that already began to stain it. "Now you've ruined my kimono."

In answer, Hanzō attacked again.

Hiro sidestepped, turned, and flung himself at Hanzō's knees. Grasping the leader's legs, he knocked his cousin backward to the ground. It wasn't a tactic he used often, but Hiro noted with irony that it seemed to work unusually well in Iga.

Hanzō lost his grip on his dagger and landed hard. The weapon dropped to the floor and rolled to a stop just out of reach.

Pressing the advantage, Hiro struggled to pin his cousin to the floor, but Hanzō thrust his hips toward the ceiling, seized the neck of Hiro's kimono, and threw him into the air like a sack of rice.

Hiro flew over Hanzō's head, careful to keep his hold on the shuriken and to block his fall with his empty hand. He rolled to his feet, but before he could stand, a blow to the back of his shoulders knocked him facedown to the floor.

Hanzō planted a knee on Hiro's back, forcing the air from his lungs.

Hiro glanced around, but Hanzō's dagger had disappeared. Expecting to feel it pierce his neck at any moment, Hiro reached his fist behind his back and slashed with the shuriken, forcing Hanzō to lean away. The pressure on his spine released for only a moment, but it was enough.

Hiro pushed himself off the floor and flipped onto his back.

Hanzō grabbed for Hiro's wrist, but Hiro spat in his cousin's face. Hattori Hanzō roared in anger, the sound cut short as Hiro punched him in the stomach. Hanzō grunted and doubled over.

Hiro rolled away. Pushing up to his feet, he faced his cousin.

A drop of Hiro's blood ran down the shuriken and pattered on the floor.

Hanzō straightened, brandishing his dagger.

Hiro risked a glance at his injured arm. Blood now streaked the kimono sleeve, and left a pattern of drops and smears across the once-pristine tatami.

Hanzō made a disgusted noise and flung his weapon to the floor.

"What are you doing?" Hiro asked, confused but wary.

"I could ask the same of you." Hanzō's face was flushed with anger. "You should have killed me easily with the first attack, and you pulled at least one other strike."

"If we're counting? I pulled more than one."

"Explain yourself!" Hanzō shouted.

"I needed to know if you would kill me."

Hanzō crossed his arms. "Do not tempt me."

Hiro picked up Hanzō's weapon from the floor and extended the handle toward his cousin.

The Iga commander accepted and sheathed his weapon. "Explain yourself, and be persuasive, or I will order you hanged at dawn."

"Who chose me to attend these negotiations?" Hiro asked.

"That is not an explanation."

"Answer my question, and I will answer yours."

Slowly, Hanzō's fury faded, though his eyes still smoldered. "Neko insisted on your presence. I did not want you here at all." After a moment, Hanzō added, "I believe you understand why."

"Because you never intended to negotiate an alliance with Koga," Hiro said. "You planned to murder the delegation, and knew that I would not cooperate."

"Wrong." Hanzō's nostrils flared. "Because I did not want my chance for peace with Koga thwarted by a willful, insubordinate man who cannot take an order without argument!"

Hiro shrugged. "Close enough."

"Iga sent you to guard that priest as a punishment, yet you wear it as a badge of honor," Hanzō snarled.

"I no longer consider protecting the priest a punishment," Hiro said. "Mateo is an honorable man, and has become my friend."

Hanzō's face turned purple. "You exceed your mandate, solving murders in Kyoto and not staying in the shadows as you should!"

Hiro saw no reason to reply. His cousin spoke the truth.

"Surely you did not come here, and provoke a fight, because you longed to discuss your personal failings," Hanzō said.

"I needed to know if you wanted me dead, and if not, why you would make me work with Neko. Surely you knew the pairing was ill-advised."

Hanzō's mouth fell open. The color faded from his cheeks. "You truly believe I ordered the deaths of Yajiro and Fuyu."

Hiro raised an eyebrow at his cousin. "Persuade me otherwise."

CHAPTER 47

"I have no obligation to explain myself to you," Hanzō declared. "Even so, I choose to answer your question. Lord Oda's recent attempt on my life made me realize Iga is vulnerable. He wants to seize control of Japan, and to do that he will eliminate everything and everyone he cannot control.

"An alliance with Koga is the only way to save not only Iga but all shinobi clans from extinction in the coming war. Only by standing together can Iga and Koga ensure the samurai who becomes the new shogun will not try to exterminate us along with his samurai rivals.

"Don't you think I know what you've been doing in Kyoto? Why would I ever bring you to Iga if I planned to murder the Koga emissaries?"

"You might have thought that Neko could distract me," Hiro said. "She's certainly trying."

Hanzō snorted. "I thought she cured you of that weakness years ago."

"You did not order her to distract me, then?" Hiro no longer suspected Hanzō of ordering the murders. Not because of his cousin's words, but because Hanzō had several chances to kill him during their fight and had not done so.

"I gave her no such order." Hanzō's forehead wrinkled in disapproval. "Would you mind not bleeding on my tatami?"

Hiro wrapped his ruined kimono sleeve around his arm to stanch the flow of blood.

"I cannot believe you suspect me of killing those emissaries," Hanzō continued. "Surely you realize Kiku must have done it."

"I have an answer to that," Hiro said, "but you won't like what I have to say."

"Do I ever?"

"Kiku may have killed the emissaries, but Neko looks equally guilty. Neither woman wants this alliance, and both have motives for wanting the others dead."

"Neko insisted on having you here. She knows you've hunted killers in Kyoto."

"Hardly proof of innocence," Hiro said. "She's been manipulating all of us since I arrived."

"Nonsense," Hanzō scoffed. "She's not that foolish."

"No, but she is that arrogant."

"Neko would never violate my trust." Hanzō shook his head. "She is unfailingly loyal and obedient to the Iga ryu . . . to me."

Hiro felt a flash of something uncomfortably close to jealousy.

Fabric rustled in the doorway.

Hanzō looked past Hiro. "Good evening, Midori."

"What's going on here?"

Hiro forced a smile and turned. "A friendly wrestling match." He tucked his injured arm behind his back. "Like we did when we were younger."

Midori did not return his smile. "When you were children, you cut his lip and he blacked your eyes on a regular basis, but I don't seem to remember you using blades." She sighed. "Have you finished your game, or should I come back later?"

"Hiro was just leaving," Hanzō said. "Come in, and we can have our meeting."

"After I see that his wound is cleaned and bandaged," Midori replied.

Hanzō nodded. "Very well. I will wait for you here."

Midori led Hiro to the kitchen, where she examined his injured arm. "This needs cleaning." She retrieved a ceramic flask from the cupboard. "Hold your arm out over the basin."

Hiro obeyed without a word, feeling suddenly five years old again.

Midori pulled the ruined sleeve away, exposing the bloody wound. Slowly, she tipped the flask and poured a narrow stream of sake over the injury. Hiro hissed. The liquid burned with a fierceness that sent weakness through his knees.

He drew a sharp breath as the odor reached his nose. "That's Hanzō's best sake!"

"A man who chooses to act like a child cannot complain when his choices cost him." Midori nodded at Hiro's arm. "I don't think that needs stitching, but you tell me if it hasn't closed tomorrow."

Hiro nodded, gritting his teeth against the pain.

Midori wrapped a strip of silk around the cut and bound it tight. "I thought you had outgrown picking fights with Hanzō."

Somehow, she always knew when he was to blame. "What would you do if an enemy threatened the life of your closest friend?"

"Hanzō is not the one who seized the priest," Midori said.

"How did you know . . . ?" He trailed off, loathing himself again for suspecting her.

Midori lowered her voice. "Not here."

She led him through the house. At the porch, they slipped on their sandals and walked across the yard.

Hiro glanced at the moon, now risen high above the trees, and wondered how long Neko would wait for him at the bathhouse.

When they reached the gates, Midori stopped in a pool of flickering golden light created by the large stone lantern just to the left of the compound entrance. Hiro hesitated, suddenly aware his mother had chosen precisely the spot where he had hidden to speak with the priest about the envelope of torikabuto.

"How do you know about Father Mateo?" he asked again. "You left before it happened."

"Hanzō sent Akiko with a message," Midori said, "though I had already heard the news from Neko. She didn't leave when Hanzō dismissed us. She hid by the door and listened."

"Why would she do that?"

"Don't be foolish," Midori said. "I know you want to save the priest, but you can't rescue him alone."

"Why did Neko stay to listen?" Hiro repeated.

"She refused to leave with you in peril."

Hiro made a derisive noise. "Neko doesn't care about my safety. She's up to something. I think she might be involved in the murders."

"Is that why you fought with Hanzō?" Midori tilted her head to the side. "Do you think he ordered her to distract you?"

"No."

"Don't lie to your mother." Midori smiled, but it faded almost instantly. "You should not be here. Didn't you get Neko's message? Was that what prompted your fight with Hanzō?"

"Message?" Hiro feigned ignorance.

"No time for games," Midori said. "Neko needed to get you a message. I told her to ask the foreigner's maid to deliver it, because no one suspects a servant."

"I got the message," Hiro replied. "What does she want—and why the bathhouse?"

"A naked person cannot conceal a blade." Midori shrugged. "Knowing Neko, she probably also hopes for something more intimate."

"As if I'd be attracted to her now?"

"Those words might persuade the priest, but you cannot fool me." Midori drew a breath, but hesitated, as if to change her mind about her words. "Go to the bathhouse. Allow Neko to explain."

"What she did requires no explanation!" Hiro stepped backward, shocked by his own vehemence. He bowed. "I humbly apologize. I should not have raised my voice to you."

"Neko cares for you," Midori said. "More truly, and more deeply, than you know."

"How can you say that? Have you forgotten what she did to me?"

Midori laid a hand on Hiro's shoulder. "Many years ago, I bound these wounds. I did not realize they festered still."

"I'm not festering." Hiro didn't like hearing the Jesuit's wisdom repeated in his mother's voice.

Midori pulled her hand away. "Neko's scars are hidden, but they run at least as deep as those you bear."

"She chose to inflict them. I did not!"

"There you are mistaken, Hiro. What she did to you was not by choice."

CHAPTER 48

"Not by choice?" Hiro searched Midori's face. "Why didn't you tell me this before?"

"If I had told you, Hanzō would have killed you, on his father's orders."

Reality, as Hiro knew it, shifted underneath his feet. Truths that he relied upon collapsed like avalanching snow. If Neko had not betrayed him voluntarily . . . "Hanzō's father ordered her to do it?"

"For the benefit of the Iga ryu." Midori spoke softly, as if to dull the impact of her words. "You were *almost* the best assassin Iga ever trained. You had one fatal weakness."

"Neko."

"No," Midori corrected. "Your trust for those you love. Neko, yes, but me as well. Hanzō—your cousin's father—believed betrayal would make you Iga's perfect weapon."

"No one is that cruel. I don't believe you." Despite his words, he suddenly knew it was true.

"I was there the night he ordered Neko to betray you."

Midori's words fell like daggers into Hiro's heart.

"You knew? And you did nothing?"

She continued as if he hadn't spoken. "Neko refused, but Hanzō said if she did not obey his order, or if you ever learned the truth, he would kill you slowly, and make both Neko and me watch him do it. His son—your cousin—was there, and Hanzō ordered him to fulfill the penalty also, if you learned the truth after your cousin assumed control of the Iga ryu." Midori bowed her head. "I am sorry, Hiro. Concealing this from you—lying to you—is the most difficult thing that I have ever done."

"Why tell me now? Did Hanzō change his mind about carrying out his father's order?"

"Neko and I decided that you need our help to save the priest. Neko has a plan, but we knew that you would never trust her . . . unless you knew the truth."

"I do not trust her anyway!" Realizing he had misdirected his anger for all these years made it flare with even more intensity.

"At least allow her to explain."

Hiro's suspicions swooped back in with a vengeance. "Suddenly, neither you nor she is worried about Hanzō killing me?"

"I'm more concerned about you killing him." Midori glanced at the gates. "Promise me that you will not."

Hiro didn't answer.

"Iga cannot afford to lose its leader with Japan on the brink of war." Midori's stare bored into him. "Your cousin is not responsible for his father's decisions—or the oaths that he was forced to take."

As usual, she was right.

Hiro exhaled heavily. "I will uphold my oath to defend the ryu."

She nodded. "If you plan to meet with Neko, you should go."

He pulled the envelope from his sleeve. "I think you dropped this as we left the mansion."

Midori examined the folded paper. "That's not mine, and you know it. Where did it come from?"

"I'm not certain. Can you tell me?"

"I can try." She accepted the envelope and carefully looked inside. Frowning, she raised the paper and sniffed its contents. "Where did you get this?"

"Someone gave it to me," Hiro said. "I can't reveal who."

"You know this isn't the torikabuto that killed Yajiro."

"It isn't?" Hiro asked. "Are you certain?"

"This is mixed with willow bark. Nothing I cooked would have hidden the taste, and no tea would disguise it either." Midori shook the envelope slightly. "Depending on where you found this, it suggests the killer plans to strike again."

"I don't know where it came from." Hiro wavered, but necessity proved stronger than suspicion. "Can you tell me anything more about it?"

Midori bent toward the lantern, looked more closely, and shook her head. "Not in this light. I could probably find out what the paper's made from, which would tell us whether the envelope was made in Iga or somewhere else."

"That may be all I need to know."

She slipped the envelope up her sleeve. "I'll let you know as soon as I can. Now go—Neko is waiting, and you have a friend to save."

Hiro cut through the forest and down the hill to the east of Hanzō's mansion, staying off the path to ensure he wasn't seen. His mind replayed Midori's words, as well as the night of Neko's betrayal—a scene he had tried to forget for years, but still recalled in excruciating detail.

As he combed his memories, the facts confirmed Midori's version better than he anticipated. By the time he reached the bottom of the hill, he had decided he believed her.

The core of anger burning in his chest made Hiro glad he hadn't known the truth before he fought with Hanzō. Given the chance again, he did not know if he could stay his hand.

Approaching the river, he smelled the distinctive odor of burning pine and noticed a column of pale smoke rising up from the chimney of the bathhouse.

Hiro shook his head. The elderly woman who owned the establishment lived a short distance away through the trees. In the past, she had often left the fire burning late at Neko's request. Apparently, some things did not change.

He remembered his frustration at learning he missed his bath that afternoon. Apparently, he would get one after all.

Suddenly, Hiro felt as if someone released a fistful of silkworms in his stomach. His cheeks grew warm as the rustling in his belly spread to his knees. Forcing the nervousness away, he started toward the bathhouse door.

No noren hung in the entry, and the lantern by the door was dark, indicating the bathhouse was closed for the night.

Even so, the wooden door swung open beneath his hand.

He passed through the silent entry and into the changing room beyond, where a brazier burned in the corner near the wall. Despite Neko's invitation, which suggested a meeting in the bath, he half expected to find her waiting for him in the changing room. However, the narrow room was empty except for a dark-colored tunic and trousers hanging on one of the hooks beside the paneled door that led to the bathing chamber.

Across from the clothing, a line of buckets, brushes, and wooden stools sat beside a metal pump that drew cold water from the river. The floor around the stools was wet. Puddles glistened near the slatted drain on the chamber floor.

Hiro tried not to envision Neko waiting naked in the bath.

He failed.

To say he had mixed feelings about the encounter was an understatement. He stared at the door to the bathing room, trying to decide if he trusted Neko enough to disrobe before entering. It was highly inappropriate to enter a bath unwashed, or wearing clothing, but taking off his clothes would make him vulnerable to attack.

Hiro started across the room. He would not strip and allow himself to be played for a fool a second time.

At the door to the bathing room, he paused.

Passing through that door with clothes on violated every rule of bathing he had known since early childhood. Refusing to disrobe would also make him look afraid.

Frustration warred with common sense. In the end, he realized a thin kimono did less to block a blade than nakedness would do to protect his honor.

Hiro stepped away from the door and stripped off his kimono, hesitating for only a moment before removing his loincloth too. He hung his clothes on the hook adjacent to Neko's, sighing at the ruined sleeve. His arm no longer bled beneath the bandage, but it had begun to ache and burn. He would have to be careful to avoid reopening it in the bath.

He crossed the room to the row of stools, grasped the nearest bucket, and held it under the pump while he worked the lever. Frigid water spurted from the tap. He shivered as a spray of droplets spattered against his shins. The fire in the boiler room heated the bath itself, but the water from the river was untreated, freezing cold.

After a deep, preparatory breath, he raised the bucket and poured the water over his head. The icy liquid forced the breath from his lungs. Teeth chattering, he reached for a brush and scrubbed his skin, moving quickly as he rubbed the blood from his arms and hands, avoiding only the spot around the bandage. He filled the bucket once again and held his breath as he rinsed his body with the frigid water.

Naked and dripping, he reached for one of the tiny, hand-sized towels sitting on a shelf above the washing station. People normally carried them into the bath to wipe away perspiration, but Hiro had a different plan in mind.

Towel in hand, he crossed the room and retrieved the shuriken from his kimono sleeve. Neko and Midori would have him believe he had nothing to fear from the bath, but he would never again trust assumptions.

Hiro closed his fist around the shuriken, letting the points protrude between his fingers. The cut on his arm protested as his muscle flexed, but he ignored the pain. He draped the little towel over his fist to hide the weapon and approached to the wooden door that led to the bath.

The silkworms in his stomach metamorphosed into moths.

He drew a breath, and then another, dispelling the unexpected weakness in his knees. He reminded himself that a fight most likely awaited him in the bathing chamber. Slowing his breathing, he paused until his heartbeat slowed, then opened the door.

CHAPTER 49

A dense cloud of steamy air flooded out of the bathing chamber like the exhalation of a dragon. The piney, slightly salty aroma suggested Neko had scented the water—confirming that, as Midori mentioned, the woman had more in mind than merely rescuing the priest.

Alert for an ambush, Hiro stepped inside . . . and found the chamber empty.

Flickering braziers lit the room, illuminating the giant cedar bathtub at its center. The tub steamed like a cauldron, filling the air with humid heat that condensed and trickled in droplets down the walls. The braziers cast an orange glow on the wood and tinted the water scarlet.

Hiro stopped and looked again.

The water in the tub *was* red.

An instant later, he noticed the ferrous odor of blood beneath the scent of piney steam. He looked more closely at the room, and froze in horror.

Bloody streaks ran down the wall beside the door, the crimson trails barely visible against the varnished wood. More blood smeared the side of the tub away from the door, suggesting a wounded person had tried to flee.

Hiro pulled the towel off his fist and dropped it to the floor. Shuriken raised, he took a step forward and peered into the circular tub.

Except for the water, it was empty.

Walking around the side of the bath, he discovered Neko's blood-streaked body lying on the wooden floor.

Crimson liquid puddled around her, partially water and partially blood. Her eyes stared sightlessly at the wall. In one hand, she clutched the edge of a bloody towel, while the other lay across her chest, index finger stained with crimson. A gaping wound in her neck and slashes on her hands and arms revealed her death was not a suicide.

Hiro dropped the shuriken and collapsed to his knees beside her body. His throat swelled closed until he couldn't breathe.

He felt for a pulse, but the stillness beneath his fingers confirmed what his eyes and heart already knew.

He felt weak. The room began to spin. He set his hands on the floor and closed his eyes until the dizziness passed. When he opened them, his stomach churned.

His breaths came far too fast, but for the first time in his life, he could not slow them. Tears blurred his vision as he lifted Neko's body in his arms. He buried his face in her hair, and the scent of jasmine filled his nose—but for only a moment, before crying closed his sinuses and rendered smell beyond him.

At first, the force of his emotions pushed out conscious thought. But as he held her, an idea seeped into his mind, soft but insistent, like a mosquito buzzing in a silent room.

This is your fault.

The assassin must have entered the bathhouse after Neko entered the tub. She would have turned when the door swung open, but slowly, expecting Hiro. Her assumption gave the killer the advantage of surprise.

If he hadn't fought with Hanzō, or delayed so long with Midori, he might have arrived in time to save her life.

An anguished moan escaped his lips. He clutched her body close, consumed by grief.

"What have you done?" Midori's cry echoed off the walls.

Hiro looked up. At the sight of his mother's horrified eyes, he realized how the scene must look: his naked body covered in Neko's blood, his shuriken on the floor nearby.

He found his voice. "I didn't . . ."

The rest of the sentence faded away as Hanzō entered the room behind Midori.

For several moments, no one spoke.

The Iga commander's lip curled in disgust. "I knew you swore to avenge yourself, but never imagined you would dare to murder her." He turned to Midori. "You claimed they had a plan to save the priest—"

"I did not kill her." A breath of cool air from the door made gooseflesh rise on Hiro's arms and chest. "Someone else—"

"How dare you deny the obvious truth!" Hanzō laid a hand on his sword. "Less than an hour ago, you accused her of murdering the Koga emissaries. Clearly, you came to accuse her, lost control, and killed her in a rage. Your petty grudge has cost me my best assassin!"

"That is not true." Hiro glanced at Midori. "You know I wouldn't—"

"Hanzō." Hiro's mother stepped between them. "Please allow him to explain."

"Stand aside, Midori," Hanzō ordered. "This does not concern you."

"He would not have killed her. Not tonight." Her voice grew grave. "He knew the truth."

For a moment, Hanzō looked confused, but realization crept across his face. "She broke her oath?"

"No." Midori straightened. "I broke mine."

Hanzō drew his sword. "The penalty for taking the life of an Iga shinobi is beheading—a traitor's death."

Hiro gently lowered Neko's body to the floor. "I swear to you, on my honor and by any gods you wish to invoke, I did not take her life. Why would I kill her when I finally knew the truth?"

"A traitor's oath means nothing," Hanzō snarled.

"Hanzō, be reasonable. Hiro would never—"

The Iga commander raised his sword. "Hattori Hiro, I condemn you to death for the murder of Kotani Neko. Have you anything to say before I carry out your punishment?"

Hiro rose. "I do not accept the penalty for a crime I did not commit."

"You are naked and unarmed," Hanzō said. "Do not attempt to fight."

"If you take my life for this, you prove yourself unfit to lead the Iga ryu."

"*Kneel!*" Hanzō thundered.

Hiro raised his chin and squared his shoulders. "No."

The Iga commander shifted the angle of his sword. "I will let you choose: kneel and die, or let your mother bear your penalty."

"Hanzō—"

As Midori tried to intervene, Hiro fell to his knees. He landed in a puddle, spattering bloody drops across the floor. He needed a plan to delay his execution, but emotions clogged his thoughts like a mudslide blocking a mountain stream.

Finally, an idea broke through.

Hiro hung his head. "Hattori-*sama*, I beg you—as a sign of mercy—summon Father Mateo here before you take my life. A samurai is allowed to bid farewell to his family, even in disgrace. My brother is not in Iga. Allow the priest to take his place."

Hiro looked up, hoping his attempt to stall for time had worked.

Hanzō scowled at Neko's body. "A man who would do *that* deserves no mercy. Bow your head and accept your fate."

CHAPTER 50

Hiro considered his odds; they weren't good. Hanzō was fully clothed and armed, while he was naked and covered in blood that made his hands too slick for a reliable grip. Worse, if he failed to take the sword on the first attempt, Hanzō would kill him, and possibly Midori too.

He would have to outsmart Hanzō, or distract him long enough to get away.

"Why would I kill Neko?" Hiro asked. "I loved her."

"Not as I did." Bitterness sharpened Hanzō's words. "And yet, she rejected me."

Hiro could hardly believe the revelation. How had he never realized that Hanzō loved Neko too? He should have, though the Iga commander normally kept his feelings well concealed.

"A fact for which you have only yourself to blame," Midori said softly. "You married another—"

"—because Neko would not have me!"

"Iga has lost a beloved daughter," Midori continued as if he had not spoken. "Do not allow your personal grief to deprive us of my son as well."

"He is responsible for her death!"

Midori took a step toward Hanzō. "Hiro will find the one who killed her."

"As he found the one who killed the Koga emissaries?" Hanzō snorted. "He has failed, and now he pays the price."

"Rescind his sentence," Midori pressed. "I ask you as a captain of

Iga, not as Hiro's mother. I acknowledge my son's imperfect record, his arrogance, and his lack of respect for authority. However, he remains our best and only chance to find the killer and avoid a war with Koga. Under the circumstances, executing him is ill-advised."

Hiro looked at Neko's body and the crumpled, bloody towel that had fallen from her hand and lay beside her on the floor. The smudges on the cloth resembled . . .

"*Wait!*" The word rang loudly through the chamber. Hiro grabbed the cloth. "Neko left a message, and it proves I did not kill her."

He raised the towel, holding it by the corners to reveal the blurry writing on its surface. Two bold characters marked the cloth. Water and the humid air had rendered the first illegible; Neko's complex strokes had run together, leaving a bloody blur. However, the second character remained distinct: a box bisected by a vertical and a horizontal line that crossed at the center.

"That's not a message." Hanzō scowled. "It's just a bloody smear."

"The first part, yes," Midori said, "but the second looks like *ta.*"

"A rice field?" Hanzō asked. "That makes no sense."

"If I had killed her, she would not have had time to write a message." Hiro pointed to the cloth. "If she had tried, I would have thrown the towel in the bath, erasing it completely."

Hanzō lowered the sword a fraction. "Still, it doesn't help us. It means nothing."

"I believe otherwise," Hiro said. "She knew I was coming, which means she wrote this message for me, expecting me to understand."

He laid the towel across his palm and used his other hand to trace the bloody strokes of the second character.

Why a rice field? What do you want to say? His thoughts reached out, as if to her, although he knew she could no longer answer.

And then, suddenly, he understood.

"I know who killed her"—Hiro looked up—"and also who killed the Koga emissaries."

Hanzō indicated the towel. "Surely not from that?"

Hiro rose to his feet. "In fact, that is precisely how I know. I will explain, but not here. The Koga emissaries have a right to hear what happened, and to know the killer's name."

"You're bluffing." Hanzō stepped backward. "A bloody cloth can't tell you anything."

"It can, it did, and I will prove it at Midori's house."

"Go with him, Hanzō," Midori urged. "I will stay and tend to Neko's body."

"She will be just as dead in an hour." Hiro felt the flash of pain that struck his entire body as he said the words. "You should be there, too, to hear the truth."

"I do not need—"

"You're going with us," Hanzō interrupted. "Neither one of you leaves my sight until I understand what happened. Hiro, dress and join us at the entrance."

As Hanzō left the room with Midori, Hiro picked up the towel he had brought into the bath. After dipping it into the tub, he bent and washed the blood from Neko's face. Despite his words, he refused to leave her body in this condition.

A single cloth did little good on her neck and bloody chest, but Hiro did what he could to clean her, rinsing the cloth in the tub between his efforts. Finally, he lay the towel down across her injured neck, folded her hands across it, and gently closed her sightless eyes.

He straightened slowly, possessed by a grief that struck him over and over again, like the waves of a typhoon against an unprotected shore.

He bowed as tears ran down his cheeks. "I am so sorry, Neko. For everything."

He began to turn away but found himself on his knees again. Lowering his face to hers, he kissed her, and found her lips still warm.

"Good-bye." The word felt small and hollow, but no others came.

He stood and wiped his tears.

Redemption had passed beyond his reach. He would have to make do with vengeance.

CHAPTER 51

After washing the blood from his body and putting on his torn kimono, Hiro joined Hanzō and Midori at the bathhouse door. Neither mentioned how long it had taken him to finish dressing.

"Do you know where Akiko and Tane are?" Hiro asked as they started toward Midori's home.

"Probably sleeping," Hanzō replied. "Grandmother doesn't stay up late."

They continued down the path. Frigid air burned Hiro's nose and made his breath plume out before him in a moonlight-silvered cloud. Iga rarely experienced snow, and never this early in the year, but the temperature made Hiro wonder whether tonight might prove an exception.

Stepping closer to Midori, he whispered, "Why did you bring him to the bathhouse?"

"I wanted to help free the priest," Hanzō answered before Midori could. "She told me you and Neko had a plan, and I insisted that she bring me here at once."

"To the bathhouse?" Hiro stared at Midori.

"I did not anticipate . . ." She shook her head. "I erred, in more ways than one."

In the silence that followed, Hiro tried to pull his thoughts together. When they arrived he would need his wits about him. Applying the facts to the evidence, the answers fell into place with ease, leaving him furious with himself for not recognizing the solution sooner—and devastated that his blindness had caused Neko's death.

Hiro forced the emotions away. He could deal with them later. For now, he needed to ensure that the killer did not escape again.

When they reached Midori's house, he left his sandals on the porch and followed his mother and cousin through the door.

Toshi and Kiku stood by the hearth, along with Father Mateo. As Hiro and the others entered, the kunoichi raised her dagger to the Jesuit's neck.

"What are you doing here?" she demanded.

"I told you I would identify Yajiro-*san*'s killer by dawn," Hiro said. "I have done it."

Her eyes narrowed. "This is a trick."

Hiro nodded toward Father Mateo. "I don't play tricks with the lives of my friends."

"Put the tanto away before someone gets hurt," Hanzō ordered.

Kiku made a derisive noise. "Forgive me, but I must decline."

Midori crossed to the hearth and knelt on the floor. Toshi looked confused, but after a brief hesitation, he knelt beside her.

"Release the priest," Hiro said, "and I will explain who killed Yajiro, and also Fuyu."

"You're bluffing," she retorted. "You don't know."

Hiro sprang.

He pushed her backward and struck her weapon hand with his open palm. She staggered but recovered her balance, keeping her grip on the knife.

Hiro grabbed for her wrist, but found her stronger and more agile than expected. Behind him, he heard the whisper of a blade releasing from its sheath. He hoped it wouldn't end up in his back.

He struggled to keep hold of Kiku's wrist as she dug the fingernails of her empty hand between his knuckles. He felt them break the skin and clenched his teeth against the stinging pain. His arm protested, searing underneath the silken bandage as her twisting opened up his other wound.

Large, scarred hands closed over Kiku's, pulling her fingernails from Hiro's hand.

She struggled, but Father Mateo held her fast.

"Kiku-*san*," the Jesuit said, "I will not hurt you, but you must stop fighting. Drop the knife."

She glared at the priest, but her thrashing ceased. She released the blade. When it fell to the floor, Hiro retrieved it and backed away.

Hanzō stood two steps away, sword in hand and scowling like a demon. At the hearth, Midori held a dagger to Toshi's neck.

"Mother," Hiro objected, then realized the young shinobi also had a dagger out—and up against Midori's side.

"Everyone put the weapons away," Father Mateo said calmly. "You can always bring them out again if talking doesn't work."

Hiro gave the priest a look.

The Jesuit shrugged. "They can."

Kiku relaxed, and the priest released her. Around the room, the others sheathed their weapons.

"Who killed Yajiro?" Kiku demanded.

"The same person who murdered Fuyu"—Hiro's voice caught momentarily—"and Neko, also."

"Kotani Neko is dead?" Toshi asked.

Hiro rounded on the younger man. "Do not defile her memory with false surprise. You know that she is dead, because you killed her."

CHAPTER 52

"Toshi is the killer?" Hanzō asked, incredulous. "I don't believe you."

The others looked equally doubtful.

"I didn't kill anyone." Toshi spoke to Kiku. "He's lying to shift the blame away from Iga. Fuyu-*san* was right. This invitation was a trap."

"Can you prove your allegation?" Hanzō demanded. "If you can, please do, so I can execute this man at once."

"I will explain everything," Hiro replied, "beginning with Yajiro's murder."

"Iga poisoned Yajiro-*san*," Toshi said, "with the tainted welcome tea."

"Curious that you say so with such certainty," Hiro replied. "In fact, a poisoned tea did kill him, but it was not the sencha Hanzō sent to the guesthouse with the cakes. Yajiro drank a second cup of tea that afternoon." He shifted his gaze to Kiku. "A willow tea."

"For his headache. . . ." Kiku's eyes grew wide. "How did you know? But I prepared that tea. It wasn't poisoned."

"On the contrary, it was. The headache you mention . . . a symptom of his opium withdrawal?"

She looked even more stunned. "Who told you?"

"Toshi did, earlier this evening, though he did not understand what he was saying. He mentioned hearing you arguing with Yajiro about another woman . . . a woman Yajiro would not leave, because of her tears."

Kiku gave Toshi a disbelieving look. "There was no other woman. Yajiro loved me—but I would not have him, because of his hunger for opium. That is what ended our relationship." She looked at Hiro. "It was not as many years ago as I led you to believe."

"I suspected that, when I realized the truth," Hiro said. "Toshi heard Yajiro say he lacked the strength to resist the tears. Headaches, sweating, irritability... symptoms of opium withdrawal, which you helped him hide with medicinal teas." He turned to the young shinobi. "Yajiro was not referring to a woman. It was *poppy* tears that he could not resist."

"It was a woman." Toshi flushed. "Fuyu-*san* confronted him about it. He confessed to the affair and begged us to keep his indiscretion secret from the ryu!"

"A convenient lie," Kiku explained, "and far less harmful to his reputation than an opium habit."

"No!" Toshi's cheeks flushed red. "Yajiro chose you for this mission because the two of you were having an affair!"

"He chose me because I knew about the opium," Kiku countered, "and could brew the teas required to dull his pain and mute his hunger for the poppy."

"Why would you agree to such a thing?" Hanzō asked.

"Because I loved him, before the poppy seized control. . . . I did not love him now as I did then, but still I helped him, for the good of the Koga ryu." Kiku gave Hiro a searching look. "You figured all this out from a secondhand comment about a woman's tears?"

"That comment made the other facts align. You told me your relationship ended years ago, yet admitted Yajiro persuaded you to join the Koga delegation and to pretend you supported the alliance. That seemed odd, especially considering your reaction to his death."

"I tried to hide my feelings."

"You did well, but the facts suggested there was more to the story than you told me," Hiro said. "Neko heard the argument between Fuyu and Yajiro, before the feast. She was hiding underneath the bedroom window."

"I knew she was a spy!" Toshi declared.

"Like everyone else in Iga," Kiku said.

"You're lying about the affair," Toshi persisted. "You went to his room every night on the journey."

"To brew medicinal teas for his headaches and massage the shaking from his muscles."

"I heard moaning," Toshi accused.

"The kind that follows vomiting, not passion." She looked down her nose at him. "If you had ever been with a woman, you would know the sounds are rather different."

"Surely you didn't realize all this from Toshi's comment about tears." Hanzō gave Hiro a suspicious look.

"Taken together, the facts revealed the truth," Hiro said. "Kiku denied the affair, but Yajiro admitted it. Clearly, one of them was lying. However, Kiku's denial sparked additional investigation—denials make people suspicious—while Yajiro's admission stopped the inquiry completely. According to Neko, Fuyu threatened to expose the affair upon their return to Koga, but did not press for any further information. Until I heard about the tears, I had no reason to believe Yajiro might be lying, but once I realized the deeper truth, I also knew the affair was likely a persuasive lie, with roots in the truth."

"None of that points to the willow tea," Kiku objected. "I carried the medicines in my box and prepared each one myself. How did you even know about that tea?"

"One of your envelopes is in my possession," Hiro said, "or was, until recently. It contained the dregs of a willow tea, tainted with torikabuto."

"That's impossible. None of the doses left my possession until he drank them."

"Are you certain?" Hiro asked. "Not even on the day you arrived in Iga?"

Realization spread across her face. "I only left it alone for a moment, when I went to stop the argument."

"Who steeped that cup of willow tea?" Hiro asked.

"I prepared the mixture, but Yajiro always steeped the teas himself when others were around. I left the envelope beside his cup. . . ." Kiku turned toward Toshi, eyes ablaze. "You poisoned it when I left the room!"

The young man raised his hands defensively. "I did no such thing. The Iga kunoichi, Neko, must have poisoned the welcome tea. He is making all this up to trick you!"

"You told Fuyu I murdered Yajiro." Kiku spoke with deadly calm. "That's why he was searching my poison box this afternoon. You tried to blame your crime on me."

"I told him to check the box because you killed Yajiro!" Toshi turned to Hanzō. "She's the murderer, not me. She murdered Fuyu-*san* because he learned the truth, and then she sneaked to the bathhouse and killed Neko while Hiro and I were moving the body."

"Impossible," Kiku said. "I was here with the priest."

"Both women cannot be guilty." Dark storms brewed in Hanzō's eyes. "And how did you know Kotani Neko died in a bathhouse?"

"I-I assumed it," Toshi stammered. "I overheard the foreigner's maid delivering a message to Hiro. She said that Neko wanted Hiro to meet her at the bathhouse." He leaned back as if in sudden realization. "Maybe Hiro murdered her himself, in a lovers' quarrel!"

Anger burst in Hiro's chest like a thunderclap, but he forced it down. When he spoke, his voice was deadly calm. "If you listened to that conversation, you also heard Ana mention that Neko had critical information for me. You believed she could identify you as the killer, so you went to the bathhouse and murdered her, to hide the truth."

"I did no such thing. I attended to Fuyu's body and then came directly here."

"His clothing bears no signs of a murder," Kiku pointed out.

"Most likely, he removed his outer kimono before he entered the bath," Hiro said. "That is an assumption, but it makes no difference—Neko identified him as the killer."

"That's not possible." Toshi paled.

Hiro spoke over him. "Neko left a message for me, in her own blood, revealing the person responsible for her death."

"That cloth did not say 'Koga,'" Hanzō objected. "Or 'Toshi,' either."

"No, because Neko realized her killer acted at the command of someone else. Someone who wants to start a war between Iga and the Koga ryu."

"Koga would never accept a commission to start a war with Iga," Kiku said.

"The Koga ryu would accept no such commission," Hiro agreed, "but a lesser son of a lesser clan, a man who would never otherwise hold significant power within the ryu, might be persuaded to sacrifice Koga—and his personal honor—for a reward."

"He is lying!" Toshi declared.

Slowly, Hiro turned. "What did Lord Oda promise you in return for setting Iga and Koga at one another's throats?"

Hanzō's eyes flew wide. "Are you telling me Oda Nobunaga is behind this?"

Midori covered her mouth with her hand. "The character . . . 'rice field.'"

Hiro nodded. "We pronounce it *ta*, and it means 'rice field,' when it stands alone, but when it follows the character 'O'—a character so complex that any smudging renders it illegible—the pronunciation changes to *da* . . . and *Oda* is the message Neko left for me to find.

"So Toshi-*san*, I ask again: what price did Oda Nobunaga give you to betray your clan and soil your honor?"

"I am not a traitor," Toshi said. "I am a loyal son of the Koga ryu."

Kiku looked from one man to the other. "Have you proof of this, aside from letters written by the dead?"

"I believe young Toshi's last assignment was in Mikawa Province," Hiro said, "a territory Oda Nobunaga now controls. Also, one of Oda's agents recently tried to murder Hattori Hanzō, and burned an Iga village in the mountains. Moreover, Lord Oda has made his intention to destroy the shinobi clans quite clear."

"I went to Mikawa to help assassinate one of Oda's retainers," Toshi sneered, "and I succeeded, even though the senior shinobi failed. Why would I do that if I worked for Oda Nobunaga?"

Hanzō snorted. "Daimyō Oda has murdered plenty of his own retainers. He could have allowed you to succeed, or helped you do it, to give Koga a false impression of your loyalty."

"I am a loyal son of the Koga ryu!"

Hiro caught the hint of desperation in Toshi's voice.

"So you've mentioned," Kiku said, "but I find it increasingly difficult to believe."

CHAPTER 53

"Why does everyone keep accusing me? She's the one with the motive!" Toshi pointed at Kiku. "She opposed the alliance, but pretended she supported it. She used her relationship with Yajiro-*san* to earn his trust, killed him, and tried to blame Hattori Hanzō for the crime."

"Coward!" Kiku hissed. "Accept responsibility for your actions!"

Toshi continued as if she hadn't spoken. "Fuyu-*san* knew she killed Yajiro. He searched her medicine box. She caught him at it and murdered him to stop him from revealing the truth!"

The door burst open.

Akiko dragged a wide-eyed Tane into the house. The elderly woman froze as she noticed the number and identities of the people in the room. She released her grip on Tane, who immediately wrapped her arms around herself and stared at the floor as if doing so would render her invisible.

"Hanzō-*kun*?" Akiko asked. "What are you doing here?"

The commander faced her. "I could ask the same of you, Grandmother."

"I came to warn Hiro-*kun* that one of the Koga emissaries is a killer." Akiko opened her hand, revealing a crumpled envelope.

"Mother!" Hiro objected. "I gave that to you!"

"And I promised to find out where it came from, if I could." Midori indicated the woman standing in the entrance. "I gave it to Akiko in the hope that she could find an answer."

"And I did." Triumph rang in the white-haired woman's voice.

"This envelope did not come from Iga. Our paper does not use this much bamboo. More importantly, Tane knows exactly where it came from. She found the envelope at the guesthouse, when she went to retrieve the tray with the welcome tea. She claims it sat beside a cup that did not smell of sencha."

She looked at the girl beside her. "Tell them."

Tane nodded but did not look up.

"She brought the tray back shortly after the feast began and left it in the kitchen. When the Koga emissary died, she worried I was responsible and hid the envelope."

"She couldn't have told you that," Toshi scoffed. "She cannot even speak."

Slowly, Tane raised her face, jaw set and fury in her eyes. She looked at each of them in turn. At the sight of Hiro she released her sleeves, gestured to Akiko, and then hugged herself. After briefly glancing at Hiro as if to ensure he was paying attention, she tapped her own chest, hugged herself again, and indicated Akiko, following the series of gestures with another, more complicated set of movements Hiro could not understand precisely, though he guessed their meaning.

"She loves you, and you love her, too," he translated. "You wanted to protect her."

Tane nodded, biting her lip as her nose turned red and her eyes filled up with tears.

"Then why deliver the envelope to me?" Hiro asked.

Tane made the sign of the cross, gestured to Father Mateo, and raised her hands in an attitude of prayer.

"She is a Christian." Father Mateo spoke as if in awe.

Nodding, Tane reached into her sleeve. A tear ran down her cheek as she removed her hand and opened it, revealing a small metal cross in her palm. Fire had charred the surface black. After only a moment, she snapped her fingers shut around the cross and clutched it to her chest.

"I didn't know." Akiko looked from the girl to the priest. "She did seem unusually excited after seeing you at the welcome feast."

Tane turned to Father Mateo, bowed, and tapped her fingers to her forehead in the gesture Hiro recognized as an apology. Then, once more, she clasped her hands in prayer and bowed her head.

"She wants—"

"Forgiveness," Father Mateo said. "God has forgiven all your sins. Of that, I'm certain. Do not be afraid, Tane."

The girl raised her tear-streaked face and smiled at the priest.

"Tane was there when Midori brought me the envelope," Akiko said. "As soon as she realized it wasn't ours, she explained where she found it. We provided no willow with the welcome tea, which means"—the elderly woman paused dramatically—"the killer is one of the Koga emissaries!"

"Thank you, Grandmother," Hanzō said. "We already knew."

"You did?" Akiko frowned. "And no one told me?"

"I deduced that Tane must have found the envelope on the tray with the welcome tea," Hiro said. "It was the only explanation that made sense. The welcome tea was delivered about an hour before the feast began, which matched the amount of time it would take for torikabuto to take effect. Therefore, I knew he must have ingested the poison at or near that time.

"Tane retrieved the tray from the guesthouse after the Koga emissaries left for the feast, meaning that she was alone with the tray and its contents. She could have seen, and removed, the envelope without anyone noticing its absence. Had she discovered the envelope elsewhere—in Hanzō's kitchen, for example—Akiko would have noticed it missing, and Tane might not have connected it with the murder."

"May I see the envelope?" Kiku asked.

Akiko closed her hand around the paper.

"It's all right, Grandmother," Hiro said.

Slowly, Akiko handed it over.

Kiku examined the envelope carefully, lifting the flap and peering inside. "This belongs to me, and this is the willow mixture I prepared for Yajiro—but I did not put this poison in it." She nodded to Hiro. "I am convinced of Toshi's guilt, but I would like to hear what happened from start to finish . . . if you know."

"I do, and I will tell you." When no one objected, Hiro said, "At some point—likely, during his time in Mikawa Province—Oda Nobunaga persuaded Toshi to join his cause and sent him back to Koga with orders to start a war between the shinobi clans. When Hanzō's invitation came, Toshi persuaded his father to let him accompany Fuyu on the mission. During the journey, he doubtless looked for each of your weaknesses, trying to decide how best to kill you. Yajiro's constant headaches, and the packets of willow tea he drank to relieve them, were an obvious place to begin."

Toshi listened silently, face unreadable.

"The afternoon the delegation arrived in Iga," Hiro continued, "the fight between Fuyu and Yajiro distracted you and gave Toshi the opportunity he needed. As soon as you left the room, he poisoned Yajiro's envelope of willow tea with torikabuto. The bitter willow would disguise the toxin's taste, and since it takes about an hour to kill, he knew his victim would drop dead at the welcome feast."

"Making it look as if we murdered him," Midori added.

"Indeed, it worked out almost perfectly, at least from his perspective," Hiro said. "Yajiro's death came close to triggering the war immediately. Even I believed, at first, that Hanzō killed him."

Father Mateo bowed to the Iga leader. "I suspected you also. For that, I apologize."

"A regrettable, but understandable error," Hanzō said.

"Unfortunately for Toshi," Hiro continued, "the other surviving emissaries agreed to an investigation, rather than simply declaring Yajiro's murder an act of war. I'll give him credit—he played the role of helpful observer unusually well, avoiding suspicion and letting the rest of the suspects accuse one another, at least until Fuyu began suspecting Kiku."

Toshi scowled.

"Isn't that why you poisoned Midori's tea?" Hiro asked. "To divert Fuyu's suspicions back to Iga?"

"How could Toshi have poisoned the tea?" Father Mateo asked. "He went to meet the priests with Fuyu, and by the time he returned, we were here. He came in right after we changed to winter kimono."

"Actually, he must have arrived before that," Hiro said. "Remember, Ana had left and the house was empty when we returned. Toshi could have sneaked into the kitchen while everyone was gone, poisoned the tea, and waited nearby for us to return before making his entrance. In fact, I suspect that Tane might have heard him in the woods—she was looking away from the door when I answered it."

"I accidentally stepped on a branch," Toshi confirmed. "I hoped the poisoned tea would make Fuyu decide to leave at once, by making it appear that Iga planned to kill us all. Unfortunately, it made him even more convinced of Kiku's guilt. I tried to persuade him otherwise, but I pushed too hard and he got suspicious."

"So you killed him," Hiro said.

"Toshi couldn't have murdered Fuyu," Father Mateo protested. "He was with me at the guesthouse all afternoon."

"Foolish priest," Toshi sneered. "Your religion makes you blind, and praying makes you deaf as well. I slipped away while you said your rituals over Yajiro's body and returned before you noticed I had gone."

"A risky plan," the Jesuit said. "How did you know I wouldn't discover you missing?"

"If you had, I would have claimed I went to the latrine. As for the plan"—Toshi gestured to Hiro—"that part was his fault. I noticed that you lose track of time when praying or talking about your foreign god. I persuaded Fuyu to agree to let you perform your Christian ritual, planning to kill you both—first him, then you—while you were praying."

"After which, you would have claimed that everyone in Iga worked together to murder your delegation?" Hiro asked.

"Exactly," Toshi said. "I would have claimed the priest was secretly an Iga agent, too. But you made Fuyu change his mind, and not attend the ritual, which meant I had to alter the plan. I waited for the priest to lose himself in meditation. Then I slipped away, killed Fuyu, and disposed of Kiku's medicine box, to ensure that if Iga escaped the blame again, I could ensure that she was held accountable. Once Hanzō executed her, I would return to Koga, the sole survivor of Iga's traitorous plan."

Kiku bared her teeth, but Toshi continued, "When I heard the housekeeper telling Hiro that Neko had important information, I thought she must have seen me killing Fuyu. I couldn't risk her revealing the truth."

He smiled at Hiro. "She thought I was you when I entered the bathhouse. Did you know she loved you? It was obvious on her face when she turned. . . . You should have seen her when I cut her throat. She tried to ask me why I did it, so I told her: She was only the first of many. Every shinobi in Iga will die, along with the fools of Koga, leaving Oda Nobunaga free to rule Japan, with me in command of his loyal shinobi spies!"

He sprang to his feet, dagger in hand.

Hiro had no time to dodge. Stepping into the attack, he focused on the young shinobi's throat and focused all his strength into a single punch.

Toshi's momentum amplified the force of Hiro's strike, collapsing his throat.

The young man crumpled to the floor. His dagger tumbled harmlessly away.

Hiro reached down and retrieved the weapon as Toshi rolled to his hands and knees, choking and gasping.

"Have you anything to say before I sentence you to death?" Hanzō asked.

Toshi nodded and raised a hand. Everyone waited silently as he struggled to control his breathing and pushed himself to a kneeling position. His choking slowed, and he opened his mouth.

"You are doomed." Toshi's voice was harsh and hoarse, barely recognizable as speech. "Lord Oda will prevail."

"On the contrary," Hiro said. "Now that we all know the truth, Iga and Koga will form an alliance. Oda Nobunaga's plan to destroy the shinobi clans will fail, and a year from now, no one outside your family will even remember that you ever lived."

"Traitor!" Kiku hissed. "How could you grovel like a dog at Oda's feet? What did he promise you?"

Toshi clutched his throat as he whispered, "Leadership . . . of the only . . . shinobi clan . . . to survive the coming war." He coughed.

"You are not only a traitor," Hanzō said. "You are a fool. Oda Nobunaga would never allow even a single shinobi to survive. Once he claimed the shogunate, you would have shared our fate."

"Samurai"—Toshi coughed again—"a samurai . . . always keeps his promise."

"True," Hiro said, "and I have one to keep as well."

He drove the dagger into Toshi's chest, feeling the blade slip cleanly between the ribs.

Toshi's eyes flew open wide, and his cough grew wet as crimson foam appeared on his lips. It stained his hand and flecked the floor in front of him.

He fell, clutching his throat and choking on the blood that trickled from his lips and pooled beneath him on the tatami. In less than a minute, he gave a final choking gasp and stilled. The blood that ran from his mouth slowed to a dribble as his heart stopped beating.

"That was for Neko." Hiro looked around the room, daring anyone to argue.

Tane touched her fingertips to her lips, bowed, and made the sign of the cross before clasping her hands in silent prayer.

"Perhaps you intended it only for Neko," Kiku said, "but you have avenged Yajiro and Fuyu also. Koga is grateful." Softly, she added, "I am grateful."

A wave of emotion crashed over Hiro, nearly breaking his control. Without a word, he turned away and stumbled from the house.

CHAPTER 54

The moon shone high above the trees, a round, white orb as cold as the ice that clutched at Hiro's heart. Despite avenging all three deaths, he felt no victory.

He headed north into the trees, less by intention than from a compelling need to move, as if by doing so he could escape the pain that dogged him from within. Fallen leaves crunched underfoot, disrupting the silence. Suddenly aware of the sound, Hiro walked with greater force, shoving his feet against the leaves in an angry attempt to increase the noise he made.

A moment later, he realized the foolishness of stomping through the forest like a child resenting the loss of a favorite toy. His emotions ran far too deep for childish rage.

Hiro stopped and drew a deep, slow breath. The frigid air smelled crisp, with hints of chimney smoke and the deeper, earthy musk of fallen leaves. Though muted by the cold, these were the smells that once meant home.

Tonight, they brought him only pain.

Overhead, an owl broke the silence with a haunting cry, and Hiro felt a bitter kinship with the bird—both cursed to ask unanswerable questions.

One thing he knew: he could not stay in Iga any longer. He had raised a blade against Hattori Hanzō, and though he believed it justified, under the shinobi code his motive did not matter.

Motive always matters. His own words echoed back to him, this time in Neko's voice.

Footsteps crunched in the leaves behind him. Hiro turned around.

Father Mateo bowed. "I'm sorry if I startled you."

"I do not startle so easily."

"Hiro . . . I am sorry about Neko."

"I do not wish to have this conversation." Hiro turned away and continued walking.

As expected, Father Mateo's footsteps scurried after him until the priest caught up. "It was a comment, not the start of a conversation."

Overhead, a wind blew through the pines and rattled the bamboo stalks.

"It sounds like rain," the Jesuit said. "The bamboo in the wind, I mean."

"It was her favorite sound." Hiro's comment slipped out unbidden.

"Perhaps because she knew the proverb," Father Mateo said softly. "'A mighty wind may fell the cedar, but the bamboo merely bends to rise again.'"

Hiro stopped and turned to the priest. "Did you come out here to be my conscience?"

"After you left, Kiku and Hanzō agreed to meet tomorrow morning and work out the terms of a treaty between the clans. Lord Oda's plot has changed her mind about the alliance." Father Mateo paused. "You did it, Hiro. You stopped a war."

"Neko did it." He took a breath and continued, "Earlier tonight, I learned that she did not betray me, all those years ago. My uncle made her do it."

"I am so sorry." The Jesuit raised a hand toward Hiro's shoulder, but withdrew it without making contact.

Hiro clenched a fist. "She died before she knew I'd learned the truth."

Father Mateo drew a breath.

"Do not apologize again!" Hiro barely managed to keep a grip on his emotions. "She is gone, and nothing will bring her back. Now, what matters is ensuring Oda Nobunaga does not succeed."

"He has already failed," the Jesuit said. "By exposing his plans, you assured the treaty."

"I was not referring to the alliance. Oda Nobunaga has injured me deeply. I intend to return the favor, by ensuring that he never claims the shogunate."

Father Mateo looked surprised. "You're serious."

"I will see you safely to Yokoseura, where you will stay until the war is over, safe among your people. If I survive, I will return. Until then, I must ask you to release me from my oath."

"Absolutely not—and I'm not sitting out the action in some Portuguese colony while you do important things. I'm going with you."

"This is dangerous," Hiro said, "and someone pays the Iga ryu—"

"—good money to keep me safe." The Jesuit crossed his arms. "I do not care about the wishes of some wealthy stranger who can't be bothered to introduce or explain himself. You cannot make me stay in Yokoseura, and I won't do it. Wherever you go, I'm going with you."

The following morning, Hiro awoke at dawn to a frosty world.

He pushed a sleeping Gato off his knees and stroked her gently before sitting up and pulling his kimono around him tightly. The garment had belonged to his father, but despite its age the smoky silk retained its sheen.

Hiro rose from his futon, careful not to wake either Father Mateo or Ana, a difficult feat, given the tiny size of the Iga guesthouse. After crossing the floor on tiptoe, he slipped outside as the rising sun transformed the frost to diamonds.

Tiny rainbows sparkled in the ice that rimed the crimson trees. The air smelled cold and clean.

A floorboard creaked behind him as the Jesuit joined him at the door and looked outside.

"It's beautiful."

"It will melt in an hour," Hiro said, "which is fortunate. It won't delay us leaving."

"We're going today? I thought you would want to stay for Neko's—"

"You thought incorrectly." Hiro did not want to hear the Jesuit say *funeral*.

"Where, precisely, are we going?"

Before Hiro could answer, Hanzō appeared on the path with Kiku at his side. She held the reins of a dark brown horse that Hiro recognized as one of Hanzō's.

They approached the house and exchanged bows with Hiro and the priest, who stepped out onto the veranda and closed the door to prevent the conversation from waking Ana.

"I wanted to say farewell in person," Kiku said, "and to thank you again for avenging Yajiro's death." She raised a leather-bound scroll. "Hanzō and I have signed a provisional treaty, which I'm certain the Koga ryu will ratify. Hattori-*san* has loaned me a horse, and I ride for Koga immediately."

Hiro noted her use of the honorific *-san*, which implied that Hanzō was closer to her equal. Apparently, even her rank was now in the open, at least where Hanzō was concerned.

"Alone?" Father Mateo asked.

"Carting the bodies to Koga would take too long. Hattori-*san* has agreed to arrange the proper funeral rites for Yajiro and Fuyu. As for the traitor"—Kiku wrinkled her nose at Hanzō—"I hope you feed that coward to the crows."

She tucked the scroll into her kimono and mounted the horse with experienced grace. The animal snorted and tossed its head as if equally eager to depart.

Father Mateo made the sign of the cross in the air between them. "May God watch over your journey and bring a lasting peace between Iga and Koga."

"Safe travels to you as well." She looked at Hiro. "Perhaps, in time, we will meet again."

She turned the horse and cantered away through the trees.

When Kiku had disappeared from view, Hanzō said, "I assume you plan to leave for Yokoseura as soon as possible."

"Who is arranging Neko's . . . funeral?" Hiro asked.

"Midori has requested that responsibility," Hanzō replied. "Iga will cover the expense, of course."

Hiro nodded but did not answer.

After an awkward silence, Hanzō said, "I have a mission for you to complete on your way to Yokoseura."

Hiro's senses sharpened. A new assignment meant that all his actions were forgiven, without reprimand. He wondered just how dangerous this task was going to be.

"I need you to travel south, to Mount Koya, and deliver a message to a spy who's stationed there. With Neko gone, I need someone I can trust to warn our agents along the Tōkaidō of Oda's treachery, and to tell them of our new alliance with the Koga ryu. After you deliver the message, take the priest and hide in the Portuguese settlement until the emperor names a new shogun."

"You want me to take a priest of the foreign god to Koya-*san*, a Buddhist mountain?" Hiro asked.

"Which part of that order was not sufficiently clear?"

"What of his housekeeper?" Hiro continued. "Women cannot enter the holy city on Koya's summit."

"She can stay at the women's sanctuary—the *nyonindo*. As for the priest"—Hanzō steepled his hands as if in prayer—"everyone knows the foreigners are curious about Japan and love to see our holy sites. No one will suspect you carry a message for the Iga ryu."

"Will the spy know who to warn along the Tōkaidō?" Hiro asked.

"You can memorize the list of names before you leave. It is not long."

"We'll do it." Father Mateo sounded far too enthusiastic for Hiro's taste.

"We will not!" He frowned at the priest. "You're not a spy."

"Saving lives and stopping wars is every bit as much God's work as preaching the Gospel," Father Mateo said. "And Hattori-*sama* is right—I have always wanted to see a sacred mountain."

"A shinobi, a priest, and an elderly maid went off to visit Koya-*san*." Hanzō laughed. "It sounds like the start of quite a tale."

"Or a terrible joke," Hiro grumbled. *Not to mention, you forgot the cat.*

"Stop worrying." Father Mateo grinned. "We're just delivering a message."

"Indeed," Hiro said, with irony. "I see no way it could possibly go wrong."

CAST OF CHARACTERS

(IN ALPHABETICAL ORDER)

Where present, Japanese characters' surnames precede their given names, in the Japanese style. Western surnames follow the characters' given names, in accordance with Western conventions.

Ana – Father Mateo's housekeeper

Father Mateo Ávila de Santos – a Christian priest from Portugal

Fuyu – an assassin (and emissary) from the Koga ryu

Gato – Hiro's cat

Hattori Akiko – an Iga assassin; Hiro and Hanzō's grandmother

Hattori Hanzō* – one of Japan's most famous ninja commanders, and leader of the Iga ryu; born Hattori Masanari, also known as "Devil Hanzō"

Hattori Hiro – a shinobi (ninja) assassin from the Iga ryu, hired by an anonymous benefactor to guard Father Mateo; at times, he uses the alias Matsui Hiro

Hattori Midori – an Iga assassin and Hiro's mother

Kiku – a female assassin (and emissary) from the Koga ryu

Koga Yajiro – leader of the emissaries sent by the Koga ryu to negotiate with Hattori Hanzō

Matsunaga Hisahide* – a samurai warlord who seized Kyoto in June 1565

Neko – a female assassin from the Iga ryu who is also Hiro's former lover

Oda Nobunaga* – a samurai warlord who wanted to become the shogun and rule Japan

Tane – an orphaned girl, discovered in a burned-out ninja village, currently in the care of Hattori Akiko

Toshi – an assassin (and emissary) from the Koga ryu

* Designates a character who, though fictionally represented, is based upon a historical figure. [All other characters are entirely fictitious.]

GLOSSARY OF JAPANESE TERMS

D

daimyō: a samurai lord, usually the ruler of a province and/or the head of a samurai clan

F

futon: a thin padded mattress, small and pliable enough to be folded and stored out of sight during the day

H

hakama: loose, pleated pants worn over kimono or beneath a tunic or surcoat

I

ichibancha: "first picked tea"—tea leaves picked in April or early May, during the first picking of the season; Ichibancha is considered the highest quality, and most flavorful, kind of tea

J

jisei: "death poem"—a special, stylized poem written by samurai just prior to death, including (but not limited to) deliberate death by seppuku

K

kami: the Japanese word for "god" or "divine spirit"; used to describe gods, the spirits inhabiting natural objects, and certain natural forces of divine origin

kanzashi: a type of hairpin worn by women in medieval Japan
katana: the longer of the two swords worn by a samurai (the shorter one is the wakizashi)
kimono: literally, "a thing to wear"; a full-length wraparound robe traditionally worn by Japanese people of all ages and genders
kunoichi: a female shinobi

M

miso: a traditional Japanese food paste made from fermented soybeans (or, sometimes, rice or barley)
mon: a traditional Japanese family crest; the symbol of a samurai clan

N

neko-te: literally "cat's claws," a weapon consisting of metal or leather finger sheaths tipped with sharpened metal blades; the sheaths slipped over the ends of the wearer's finger, allowing the blades to protrude like the claws of a cat
noren: a traditional Japanese doorway hanging, with a slit cut up the center to permit passage
nyonindo: the "women's hall" on Mount Koya where women stayed to pray and meditate during the feudal era, when women were not allowed on the summit of the sacred mountain

O

obi: a wide sash wrapped around the waist to hold a kimono closed, worn by people of all ages and genders
oe: the large central living space in a Japanese home, which featured a sunken hearth and often served as a combination of kitchen, reception room, and living area

R

ronin: a masterless samurai
ryu: literally, "school"; shinobi clans used this term as a combination identifier and association name (Hiro is a member of the Iga ryu)

S

sake (also "saké"): an alcoholic beverage made from fermented rice

-sama: a suffix used to show even higher respect than *-san*

samurai: a member of the medieval Japanese nobility, the warrior caste that formed the highest-ranking social class

-san: a suffix used to show respect

sencha: a type of Japanese green tea, prepared by steeping whole tea leaves in water

seppuku: a form of Japanese ritual suicide by disembowelment, originally used only by samurai

shinobi: literally, "shadowed person"; *shinobi* is the Japanese pronunciation of the characters that many Westerners pronounce "ninja," which is based on a Chinese pronunciation

shogun: the military dictator and commander who acted as de facto ruler of medieval Japan

shogunate: a name for the shogun's government and/or the compound where the shogun lived

shoji: a sliding door, usually consisting of a wooden frame with oiled paper panels

shuriken: an easily concealed, palm-sized weapon made of metal and often shaped like a cross or star, which shinobi used for throwing or as a handheld weapon in close combat

T

tanto: a fixed-blade dagger with a single- or double-edged blade measuring six to twelve inches (15–30 cm) in length

tanuki: the Japanese "raccoon dog" (*Nyctereutes procyonoides viverrinus*), which, though neither a raccoon nor a dog, has been present in Japan—and in Japanese folklore—since ancient times

tatami: a traditional Japanese mat-style floor covering made in standard sizes, with the length measuring exactly twice its width; tatami usually contained a straw core covered with grass or rushes

tokonoma: a decorative alcove or recessed space set into the wall of a

Japanese room; the tokonoma typically held a piece of art, a flower arrangement, or a hanging scroll

torikabuto: the Japanese name for *Aconitum sp.*, a highly poisonous plant also known in English as aconite, wolfsbane, and monkshood; the leaves, stems, and roots are highly toxic, causing death within one to four hours after ingestion

torikatsu: fried chicken (in modern Japan, pounded, breaded, and normally deep-fried)

W

wakizashi: the shorter of the two swords worn by a samurai (the longer one is the katana)

For additional cultural information, expanded definitions, and author's notes, visit http://www.susanspann.com

ACKNOWLEDGMENTS

Most people don't bother to read the acknowledgments section—so if you're reading this, I appreciate you "listening" as I thank the people who helped me make this book a reality.

First and foremost: thank you, the reader, for choosing this book from the millions of others clamoring for your attention. I deeply appreciate you spending your valuable time with Hiro and Father Mateo, and with me.

Thanks to my agent, Sandra Bond, for your eagle-eyed editing, thoughtful comments, and hours of work on my behalf. You are the best business partner, and friend, an author could hope to have.

Thanks to Dan Mayer, my editor; your input made this novel stronger and prevented both Father Mateo and me from wandering off with egg—and worse—on our faces. And thanks to Jill Maxick, Jeff Curry, Nicole Sommer-Lecht, Lisa Michalski, Hanna Etu, and everyone else at Seventh Street Books who contributed to making this book a reality. I am truly blessed and honored to work with each and every one of you.

Thank you to Heather, Kerry, Julianne, Chuck, and Rae for your help, support, and constant reinforcement. To Steve, Wing, Peter, and the rest of Blood Vigil of Feathermoon—thank you for helping me escape to the World of Warcraft. To each of you, and to all of my friends: I love you and could not do this—or anything else—without you.

To Michael and Christopher: thank you for helping me keep my dreams in the air, my feet on the ground, and my butt in the chair. And to Paula, Spencer, Robert, Lola, Spencer (III), Gene, Marcie, Bob,

Anna, and Matteo: words alone are not enough to thank you for all you are and do.

If you've made it this far, I thank you again for reading this page—and this book—to the end. If you like this novel, or any other, I hope you'll consider telling a friend. Your praise and your recommendation are the greatest rewards an author can receive.

ABOUT THE AUTHOR

Susan Spann is the author of four previous novels in the Shinobi Mystery series: *Claws of the Cat*, *Blade of the Samurai*, *Flask of the Drunken Master*, and *The Ninja's Daughter*. She has a degree in Asian studies and a lifelong love of Japanese history and culture. When not writing or practicing law, she raises seahorses and rare corals in her marine aquarium.